LOST MEMORIES

BY

SUZANNE FLOYD

COPYRIGHT

This is a work of fiction. All characters in this book have no existence outside the imagination of the author. Names, characters, places and events are either the products of the author's imagination or used in a fictitious manner. Any resemblance to actual persons, living or dead, or actual events is purely coincidental.

Cover by Bella Media Management

This book is dedicated to my husband Paul and our daughters, Camala and Shannon, and all of my family. Thanks for all your support and encouragement.

"Once Lost, now found. Eternally thankful!" Our Daily Bread

PART ONE
CHAPTER ONE

He slammed his beefy fist on the desk causing the smaller man to cringe. "Why the hell didn't you finish the job?" he growled menacingly, enjoying the younger man's discomfort.

"I didn't think she'd live." The younger man's voice shook as he faced the anger in the big man's eyes. "A few more hours in the desert, and she wouldn't have. I didn't think anyone would ever find her." His voice took on strength as he tried to defend his actions.

"Oh, is that how it was *supposed* to happen?" the big man questioned. His voice was all the more menacing for the mild tone. "The desert is lousy with kids on dirt bikes and four wheelers. Did you think they only went on regular trails, and wouldn't go exploring around? I told you to take care of her, not leave it to chance." He stood up, walking around the desk.

The younger man seemed to shrink as he stared up at the man towering over him. "She was almost dead when I left her out there," he whined. "The sun would have finished her off if those kids hadn't found her. I...I just couldn't kill her," he finished in a lame voice.

"It's a little late to start getting squeamish." The big man began pacing around the office. He could feel the walls closing in on him. "I don't think you realize what it means to both of us if she lives." He looked down at the newspaper on the desk. "It says she's in critical condition, and hasn't regained consciousness, but nothing else."

The chair groaned under his weight as he sank down again. He was big, but there wasn't much fat on his bones. Resting his chin on his hand, he read the newspaper article again. "They don't know who she is yet. That could work in our favor. At least you had enough sense not to leave her purse with her. She wasn't wearing anything that could be traced to who she is either."

"What if the hospital reports her missing?" If someone filed a missing person's report on her, the sheriff's office in

Phoenix would be able to identify her. Had anyone else seen her at the hospital, he wondered?

The big man gave him a look of disdain. "Unlike you, I don't leave things to chance. I sent an email to the administrator from our good Doctor Sanders. Due to a 'family emergency,' she wasn't able to come to Arizona as planned. She had to resign her position even before she started."

"What about her family? Won't they file a report?"

He'd managed to hack into the system and pull her personnel file, he was safe there. "She has no family, now stop asking questions. I need time to think."

For several long moments, both men were lost in their thoughts. "All I have to do is make sure she doesn't wake up." He was speaking more to himself than to his companion.

"How are you going to do that?" The younger man stared at him in disbelief. "She's in the hospital in Phoenix."

"I should send you up there to finish what you left undone." The big man paused, letting the veiled threat sink in. "Unfortunately, I wouldn't trust you to walk my dog now."

A sigh of relief escaped the younger man's lips before he asked quietly. "What are you going to do? She's in ICU. They aren't going to let a stranger walk in there without asking a lot of questions."

"I'm aware of that, you idiot!" Again they fell silent, each considering the problem. "As much as I dislike the idea of working in Phoenix again, I think that might be the best move right now." Thinking out loud helped his thought processes. He'd forgotten the young man was still in the room with him. "I still have contacts up there. I even know the old coot in charge of that hospital. I think I'll give him a call, and see if he'd like to have me on his staff again." Time was of the essence. He had to take care of this little matter before she woke up.

"But you'll get caught if you try anything," the young man protested. "Can't we just wait and see what happens? They don't think she's going to live, so why risk it?"

Cold steel glared back at him. "You might not mind

spending the next twenty years in prison, but I'm not spending so much as one night behind bars. And I'm not sitting around waiting to see if she wakes up so she can nail me to the wall."

The young man dropped his eyes, unable to meet the contempt in the older man's gaze when he glared at him again. "I made the mistake of letting that damn broad walk in on me. I don't plan on making another by letting her live to accuse me of anything." A cruel smile twisted his usually handsome features. "She doesn't know my name, and can't swear that I'm the one who hit her. All she can really pin on me is stealing drugs, possibly assault. But you're the one who left her out there to die in the heat. It will be attempted murder for you. Are you willing to wait and see if she'll live to accuse you of that?"

The young man blanched. "N..no, no," he stammered. "I was just doing what you told me to do." He regretted his words the minute they were out of his mouth.

The big man leaned over the desk, his face menacing. "Don't even think about double-crossing me." His voice was dangerously low. "It would be the last thing you ever did." The young man's narrow face and emaciated body reminded him of a weasel. Even his furtive movements were weasel-like. Glaring at him now, the bigger man enjoyed making him cower.

Silence filled the small room for several minutes before the young man asked again, "How do you plan on doing it? She's in intensive care. Even if your friend can get you on staff before she wakes up, you won't be able to get at her. There's always a nurse on duty in the ICU."

"Don't tell me how a hospital is run, damn it! Right now my only plan is to get up there as fast as possible. Once I'm there I'll think of something. I'm not sitting here waiting for the roof to cave in, and I'm not spending even one night in jail, let alone years in a prison cell." The last words were made as a vow to himself.

He resumed pacing, thinking out loud as he tried to put some order to his thoughts. "Right now there is no reason to connect her with Tucson or this hospital. If she dies before the police broaden their search, I'm home free." Only a small article appeared on the front page, the rest was buried on page three. No pictures accompanied the article. There was no reason for anyone in Tucson to connect that woman with Doctor Brianna Sanders, the new doctor scheduled to start work on Monday. She didn't have any business being in the hospital in the middle of the night before she began working here. That would work as a plus for him.

In his mind's eye he saw the entire event unfold again, his anger building just as it had then. She had walked into the pharmacy early Sunday morning, introducing herself as Doctor Brianna Sanders, the new doctor on staff. Her voice was soft and sexy. She apologized for the interruption, explaining that she was just trying to get a feel for the hospital before starting work there in the morning. The explanation died on her lips as her mind registered what he was doing. "What are you doing with those drugs?" Her Southern accent was no longer soft or sexy.

He'd glibly spun a story about running a clinic to help out the poor in the area, a clinic financed by the medical center. He was getting his supplies ready for the coming week.

She might have bought it if that damn little weasel hadn't barged in right then, telling him to hurry before they got caught.

Trapped between the two men, there had been little chance of escape. Still she tried to run. He had to admit she put up quite a fight, but there was little doubt about the outcome. The rest was a blur in his mind. He knew he'd hit her, he could still feel the rush, the excitement. After that first blow, he couldn't seem to stop himself, nor did he want to. If that damn weasel hadn't pulled him off, he would have finished the job himself, and he wouldn't be in this fix right now.

Casting a dark glare at the younger man, he decided when the time came he was going to enjoy getting rid of the interfering little bastard.

She wasn't officially on staff at the hospital until Monday, which worked in his favor. As far as anyone at the hospital will know, she simply never arrived. If anyone in her past questions why they haven't heard from her, they won't be able to connect her disappearance to him.

The young man watched his boss pace the room like a caged tiger. *Whatever possessed you to get mixed up with this nut*, he questioned silently? Money and drugs were the answer, of course, only now they weren't much consolation. He would be tried for murder if she died, and there was little doubt that she would, one way or another.

CHAPTER TWO

The silent figure on the bed stirred slightly, causing the nurse to look up from the chart she was reading. It was the first outward sign of life in over three weeks. Her condition was listed as critical but stable.

By the next day, she was moving around more, moaning with each movement. "She's moving more regularly now and mumbling some, but nothing makes sense." The duty nurse spoke quietly to the doctor beside her. "She's lucky to be alive."

The doctor nodded solemnly, but didn't speak as he watched the unconscious figure on the bed. Moving away, he spoke over his shoulder. "Let me know if there's any significant change. Her medication stays the same."

Janice Able walked back to the nurses' station, looking through the chart in her hand. "It's amazing she's still alive," she commented with a shake of her head. "The odds certainly weren't in her favor. I know Doctor Weber didn't expect her to pull through."

Nurse Barbra Johnson smiled wistfully. "She's certainly receiving a lot of attention. I wouldn't mind trading places with her for a little while."

"What!?" Janice's head snapped up to stare at the younger woman. "She's been more dead than alive for weeks, and she still might not make it. We won't know how much brain damage she sustained unless or until she wakes up."

"And she has every good-looking doctor in this hospital dancing attendance on her; even the med students and interns have been checking her out. I can't believe the amount of attention she's getting." Barbra sounded almost resentful.

"I don't know how you can even joke about trading places with that poor girl," Janice Able said disdainfully. "She may never regain consciousness. If it weren't for Doctor Weber's caring concern for his patients, she would have been transferred to one of the county facilities weeks ago. Would you want something like that just so you could get the attention of some good-looking doctor?"

"Oh, that's not what I meant," Barbra dismissed Janice's argument with a wave of her hand. "I'd just like to have the attention she's been getting. If you were honest, you'd agree with me."

"I'd do no such thing," Janice answered hotly. "If you'd think less about the doctors and more about your patients, you would be a much better nurse. Marrying a handsome doctor isn't a good reason to become a nurse."

Barbra laughed, "Maybe not, but it's certainly better than most. My mother always said it was just as easy to fall in love with a rich man as it is a poor man. Being a nurse puts me in the right place to meet that rich man. Besides, it will give us something in common later in life."

The older woman sniffed disapprovingly. "I became a nurse to help people, not to find a rich husband. Right now we have patients who need tending, so let's get busy." She turned and walked away, her rigid back expressing her disapproval. If this was a prime example of the new breed of nurses, the profession was in a lot of trouble.

Barbra watched her walk away, unconvinced that the only reason Janice Able had become a nurse was to help people. More than once she'd seen the older woman staring after Doctor Weber, hunger written all over her face. *The man has to be as blind as a bat if he doesn't know how Janice feels about him,* she thought. *Why she doesn't just tell him is beyond me.*

Barbra enjoyed the influx of new doctors that were always coming to work and learn from Doctor Weber, but she needed to find the right one soon. She wasn't getting any younger, while the doctors fresh out of med school seemed to be getting younger and younger. There were two who had caught her eye, and they weren't among the baby-doctors as she called the interns who rotated through the hospital.

Doctors Dean and Riley were prime examples of what she

was looking for. They already had their careers established, and weren't burdened by a wife. She would love to become either Mrs. Dean or Mrs. Riley. She shrugged. It really didn't matter which to her. Then she wouldn't have to put up with the likes of Janice Able who insisted the only reason to become a nurse was to help people.

Both men had recently come to work and learn from Doctor Weber. Barbra was hoping to capture the attention of one or both of them. She gave a wistful sigh. It would be ideal to have both men dancing attendance on her.

Helping people is all well and good, Barbra thought, but in reality, nursing is plain hard work with very little appreciation. People need incentives and benefits to do the job. For her, marrying a doctor was the benefit and the incentive all rolled into one.

"She's got quite an attitude going there." Someone behind her spoke up.

Barbra whirled around, staring at the man standing in the shadows. "You startled me. I didn't see you. You shouldn't sneak up on people."

He laughed. "Didn't sneak, I've been standing here watching. Most people can't miss me. Wish I wasn't quite so big."

Her light eyes skimmed over his large frame. Sure, he was big and good looking, and he was a doctor. But after one date, he hadn't asked her out again. At first she had wondered what she'd done wrong, but that seemed to be standard operating procedure for him. In the short time he'd been at the hospital, he had asked every unmarried nurse out, even a few of the married ones. She hadn't heard of anyone he'd asked out a second time. What, or who, he was looking for was a mystery, and she'd given up trying to figure it out. There were more fish in the sea. She wasn't going to waste time on someone who wasn't interested.

"Well, I need to look, um, keep busy," she changed her wording, "before Janice comes back. I don't have time to visit with you." He chuckled again, but didn't argue. "What are you doing here? Is there something you need? I didn't think you had any patients on our floor."

He shrugged away from the wall he'd been leaning against. "I like to get an early start on the day. Just because I'm not a neurologist doesn't mean I won't be working with some of the patients on this floor, including Jane Doe once she comes out of the coma. I thought I'd check on her as long as I was here. So tell me, how's our Jane Doe doing?" As an orthopedic surgeon, Jerry Edmonds had been one of the many doctors who worked on her when she was first brought to the hospital. It was still to be determined whether she would need more surgery.

"She's beginning to move around some. Doctor Riley isn't sure whether that's a good sign or not." She picked up Jane Doe's chart.

"Well, I hope the poor girl makes it," he commented, before moving down the hall. "See you around, Barb."

"It's Barbra!" she snapped at his retreating back. It was bad enough her mother had given her such a common name, but she hated when people shortened it. She dismissed him with a shake of her head. She was unsure what his game was. He made her nervous, and she didn't know why.

Looking at the chart in her hand, her mind returned to her patient. The girl certainly had enough people working to make sure she pulled through. With the publicity she first got, nearly every employee in the hospital, from the top doc right down to the lowliest custodian, had stopped by at one time or another to check on her. They were all pulling for her. Putting the chart down, she dismissed Jane Doe from her mind along with Doctor Jerry Edmonds.

Morning rounds would begin soon; the hospital was coming alive. If she didn't follow Janice Able's directive to get busy, the woman would be back to assign a *very* menial chore. It was best to pick out something she'd rather be doing. She walked in the opposite direction Janice had gone, hoping to avoid the other woman for the rest of her shift.

Before her shift ended, Doctor Collin Riley walked up to

the desk where she was working. Her heart gave a small leap. Doctor Collin Riley ranked right up at the top of her list of possible husbands. Barbra skimmed her hands down the sides of her uniform, smoothing out any wrinkles that might have appeared while she sat behind the desk.

She chose not to wear the more comfortable, sexless scrubs that most floor nurses wore for the more traditional uniform. But the only thing traditional about Barbra's uniform was the color white. The short, formfitting dress clung to her trim figure, showing off her enhanced curves.

Her makeup was understated, but clearly applied by an accomplished hand. In all, she looked like a high fashion model instead of a nurse. That was exactly the image she wanted to present to the world. She had even changed the spelling of her name to match Barbra Streisand's to draw more attention. The fact that she had a nursing degree was a minor detail in her mind; one that was only for the purpose of putting her in the right place to meet the doctor of her choice.

Unfortunately Barbra's bitchy attitude was etched on her face for all to see even the very doctors she was trying to impress. Most of them kept their distance from her.

"Any change?" Doctor Riley didn't bother looking up or clarifying who he was talking about. Every doctor on staff wanted to be part of Jane Doe's recovery, if in fact she did recover.

"Very little change, Doctor," Barbra kept her voice businesslike as her eyes devoured him hungrily. "She's still moving around some, but she hasn't regained consciousness."

He picked up the chart, walking briskly down the hall to Jane Doe's room. For a long moment he studied her face. Even after all this time, swelling still left her features slightly distorted, the bruises that had been a dark purple, almost black, were fading so only a slight yellowing showed under her pale skin. Her jaw had been broken in three places and was now wired shut. The wires could be removed, but as long as she was unconscious it didn't matter one way or the other. The nurses had tried to get the dirt and dried blood out of her hair, but the exact color was still hard to distinguish.

Moaning softly, the girl moved her head against the pillow. Doctor Riley leaned closer as she mumbled, hoping to catch what she said.

"Did you understand her?" Barbra had followed him into the room, and stood beside him, looking up into his handsome face. "She's mumbling a lot now, but we can't make out what she's saying."

He shook his head. "It's just sounds. We'll have to wait until she wakes up to get anything else."

"Then you're sure she's going to pull through?" Until now, no one would venture a positive guess.

The doctor briefly glanced at Barbra before returning his gaze to the girl in the bed. "I'm not sure about anything where she's concerned. She shouldn't have made it this far, but she has. She still might have some brain damage. We'll just have to wait and see." A worried frown creased his dark brow.

Barbra watched him thoughtfully as he left the ward a few minutes later. *Why can't he be that interested in me,* she questioned silently? *I can do a lot more for him than that girl.* Her thoughts weren't so charitable toward the unconscious woman now.

"Wipe your chin, Barbra, you're drooling." A teasing voice spoke from behind her.

Turning sharply, Barbra glared at the other woman. "Knock it off, Courtney. I wasn't drooling."

"If you say so." Courtney Crammer's teasing fell flat. Barbra was good at teasing others, but didn't like it when the tables were turned on her. "I happen to agree with you though. He is one fine hunk."

"I didn't think you'd notice," Barbra retorted, "since you're still carrying a torch for your ex-fiancé." Her grin was malicious as she watched Courtney's lips thin in aggravation. "What are you doing down here anyway? Shouldn't you be working?"

Courtney chose to ignore Barbra's taunts. Retaliating would only cause more trouble. For now, she had to get along

11

with the woman. "We get to take breaks, even in ICU. I just came down to see how our favorite patient is doing."

Barbra glared at her again. "I told you it wasn't necessary to keep running down here all the time. I'll let you know if there's any change. I can take care of her just fine without you checking up on me."

"Oh, get over yourself, Barbra, I'm not checking up on you. She was my patient for two weeks in ICU. I just like to see if she's improving."

Barbra continued to glare at Courtney for a long moment. Then her bad mood evaporated as quickly as it started. "I'm sorry; it's been a rough night." She smiled sweetly.

Courtney looked around to see if someone had walked up behind her. That sweet smile was put on display only when a handsome man was around, or when she wanted something. Since they were alone, Courtney knew it meant Barbra wanted something from her. She didn't have to wait long to discover what it was.

"Ted called earlier. He wants to spend the day with me. I invited him over for breakfast. I didn't think you'd mind finding something to do for a little while."

Courtney clenched her jaw, biting back an angry retort. When Barbra first moved to Phoenix six months ago, Courtney had invited her to share her apartment. At the time, it seemed like a godsend. She had been struggling to make ends meet after her fiancé walked out, leaving her with a stack of bills and the entire rent to pay on the lavish apartment he'd insisted they have. She was glad to be rid of the bum, but Barbra wasn't proving to be such a prize either. Granted, she paid her half of the rent and utilities, and wasn't running up credit card bills Courtney would eventually have to pay. That was the extent of their compatibility though.

Barbra had taken over the apartment like it was hers, treating Courtney like an unwanted guest. Now that they were on the same shift, she drove Courtney out of the apartment with one excuse or another several days a week. It was going to come to a screeching halt! "Damn it, Barbra," she finally answered in a low voice. "This is the third time this week you've come up with a reason I can't go home to my own apartment. I'm getting tired of it."

"I know, and I'm sorry." Barbra's New York accent became more pronounced when she poured on the charm, aggravating Courtney even more. "I wouldn't ask again, but you know how hard it is for me to say 'No' to Ted." Soft pink stole up her cheeks. She was the only person Courtney knew who could blush on command. "You can join us, if you want."

Courtney snorted. "No thanks, I'm not into that sort of thing. This is the last time, Barbra; remember I live there, too." Without waiting for a reply, she stormed away. Courtney hated being used, but short of kicking Barbra out she didn't know what else to do.

If only Barbra would marry Ted, that would solve the problem. The thought gave her a moment of unrest, and she quickly pushed it aside. Besides, she knew Barbra didn't want to marry Ted. He wasn't a doctor or lawyer. In fact, he isn't a professional of any kind. Ted built houses, which isn't a bad thing, unless you happen to have your sights set on a doctor.

Men can be so blind, she thought irritably. He ignored Barbra's manipulative nature, choosing to see only the sweet side she presented to the men who came into her sphere. But Barbra couldn't maintain her sweet act forever. She was always on the prowl for a rich doctor to marry. When one finally paid her the attention she thought she deserved, she'd dump Ted in a heartbeat. Then he would see the real Barbra.

Courtney sighed, "Why do guys who are genuinely nice always fall for women who use them for a doormat?" she wondered out loud.

~~~

Jane Doe's chart read like a medical textbook: Fractured skull, hematoma, broken jaw, broken arm, three fractured ribs, a ruptured spleen, a multitude of cuts and bruises. Not to mention dehydration and near heat stroke when she was first brought in. To get her this far, she'd had two operations and there was no telling how much, if any, brain damage had been

13

done. Any number of these things should have killed her. Damn it! "What does it take to get rid of you?" *he muttered softly as he stared down at the woman in the bed. Something had to be done before that little pipsqueak panicked, giving them away. When this was all over, he was going to enjoy doing away with him. Until then, the little bastard had his uses, and it wasn't all that hard to keep him in line. Replacing the chart, he quietly left the floor.*

~~~

"You've got to do something." The slight man's voice squeaked nervously. "She's beginning to wake up. I thought you wanted to prevent that."

"I do, damn it," the big man growled. "But I can't just walk in there and snuff her. There are too damn many nurses around. I have to be careful. I'm not going to get caught."

Swallowing the fear in his throat, the young man pushed on. "But you've been here long enough, you should do something. I've seen you go into her room, and no one stops you. You even talk to the other doctors and nurses about her? What are you waiting for?"

"I'm waiting for the right opportunity. It would have looked rather suspicious if something happened to her the minute I start working here. If I plan this right, she can have a relapse, and no one will suspect a thing."

"How...how do you plan on doing it?" He was anxious to know the details, yet repelled at the same time.

"It's got to look natural or at least like an accidental mix up in her meds. I'll have to see what comes up." He enjoyed watching the young man shudder.

The opportunity presented itself just two nights later.

~~~

Alone at the nurses station, Barbra propped her feet on a desk drawer, leaning back in the chair to relax. Everything was peaceful and quiet, just the way she liked it. Patients were settled in, visitors were long gone, and doctors' rounds didn't start for several hours. Even Janice Able managed to relax a little during the wee small hours of the night. As long as

14

Doctor Weber isn't around, Barbra corrected herself with a mocking grin.

Before Barbra could get too comfortable, Janice stepped out of a room down the hall. "Barbra, I need you down here, STAT." Without getting up, Barbra turned to the bank of monitors on the wall. Everything was as it should be. Patient call buttons weren't even lit, so what's Able up to now? she wondered. Barbra knew better than to ignore the summons though. Janice could cause all sorts of trouble for her. Setting down the can of diet Coke, she slowly headed down the hall.

Stepping quietly out of the stairwell, the shadowed figure watched silently as the nurse disappeared into a room. He couldn't believe his good fortune. The damn little weasel was right, he thought, time was running out. He had to do something, and do it soon. With cat-like steps, he hurried to Jane Doe's room. He didn't know how much time he had, but he had to try something. If someone saw him, he would just explain that he'd come in to see a patient on another floor, and decided to check in on Jane Doe. No one would question him.

"For one small lady, you've caused me a lot of trouble," he whispered to the unconscious figure in the bed. "After tonight, I won't have to worry about you any longer." He pulled a syringe from the deep pocket of his lab coat, injecting insulin into the IV tube already in her arm. "Sweet dreams, sweetheart," he said in his best Bogart impression.

The nurse's station was still empty when he slipped out of the room minutes later and hurried silently back to the stairs. She was still in a coma; this would finish her off. Maybe the nurse would stay away from the station long enough to miss any warnings the monitors might issue. He'd thought about disconnecting them, but that would be too obvious. Even if the nurse returned in time to notice the monitors, he didn't think there would be enough time to save her.

The door to the stairs clicked closed as Barbra returned to the nurses' station. "Some emergency," she grumbled, too angry at Janice to notice the soft sound. "She could have handled that by herself. She's going to cry wolf one too many times, and no one's going to answer." Picking up her pop can, she took a deep swallow. "She just likes to throw her weight around." She snickered. "She has plenty to throw, too." A nasty smile curled her lips.

Janice Able wasn't fat, just "pleasingly plump", but Barbra enjoyed making fun of the extra roll she carried around her waist. Behind Janice's back, of course. Barbra was openly contemptuous of almost everyone, but she wouldn't openly make fun of her boss. She wouldn't take chances with her job.

When a monitor set up a racket, she slammed the can down hard enough that Coke splashed out of the spout. "Now what!" She turned to the bank of monitors. Jane Doe's cardiac monitor was squealing. This time Barbra moved quickly. Since being moved from ICU her condition had remained stable. Barbra didn't want that to change on her shift.

"Get a crash cart!" Janice reached the room just ahead of Barbra. "Get a doctor up here, and call Doctor Weber."

Rushing back to the station, Barbra cursed her bad luck. "If something happens to that girl now, they'll blame me." She placed the call to Doctor Weber first. This was his star patient, he'd be furious if he wasn't called immediately. Then she called down to emergency. At two in the morning, the only doctors on duty were in the ER. Emergency codes sounded in the hall bringing several nurses rushing to help. No one wanted to lose Jane Doe now.

Doctor Bakker from the ER worked furiously alongside Janice, each issuing orders to the others in the room. Blood was drawn in an attempt to pinpoint what had happened. Only minutes had passed since Barbra's call, when Doctor Weber charged into the room taking over the proceedings. "What happened here? When I left tonight, she was fine."

Before anyone could answer a nurse stepped into the room with the results of the blood tests. "This doesn't make sense," she announced to the room in general, a bewildered frown creasing her forehead. "Her blood sugar is down to twenty."

"They made a mistake, tell them to run it again," Doctor Weber barked, not bothering to look up.

"They ran it twice, Doctor, there's no mistake."

Both doctors spoke at once. "Insulin!"

All eyes shifted to Barbra. "Don't look at me! I didn't do anything to her."

Doctor Weber looked at her a moment longer, then turned back to the unconscious woman on the bed. "I want a glucose IV, STAT." For the moment they forgot about Barbra, but she was certain as soon as Jane Doe was stable again, Doctor Weber would accuse her of trying to kill his patient.

As the glucose began to work, Jane Doe's heart rate and blood pressure climbed back to normal, her breathing became less labored. Doctor Weber continued to watch her for several long minutes, wondering who would do this and why. She'd been improving, and this could set her back. He was still uncertain if she would ever regain consciousness.

Finally satisfied that she was stable, at least for now, Doctor Weber led the others from the room. Turning to Barbra, he asked the questions plaguing him. "How did someone get in here and fill her full of insulin? Where were you tonight?" He fired off his questions without giving her a chance to answer.

"I don't know anything about it," Barbra snapped. "I didn't do anything wrong." Her face was flushed with anger.

With an effort, Doctor Weber calmed down, telling himself he'd learn a lot more if he were friendly. "Now, don't go getting your back up. No one is accusing you of anything. We're just trying to find out what happened. She almost died."

"I know that, but it wasn't my fault. I didn't do anything wrong." Barbra was still on the defensive, and looking for someone else to blame.

"Well, you might want to stop protesting so much. People might think you have something to hide." His voice held an edge of suspicion behind the teasing words. "Just tell me what happened. Did you see anyone on the floor any time before she crashed?"

Her lips clamped tight, Barbra shook her head. She hated being grilled. "I stepped away from the desk to help Janice with a patient. When I came back the monitors started going crazy." She started to repeat that she'd done nothing wrong, but stopped herself in time.

"Has anyone been asking questions about her?" Doctor Weber pressed.

"You mean other than the entire hospital staff, half the police department, and a dozen or so reporters? Even on the graveyard shift, people stop by to see how she's doing."

He ignored her sarcasm. She wasn't stupid enough to fill her own patient with insulin while she was on duty, but maybe she saw or heard something without realizing it. The police needed to be called, but he didn't like them haunting his halls. "Who came around tonight asking about her? Anyone you haven't seen before?"

Barbra thought for a moment. "I don't think anyone stopped by tonight. It's been very quiet. At least, it *was* quiet." Something tugged at the back of her mind, but anger wiped the thought away.

CHAPTER THREE

Three hours after leaving the hospital, he returned, feeling smug and confident. He was a little early for his shift, but not enough to draw attention. Checking on patients was always a good excuse if anyone questioned him.

After leaving the hospital the night before, he'd been unable to sleep, planning his next move. With her out of the way, he could begin his money-making endeavor again. This time he'd leave that little weasel out of the equation.

Giving himself a mental shake, he pushed the elevator button. He had to remember to act surprised and upset when told about what had happened to 'Jane Doe'. I should get an Oscar for that performance, he told himself.

Lost in his own thoughts, he paid little attention to the conversations as people entered the elevator behind him. Finally their words penetrated his thoughts, jarring him out of his reverie.

"I can't believe someone actually tried to kill her, right here in the hospital," a young intern was saying. "They don't have any idea who did it either."

"I heard Doctor Weber is on a rampage," his companion put in. "He's got a guard posted, and no one goes in her room without Weber's okay."

He couldn't believe his own ears. Rage boiled up inside him. How could this be true? He didn't need to be told who they were talking about. Only Jane Doe received this kind of attention. She was still alive, and still a threat to him.

At the next floor, he escaped the confines of the elevator. If he didn't get away from these people, he'd go mad. An empty room provided the privacy he needed, and he paced around the bed trying unsuccessfully to calm down. "She's like a damn cat with nine lives," he whispered fiercely. "She's going to run out of them real fast, and I'm going to be the one to help her."

This did complicate things though. Ben Weber wouldn't

take kindly to this sort of thing happening in his hospital. From now on she'll be well-guarded, making it difficult to reach her a second time. *But I've always loved a challenge*, he thought, *I'm not through with you yet, Doctor Brianna Sanders.*

~~~

A security guard was temporarily stationed outside Jane Doe's room. Only those authorized by Doctor Weber were allowed to enter her room. Barbra hoped the woman didn't have another emergency. No one would get past the guard in time to save her.

Within minutes, the entire hospital had known of the attempt on Jane Doe's life. Once again she was the object of everyone's curiosity and concern. People stopped by the ward just to see how she was.

Fuming, Barbra stomped into the breakroom to escape for a minute. She was a victim as much as Jane Doe. Whoever did this left her holding the bag. She'd seen the questioning stares as people wondered what part she'd played in this little melodrama. *Jane Doe had survived, but I'm still looked at with suspicion,* she continued to seethe. In her eyes, that made her the real victim. This could hurt her career, but more important, it could hurt her chances of marrying one of the doctors. They wouldn't look kindly towards her if she were accused of trying to harm a patient.

Offense was the best defense, she decided, complaining to anyone who would listen. "I can't believe someone could get through security so easily. No one is safe here. If I hadn't been called away from the station, I probably wouldn't be here to talk about it now." She gave a delicate shudder. "If he wanted to hurt Jane Doe that bad, he wouldn't let the fact that I was there stop him. Something needs to be done about security during the middle of the night. We can't let every kook walk in here any time of the day or night."

Placing the blame on someone else had always worked for her, now should be no different. *Maybe Janice Able was working with this murderous person,* she thought. *After all, she had called me away at just the right time so this other person could administer the lethal dose of insulin. She couldn't put that theory out, but it was something to think about. Maybe Janice needed watching.*

~~~

Courtney heard about the attempt on Jane Doe shortly after it happened, but she wasn't able to leave ICU until the end of her shift. She hurried out to the car so she could get Barbra's first-hand account. As she drew closer to the car, Courtney could see the haggard expression on Barbra's face, her light blue eyes brimming with tears. Nearly losing a patient was hard, but to have someone attempt to murder your patient almost under your nose would be devastating. Feeling responsible was an emotion Courtney would never have attributed to her roommate though. Barbra hid behind a mask of unconcern, acting totally self-serving. This was the first time Courtney saw the human side of her.

"Hi, kiddo. How are you holding up?" She patted Barbra's shoulder sympathetically. With anyone else, she would have given her a hug, but a pat was as personal as she could get with Barbra.

Sighing heavily, Barbra shook her head. "I can*not* believe this night. I don't know where security was when this guy got through, but they really screwed up." Her harsh tone of voice belied the shattered appearance she put forth.

"It could have been much worse," Courtney said. "You were there when the monitors went off. That's what counts."

"Oh, I know, but no one else sees it that way. Doctor Weber even tried to blame me."

"Barbra, this isn't about you!" Courtney stated in disgust. "Somehow, someone got into *our* hospital, and tried to kill that girl."

Barbra looked at her briefly before returning her gaze to the ground, tears swimming in her eyes again. "Don't you think I know that? Whoever did this was on *my* floor, on *my* shift. Jane Doe was *my* responsibility. How could this happen?" Once again it was my, my, my.

21

Courtney reached over, giving Barbra's arm a brief squeeze of support. She's human after all, Courtney thought. Maybe, she qualified. "You did everything you could. Now it's everyone's job to make sure this monster doesn't get back in to try again."

"Damn straight about that!" Barbra snapped fiercely, her spunk returning with a vengeance. "I'm not taking the blame for this happening again. It could cost me my job!"

That's more like the Barbra I've come to know, Courtney thought. Barbra's concern was only for herself. "I heard Doctor Weber put a guard outside her room, and I'm sure the police will put one on her as well. No one is going to be able to do this again. It's over now. Relax today and try to forget about everything."

"That's exactly what I plan on doing," Barbra agreed. "I called Ted, and he insisted on coming over. He felt so bad for me." She turned to Courtney, putting on that phony charm. "I knew you wouldn't mind if he came over after everything I've been through tonight."

Courtney released a heavy sigh. *You walked into that one*, she told herself. "I've had a long night, too," she said, refusing to be kicked out of her own apartment again, "As soon as I get something to eat, I'm going to bed, so I won't bother you." She shot a glance at Barbra, daring her to argue.

Barbra considered putting up a fuss, but quickly reconsidered. "That's fine. We might not stay there anyway." Her New York accent grated on Courtney's already frayed nerves.

Ted was waiting for them when they drove into the apartment parking lot. Barbra leaped out of the car before Courtney shut the engine off. "Oh, Teddy, I'm so glad you're here." She rushed up to him, wrapping her arms around his neck, crushing herself against his broad chest. For a slight moment, he paused before closing his arms around her.

Courtney followed slowly behind, embarrassed by the way Barbra draped herself all over the man. Another more elemental emotion reared its ugly head, but she pushed it aside without examining it too closely.

Looking uncomfortable, Ted patted Barbra's back. "It's all over now, Barbra. She's going to be all right. You got to her in time."

Courtney raised an eyebrow. That wasn't exactly the way it happened. But who was she to disillusion the poor guy. If he wanted to believe his girl was a hero that was fine by her.

"It was just awful, Teddy. I'm going to have nightmares for weeks." Barbra shuddered delicately. Courtney didn't miss the man's grimace. Maybe things weren't as rosy as Barbra let on. "I don't know if I'll be able to sleep at all. A killer was actually on my floor! If I hadn't left the desk for *just* a minute, he might have killed me before going into her room." A single tear squeezed out between her dark lashes. "I'll never be able to sleep without you." Her stage whisper was loud enough to reach Courtney.

Ted actually blushed as he met Courtney's gaze over the top of Barbra's head. "I can't stay with you today. I told you that on the phone. I have to go to work."

"But you're the boss, Teddy," Barbra protested. "You can do whatever you want."

"That isn't the way I run my business. I said I would stop by on my way to the next job, but I have to work."

"That's what employees are for," Barbra whined. "You don't have to watch them every minute. I need you."

Ted sighed wearily. "I own the company; it's my job to make sure each job gets done right, and on time. I'm on my way across town now."

"Oh, Teddy," she pouted. "You can't abandon me." She clung to him like a small child.

Ted cringed, gritting his teeth in aggravation. Even his mother didn't get away with calling him 'Teddy' any longer. But Barbra thought she was being cute, and it would help her to get her own way. He tried again to extricate himself from her cloying embrace. "I'm sorry about what happened last night, and I'm glad nothing happened to you, but I can't stay."

Courtney headed for the apartment, whistling a happy

tune. She'd heard enough to boost her spirits for an entire month. Ted wasn't as enamored with Barbra as she claimed. She should be madder than hell. Not only did Barbra continually use her, but she lied as well. Somehow she couldn't quite force any anger to the surface. She wondered how many times Barbra told her Ted was coming over to spend the day when he was actually there only a few minutes.

Okay, so that makes me mad, she thought, but Ted wasn't begging Barbra to marry him. In fact, Courtney doubted he had even brought the subject up. She couldn't stop the happy giggle from bubbling out. She didn't stop to analyze or question her feelings. For now it was enough just to be happy about something.

~~~

"You didn't finish her off either," the younger man stated with a gleeful smirk on his face. The big guy wasn't perfect after all, he thought with satisfaction. This should put him in his place. "You should have stayed around to make sure she was finished. I guess I'm not the only one who's a little squeamish about murder."

In three giant strides the big man was across the room, his beefy hand gripping the younger man's throat. "Would you like me to show you just how squeamish I am?" he asked softly. "It wouldn't take much to snap this scrawny little neck of yours." His fingers squeezed tighter with each word. They were in one of the empty rooms where no one would interrupt them for the moment.

The young man's eyes bulged as his fingers clawed at the big hand gripping his throat. Garbled sounds came out of his mouth. Slowly the fingers relaxed, and he was able to gulp air into his lungs as he collapsed against the wall, sliding down to sit on the floor. He could feel the hard glare of his boss as he stood over him.

"She would have died if that damn nurse had stayed away a few minutes longer," he snarled. "I had no control over that. That damn monitor!" he muttered. Turning it off would have been a dead giveaway that someone had tried to kill her again.

As it turned out, they knew anyway. He'd wanted it to look like a relapse, but that wasn't going to happen now.

The other man was temporarily forgotten as he paced around the small room. He had to make sure she died, but getting at her was going to be twice as hard now. Staying around to make sure she was dead wouldn't have been a good idea, but the little bastard is right, he told himself. He should have done something different. The admission only fueled his anger against the other man.

Shifting his attention back to the man still cowering on the floor, his dark eyes large with fright, power flowed through him. This was what he liked to see. For now though, he needed the little weasel to be his eyes and ears. People tended to overlook the guy. He could learn all sorts of useful information if he'd only try. There was plenty of time to get rid of him later.

Reaching out a helping hand, the smaller man cringed away, anticipating a blow. "I'm sorry I lost my temper. The two of us have to stick together. We've been in this right from the start, and two heads are better than one, so let's work together and figure out a way to finish her off permanently."

~~~

Three days later, six weeks after being brought into the hospital more dead than alive, Jane Doe opened her eyes!

25

CHAPTER FOUR

For several long minutes she laid still, only her eyes moving around the unfamiliar room. The nurse's aide worked silently giving her a sponge bath, unaware her patient was no longer unconscious.

"Could I have a drink of water?" The voice was a hoarse croak, sounding like a machine badly in need of lubrication.

The young aide jumped at the sound, splashing soapy water over the woman in the bed. "Oh, my God!" She clutched her chest as if to keep her heart from jumping out. "Oh, oh, oh." She seemed to run in place for a moment before running from the room and shouting for a doctor.

Confused and startled, Jane Doe tried to call out to the young girl, but something prevented her from opening her mouth. The beginning of panic gripped her. What was wrong with her? Why couldn't she open her mouth?

Before hysteria could set in, doctors and nurses rushed into the room, all of them talking at once. "How are you feeling?" "Do you need anything?" "Can you tell us your name?" With just a look an older man silenced them, before turning to her. "I'm Doctor Weber. How are you feeling?"

Her mouth felt like it was stuffed with cotton, and she still couldn't open it. She wanted to tell him that, but when she tried to speak the only sound that came out was a hoarse croak. She didn't know who all these people were, but since he was a doctor she assumed she was in a hospital somewhere.

"Get her some water!" The doctor snapped, and several people rushed to do his bidding. Within minutes a pitcher of ice water, a glass and straw were produced. Doctor Weber took the glass from the nurse. Fitting the straw between the wires holding her jaws shut, he cautioned her softly, "Just sip a little bit at a time." There was a chuckle in his voice as she tried to empty the glass in a single gulp. "There's plenty here." Draining the glass, she pointed to the pitcher again, not yet

26

trusting her voice.

With her thirst temporarily quenched, Jane Doe laid back against the pillow. The small exertion left her drained.

Doctor Weber watched her for a long moment as her eyes drifted shut. Medical training told him she was just resting, and hadn't slipped back into the coma. Still, he was reluctant to leave for fear she wouldn't wake up again. Finally he turned to the others in the room. "We'll let her sleep for now." His gruff voice was choked with emotions. "When she wakes up again we can talk to her." He started to leave the room.

"Wait!" The mumbled word stopped him from letting the door close. He stepped back into the room to see his patient awake, her eyes wide with fright.

Doctor Weber came back to her bedside. "You're going to be all right now," he assured her. "We're taking good care of you."

"Where am I? Why can't I open my mouth?" The questions tumbled out on top of each other. Her words were muffled and slightly garbled.

"Your jaw was broken; we had to wire it shut allowing it to mend. Do you remember what happened to you?"

Jane Doe searched through her blank memory, trying to remember something. Finally she shook her head, panic setting in again.

Doctor Weber heaved a weary sigh. It wasn't unusual for a victim to block out the traumatic events. All the same, he had been hoping she could name her assailant. He wanted the bastard caught. That would come in time, he assured himself. He didn't want to push her today.

Trying to lighten the mood, he patted the young woman's hand. "What's your name? Is there someone we can call for you?" In the time she'd been in the hospital, no one had come forward to identify her.

She didn't answer immediately as she tried to remember something, anything. Panic tightened its grip on her when she realized there was nothing to remember. Her memory was blank. Tears swan in her large turquoise-colored eyes as she looked up at him. "I don't know my name! What happened to me? Why can't I remember anything?" She clutched at his hand.

Another disappointment. Doctor Weber patted her hand consolingly. "Your memory will return," he assured her. "Don't try to force it. You've only been awake for a few minutes. Try to get some sleep. Things will look better when you wake up again." He would have walked away from the bed, but she continued to cling to his hand.

"Please! Tell me what happened. Where am I?"

Postponing the inevitable until she was stronger was not an option. Her rising panic wasn't good for her either. "You were found in the desert, and brought to the hospital in Phoenix. You had no identification on you so we couldn't call your family." This was a fairly safe version of the truth.

"Was I in an accident? How did I get in the desert?" Why was she in the desert in the dead of summer? Somehow she knew it was summer.

"We don't have any of the details. You were left there." Again, this was the truth as far as it went. He was omitting a great deal.

"Why was I left in the desert? Who would do that?" He wasn't making any sense.

Doctor Weber patted her hand. "There's plenty of time for all your questions, right now you need to rest." Already her strength was ebbing away, her grip little more than a feathery touch on his hand. He disentangled his fingers from hers. Before he was out the door, Jane Doe had drifted into an uneasy sleep, her mind struggling to put the pieces together.

~~~

He could feel the excitement as he walked down the corridor from surgery. It only took a few minutes to discover the cause. 'Jane Doe' was awake. A light sweat broke out on his forehead, his hands balled into fists to keep them from shaking.

"Why can't the damn bitch just die?" he muttered as he hurried to the doctor's lounge. But there wasn't time to think

28

about that right now. Depending on how much she could tell them, the police could be looking for him at any minute. He needed to get out of there as quickly and inconspicuously as possible. He had no intention of being anywhere near the hospital when the police decided to have a little talk with him. In fact, if he hurried, he would be out of the country before they realized he wasn't at the hospital.

Quickly changing out of his scrubs, he headed for the elevator, forcing himself to walk slowly. It wouldn't be good to draw attention now. He had always known she might wake up before he could finish her off, and had planned accordingly. As long as he could make it to the airport, he was home free. No one knew he had a pilot's license and airplane of his own, not even that damn little weasel. When they came looking for him, they wouldn't find out about them either. The plane was safely registered under another name, the same name he had used on his pilot's license and passport.

He congratulated himself on his foresight. Few people would have thought ahead as he'd done three years ago when he got his license. Now he could escape this mess without anyone being the wiser. He regretted the fact that he couldn't finish off that little bastard first though. He gave a fatalistic shrug. He couldn't have everything.

Reviewing his plans to leave the country, he paid little attention to the excited babble going on around him. Everyone was excited about 'Jane Doe'. Everyone, that is, but him.

"Sure is a shame about that Jane Doe, isn't it doc?" An elderly janitor stopped beside him at the elevator capturing his attention.

"Shame?" One dark brow lifted inquiringly. *Damn straight it's a shame*, he thought, but he didn't think anyone else would agree.

"You haven't heard then?" He enjoyed being able to tell a doctor something. After a meaningful pause, he gave his gray head a sad shake. "I was cleaning up outside her room when I heard Doctor Weber tellin' Ms. Able that poor girl doesn't know who she is or what happened to her." He gave his bushy head another shake. "I sure do feel sorry for her."

Relief flooded through him, causing his knees to go weak. Her death would be better, but this reprieve gave him some breathing room. "That really is too bad." He managed to keep the relief out of his voice. "I've been in surgery all morning. Thanks for telling me." With an absent nod to the old man, he walked off, no longer in a rush to leave the hospital.

~~~

Doctor Weber was standing at the nurses' station going through several charts when Sergeant Booker stepped off the elevator. Growling with frustration, Rex Booker started down the corridor, his long strides eating up the distance. "Doctor Weber, I'm a very busy man," he started without preamble. "I don't have time to play games."

"Nor do I, Sergeant. What's on your mind?" Doctor Weber filed the charts he was working on, and walked away from the station, forcing the Sergeant to follow him.

"You called me, Doc. Remember? You said Jane Doe had regained consciousness. I dropped everything so I could get down here to talk to her. Now your nurses tell me I can't see her. What kind of game are you playing?" By the time he finished speaking, his face was red with anger.

"I said Jane Doe is conscious, which she is. Right now she is asleep, as in taking a nap. I'm sure you've taken one of those a time or two." He enjoyed needling the policeman. Even though they were technically on the same side, the two men didn't see eye to eye on the treatment of victims or suspects.

Sergeant Booker drew a deep breath through gritted teeth, trying to quiet his already jagged nerves. Too much coffee, he thought, before speaking again. "All right, Doc, when can I talk to her?" His voice was deadly calm belying the dangerous mood he was in.

Through toying with the younger man, Doctor Weber drew to a halt, his steely gaze held the Sergeant's. "She fell asleep before I called you." He consulted his watch. "That was over an hour ago. I think it's a safe bet she'll wake up before too much longer. We have a few things to discuss before then. Let's talk in my office." He strode off again preventing the Sergeant from objecting.

Settled in the doctor's plain office, Sergeant Booker examined his surroundings, nodding approval at the no-nonsense decor. The desk was made of mahogany and obviously expensive. It was also twice the size of his metal desk at the station. Nearly every inch of the glossy surface was covered with papers, files, X-ray envelopes, and other paraphernalia he couldn't identify. The rest of the office wasn't ostentatious as some of the doctors' offices he'd been in.

Turning his attention back to the doctor, Rex ignored the fact that the doctor studied him as thoroughly as he had been studying his surroundings. "You had something you wanted to discuss with me?" One light eyebrow lifted slightly.

"When she regained consciousness, she didn't remember anything of her past, including her name." Doctor Weber picked up the forgotten coffee cup on his desk, ignoring the fact that the coffee was several hours' old and stone cold. He lifted the cup in a silent question to the Sergeant who shook his head.

"You told me that on the phone, Doc. You also said it was probably just temporary. I checked with a doctor friend of mine; he agreed that in time, she will probably regain her memory. She could wake up from this little nap, and remember everything."

"Almost everything," Doctor Weber qualified. "The attack and what led up to it may never come back to her. That isn't unusual."

"He told me that too, but I have to ask the questions anyway. I have to find out what she does and doesn't remember. I'm guessing she knew who did this to her."

"That's what I wanted to discuss with you. I was hoping she could tell us who did this and why. I want the SOB who tried to kill her right here in my hospital. When she couldn't remember anything I didn't give her the details of what happened."

The sergeant nodded understanding. "That's fine; I'd rather be the one to tell her. If the details shake lose any memory, I want to see her reaction."

"Precisely my point, Sergeant," Doctor Weber stated. "The details might not be so good for her right now. She isn't strong enough to handle too many shocks, and I don't want her to have a relapse."

"Neither do I Doc, but we can't keep the details from her. She needs to know that someone tried to kill her." He paused for effect. "Twice. Now that she's conscious, it could push that bastard to even more desperate measures."

"How much more desperate do you want?" the doctor snapped. "He had the balls to come into a hospital room, and attempt to kill her. Any number of people could have walked in on him."

"At two in the morning?" Sergeant Booker left the question hanging for only a moment before answering his own question. "I'd say he felt pretty safe. It doesn't take a mental giant to know there's very little activity going on at that hour."

Reluctantly, Doctor Weber agreed. Any other time of day or night there would have been staff around as well as visitors coming and going. Midnight until three or four in the morning was the slowest time possible. "That time of night, the main doors are locked. You can only enter through the ER. So why wasn't he stopped by security or one of the staff?" The question had been plaguing him since the attempt on Jane Doe. No one had been able to answer it though.

"Not if he fit in around here." The Sergeant's voice interrupted his dark thoughts.

Doctor Weber nearly came out of his chair. "Are you suggesting it was one of my employees?! That's..."

"Relax, Doc, I'm not saying one of your people did it, although I don't rule them out either. I'm just saying that it wouldn't be very hard for someone to dress up like a doctor, nurse, or any other hospital worker, and just waltz in. No one would stop them. Just because the rest of the hospital is quiet in the middle of the night, the ER is still busy. Someone looking like they belong would go unnoticed."

Doctor Weber frowned. "If someone unknown came in here in the middle of the night, I'd like to think they would at least be challenged."

"So you're saying your security team knows every single person who is authorized to do business here?" Sergeant Booker asked, lifting one light eyebrow. "That's some team you have. I'd be interested in hiring them for the sheriff's department."

"I get your point," Doctor Weber sighed wearily. "I just never considered this place unsafe for our patients before."

"For the right amount of money, a witness isn't even safe in protective custody." Even he could hear how cynical the words sounded. Shaking off the dark mood that had descended upon him, he turned his attention back to the matter at hand. "Until Jane Doe regains her memory, she's pretty much at the mercy of the people around her. How long do you think this amnesia will last? What can we do to make her remember?" He didn't want the SOB running loose any more than Doctor Weber did. Until he was in custody, she wasn't safe.

Ben Weber ran his hand across his face. Damn, he was feeling old, defeated. Even after all the progress medical science had made over the last one hundred years there was still a great deal that was a complete mystery. "I don't know how long the amnesia will last," he finally answered. "As I said earlier, she could wake up and remember everything, or..." His voice trailed off without finishing his sentence. "There isn't anything we can do to hurry it up. We'll be running tests to see if there is any permanent brain damage. Until we know more, I can't make any prognosis."

"You're supposed to be one of the best neurologists around. Why don't you know?" Frustration made Sergeant Booker's voice harsh.

"In case you haven't noticed, Sergeant, medicine isn't an exact science. The brain is one of the least understood organs of the body. I'm betting she will regain her memory, but I won't put money on when."

"I've seen accident victims who were unable to remember anything about the crash or immediately before and after," the Sergeant put in thoughtfully. "They don't forget the rest of their lives though."

Doctor Weber nodded agreement. "The mind tends to block out the traumatic event as a form of self-protection."

"So why is this different?" Sergeant Booker questioned. "Why doesn't she remember anything?"

"It could a combination of this self-protection along with swelling of the brain from her injuries. She may never remember the beating itself. I believe she will eventually remember who she is along with the rest of her life."

"But you can't guarantee that." It was more a statement than a question.

"There are no guarantees," Doctor Weber admitted reluctantly.

They sat in brooding silence for several moments before Doctor Weber turned back to the Sergeant "I'll let you tell her what happened, but I'm going to be there. If she gets too agitated, you'll have to stop."

Winning the first battle, Sergeant Booker didn't argue with the older man. He would push just as hard as he needed to break through the mental block holding her prisoner. He wanted the bastard.

CHAPTER FIVE

Jane Doe stared up at the ceiling, willing herself not to think because thinking would bring on the panic. In spite of her best efforts, her thoughts returned to the bits and pieces Doctor Weber had told her. She'd been found in the desert, and brought to the hospital in Phoenix. How long had she been in the hospital? Why had she been in the desert? How had she gotten hurt?

Doctor Weber hadn't confirmed her assumption that she'd been in a car accident. He only said no one else was hurt. So why would she go out in the desert alone when she didn't know anything about the desert? But did she know anything about the desert? Once again, she came up against a blank wall. Her thoughts were traveling in circles bringing her back to square one. She didn't know who she was or how she'd been injured.

She had only questions without any answers. Doctor Weber said he would be back to see her, so where was he? Tentatively, she touched the patch of stubble where her head had been shaved. The rest of her hair was much longer. *I need to get my hair cut so I don't look like a freak,* she thought irrelevantly. *Am I that vain,* she wondered? Why do I care what I look like when I don't even know who I am?

The fact that they had to shave part of her hair off meant she'd had a head injury. That could account for the amnesia, she told herself logically. But she didn't know what kind of injury or what other injuries she'd sustained. Running her hands over other parts of her body, they rested on her tender abdomen. Pulling up the hospital gown to look, she gasped at the long incision. She must have had internal injuries as well. A ruptured spleen wasn't uncommon in a car accident, she reasoned, not questioning how she knew this.

A car accident would also account for the yellowing bruises that covered much of her body and the slight swelling left on her face. There was also a small scar on her lip. Had she had a split lip? Was it a result of what happened to her? If she hadn't been in a car accident, how had she been injured? She fingered the small scar.

Before her mind could take her down another path, the door opened to admit Doctor Weber. Relief flooded through her. Maybe now she could get some answers.

"Well, hello there." Doctor Weber smiled at her. "How was your nap? Are you feeling any better?"

"I still don't know who I am, if that's what you're asking." Her words were still mumbled because of the wires holding her jaws immobile. Her gaze drifted to the man who followed Doctor Weber into the room. Instead of a white lab coat or green scrubs, he was wearing tight fitting jeans and a western shirt with the sleeves rolled up to reveal deeply tanned, well-muscled arms. In place of the traditional tie, he wore a western bola tie with a large turquoise stone that matched the one on the belt buckle at his narrow waist. Her pulse quickened when she looked in his silver-gray eyes.

"I'd like you to meet someone." Doctor Weber sat down on the edge of her bed. His tone matched the grave expression on his face.

Her heart began a thundering tattoo in her chest. "Do you know me?" she whispered hopefully. Maybe the roughly handsome man was her... What? She didn't even know if she was married.

Before the man could answer, Doctor Weber spoke again. "This is Sergeant Booker; he's with the Maricopa County Sheriff's Office."

She swallowed the fear suddenly threatening to overwhelm her, forcing herself to meet those gray eyes. "Are you going to arrest me? Have I done something wrong?" She couldn't come up with any other reason a policeman would want to talk to her. Maybe she was a criminal. No! Her mind screamed its denial.

Rex Booker wanted to kick the doctor. If he thought he was being subtle, he missed by a mile. Sergeant Booker found it difficult to speak while looking into those incredible eyes.

Their turquoise color nearly matched the large stone on his belt buckle. During the six weeks since being brought to the hospital, she'd been just another victim of a violent crime. For the first time, he saw her as a woman. And what a woman!

He offered what he hoped was a reassuring smile. She looked like she wanted to run and hide, but forced herself to stay put. "I'm not going to arrest you. I just need to ask you some questions." His voice cracked twice before he managed to get it under control.

Relief flooding through her, she sagged back against the pillows. "I don't have a lot of answers right now, Sergeant." She tried to make light of the situation. He looked almost as tense as she felt. His light eyes contrasted with the bronze skin of his face and arms. Sandy brown hair flirted with the collar of his shirt. He was a head taller than Doctor Weber putting him well over six feet tall. Broad shoulders stretched his shirt tight across his chest, straining the seams. There didn't seem to be any fat on his big frame. She guessed him to be thirty-something.

"Maybe my questions will help jog your memory," he answered, remaining serious. "Can you think of any reason why someone would do this to you? A boyfriend or husband maybe?" he suggested.

Was she married, she wondered? For a long moment she considered his questions. There were no rings on her left hand, not even a pale circle around her finger to indicate she had ever worn one. "I'm sorry, Sergeant, I don't think I'm married, but I don't know for sure. I don't even know what happened to me. Was I in an accident of some kind?" It was the only explanation she could come up with for her injuries.

"You weren't in an accident," the Sergeant answered, letting that thought sink in. "Someone left you there."

"Why would anyone do that? How did I get hurt?" Instead of answers, he left her with more questions.

"Someone beat you, and left you in the desert presumably to die." The Sergeant's soft words were like a physical blow, knocking the wind from her lungs.

37

Gasping for breath, she whispered softly, "Who would do such a thing? Who hates me that much?"

"That's what we're trying to find out. Anything you can remember will help."

"I don't even know my own name! How can I tell you who did this?"

Doctor Weber gave her hand a comforting pat. "Amnesia after a serious head injury isn't uncommon, and it's usually temporary. You could wake up tomorrow morning, and remember everything. Then we'll catch the bas…the person," he amended quickly, "who did this to you."

"Or I could remember nothing," she added what he deliberately left out. "I might never remember, right?"

"That is a remote possibility," he acknowledged. "But not very likely. From the tests we've already run, you don't appear to have any brain damage, so it's unlikely your amnesia is permanent."

"No brain damage?!" She was incredulous. "How can you say that? What do you call amnesia?"

Doctor Weber smiled slightly. She was a fighter, and that was good. Someone out there wanted her dead. She was going to need all the fight she could muster until they found him. "There are a number of causes for amnesia. The trauma of what happened is enough for your mind to block it out. I'm confident that in time you will remember nearly everything about your life."

"Nearly everything?" she asked. "But I may never remember who did this or why." It was more a statement than a question.

Doctor Weber considered his answer for a moment, afraid of saying too much, and adding to the fear she already felt. "Chances are you won't remember the actual attack, but you will remember who did it. If you knew your attacker, that is." He didn't buy the sergeant's theory of a domestic dispute. This felt far more sinister.

Sergeant Booker had allowed Doctor Weber's interference, carefully watching her reactions. So far, there was no flicker of memory on her face. An extremely pretty face, he thought, now that the swelling had gone down, and the bruises were fading. Tomorrow he would put out a bulletin with her picture, hoping someone, somewhere, had filed a missing person's report. After listening to her, he even had a starting point for that search.

Sitting down on the foot of her bed, he took command of the conversation again. "You aren't from around here, at least not originally. My guess is South Carolina, Tennessee, or Kentucky. Do any of those sound familiar?"

"Of course!" She looked at him indignantly. "They're southern states. I've lost my memory, Sergeant, not my intelligence."

Coloring slightly, he glanced at the doctor. The other man was enjoying his embarrassment. Clearing his throat, he rephrased his question. "Even with wires holding your jaws shut, I can tell that you have a southern accent. Do any of those places jog your memory?"

Doctor Weber frowned, staring hard at Jane Doe. "I'll be damned," he whispered. Until now he had overlooked the softly accented voice as a clue.

Jane stared at the sergeant before turning to Doctor Weber. "Is he right?" she questioned softly. She didn't hear the accent in her own voice.

"Yes, and I'm ashamed to say I didn't notice."

She turned back to the sergeant, excitement bubbling inside her. "Can you find out who I am now?"

"It's a start," he answered cautiously. "Does anything about the south seem familiar? Other than what you learned in school." He added quickly. "Any place in particular?"

For a long moment there was no sound in the small room as she searched what memory she had. Fleeting shadows teased at the edges of her mind, but she couldn't grasp anything long enough to examine it. She didn't know if her impressions were something from her past or something she had read about.

Frustrated and disappointed, she shook her head. "I can't

tell you anything more than the average person who has read about the south." Pictures of small country towns and open fields flowed through her mind. A peaceful feeling settled over her. She could almost smell the flowers and the damp grass. Just as quickly the impression faded again, adding to her frustration.

Further questions failed to reveal anything more. Pushing wasn't the right tactic. Standing up, Sergeant Booker smiled down at her. "This is a start. I'll have a photographer come in to take your picture for bulletins to be sent out to all the southern states. If someone filed a missing person's report, we'll know it before long."

"And what if no one has?" Her voice was small and worried.

"We'll cross that bridge when we come to it," the sergeant answered gently. "We've already sent your fingerprints to the FBI, turning up nothing."

"I guess I should be happy about that. At least I'm not a criminal." She gave a weak smile.

With fierce determination, she pushed away all thoughts of self-pity. She was a take-charge, no-nonsense person. At least she thought she was. If she hadn't been before, she would be from now on. "How long have I been in the hospital?"

"Six weeks," Doctor Weber answered softly.

"Six weeks? And no one has filed a missing person's report? Doesn't anyone know me?"

"Like I said, I'm going to be sending your picture to different states now that we know where you're originally from." Sergeant Booker tried to sound positive. "Maybe you recently moved to Arizona, and don't know anyone here."

"If I just moved here, why would someone want to kill me? Do you think whoever did this will try again?" She posed the question to both men, looking at them expectantly.

For a long moment neither man spoke, each trying to formulate an answer. They finally spoke at the same time, "We have to assume that he will." "He already has."

Jane Doe frowned. Which was it? Her face blanched as she

realized the truth. The doctor tried to protect his patient by hedging the truth, but the sergeant was right in there with reality.

Doctor Weber glared sharply at the other man, but Sergeant Booker ignored him. "He's already tried here in the hospital. You're the only one who can identify him so it's safe to say he'll keep trying."

Questions pounded in her mind, but she couldn't force them past her frozen lips.

Doctor Weber gently picked up her hand, giving it a reassuring squeeze while glaring at the sergeant again. The man had no tact or compassion. "We're doing everything possible to keep you safe. Hospital security has been increased, and now that you're awake you can..." He'd been about to say she could tell them who had done this to her. For now, that wasn't possible.

She couldn't believe someone hated her so much they would risk discovery right here in the hospital. What had she done to this person? "What did he do?" she whispered hoarsely.

Doctor Weber explained in simple terms about the insulin, trying to make light of what really happened.

"I went into cardiac arrest," she concluded correctly. "But how did he get in the hospital?"

Sergeant Booker answered before the doctor could say anything. "This isn't a secured wing, and you weren't under guard at the time. He took a risk, but not as big as he would now. We're taking every precaution so that nothing more will happen here."

But once I leave the hospital, and the protection is gone, I won't know whom to trust, she thought grimly. *I have to remember who did this to me so I can identify them, or I'll never be safe.*

As if reading her thought, the sergeant continued. "Since you can't remember anything, you aren't an immediate threat to him. Until we catch this Son..." He stopped short when Doctor Weber cleared his throat. "You need to let me, or

41

someone in the sheriff's department, know if you remember anything, no matter how small." Satisfied that she couldn't shed light on her past for the moment, Sergeant Booker left, reminding her once again to call him immediately if she remembered anything. He tapped the business card he left on her tray table. "You can reach me at any of these numbers."

When both men were gone she tried again to recall something, anything, about her life. Not only had she been beaten so badly she lost her memory, but the maniac was bold enough, and confident enough, to try again, right here in the hospital. *And you're a sitting duck as long as you stay in this bed*, she told herself.

Determined not to remain a victim, she lowered her legs over the side of the bed. The next person who came through the door could be the killer. If she didn't want to be an easy target, she needed to be able to move around.

Placing her feet on the floor, she eased off the bed. Her knees buckled under her weight. Gripping the side of the bed, she willed herself not to fall. Using the mattress as support, she took several hesitant steps. Her heart pounded like she'd just run a marathon. Had she always been such a weakling?

~~~

When Courtney and Barbra came on duty at midnight, the hospital was still buzzing with the news about 'Jane Doe'. Courtney's heart went out to the young woman who had been her patient for two weeks. "How much more does she have to go through?" She spoke softly as they stepped into the elevator.

"She'll be the center of attention again," Barbra stated caustically. She made it sound like the young woman had done all this just to gain attention for herself.

Courtney ignored her; it would do little good to argue. The two women had spoken very little since the scene with Ted in the parking lot. Courtney wished Barbra would move out, but until that happened she would just have to make the best of a bad situation. For the moment, ignoring her worked the best.

CHAPTER SIX

"She can't remember anything, she can't remember us, so we're in the clear," the young man whined. "Let's just cut our losses, and get out of here."

"With attempted murder hanging over our heads?" A dark brow lifted sardonically. "I don't think so. Just because she doesn't recognize us now, doesn't mean she won't the next time she sees us. She could remember everything tomorrow."

"Or never, everyone is saying that, even you." He received a dark glare for his efforts.

The big man relaxed back in the chair, his hands clasped behind his head. "If you're turning chicken, you go ahead and run. I think I'll stick around for a while." A cold smile spread across his face. "It could be fun teasing her with bits and pieces just to see what happens." If he'd known she would have amnesia, he could have claimed she was his wife or something, he thought. He could have had some fun with her before finishing her off.

The young man's face blanched, his mouth worked wordlessly for several seconds. Gulping air into his lungs, he finally managed to whisper, "You're kidding, right?"

The big man gave a careless shrug. Pushing the weasel was an amusing pastime while he waited for the opportunity to finish off that damn bitch. It could also be dangerous, he reminded himself. The idiot was unstable, panicking at every little thing. He might crack under the pressure. Controlling that panic would be an interesting challenge. When this was all over he would rid himself of the little bastard slow and easy. It was a promise he made to himself as a last reward before leaving the country with his profits.

"Right, kid, I'm only kidding." He smiled. "We've got to be careful not to show our hand."

The young man slumped in his chair, wiping beads of nervous sweat off his forehead. "We really should get out of here before she remembers everything. That way we'd be safe.

If we go back to Tucson, she'll never be able to identify us."

"We're safe only as long as she doesn't remember what happened to her and where. The old man's right about one thing; there is no predicting what might trigger her memory, or if anything ever will. I think we're just going to have to stick around, and make sure it doesn't happen." He was never going back to Tucson. He'd already burned his bridges there.

Thinking of how she had slipped through his fingers twice made his hands ball into fists. He was going to get another whack at her, and by damn he'd make sure nothing screwed it up this time.

~~~

'Jane Doe' silently watched the nurse as she worked across the room. At five-thirty in the morning, the hospital was just starting to come awake. Soon breakfast trays would be distributed, baths begun, and morning meds passed out. For all the attention Barbra was paying her patient, she might still be in a coma.

After several minutes of being ignored she cleared her throat to let the other woman know she was awake. Barbra didn't bat an eye. Unsure exactly what she was doing across the room besides a whole lot of nothing, Jane accepted the silent challenge. She coughed, then gave a phony sneeze, only to be ignored further. What did it take to get the woman's attention?

"What time does Doctor Weber start rounds?" She finally spoke, posing her question to Barbra's back.

"He'll be in as soon as he can. He's a very busy man." Barbra answered without turning around.

"I know he's busy," Jane Doe gritted her teeth in frustration. "I just wanted to know when he started rounds." She waited for an answer.

"Not until after breakfast." Barbra finally answered the question, but still didn't look at her patient.

Frustration propelled her from the bed, giving her added strength. Sensitivity training and classes in bedside manners should be required courses for all health care professionals, she decided. And this one should be the first one to sign up, Jane thought angrily.

"You aren't supposed to be out of bed." Barbra's voice held emotion for the first time since their conversation began. "I don't want you to fall and get hurt." She stopped herself from adding "on my shift." After that fiasco earlier in the week, a fall while she was right in the room would probably mean her job, even though it wouldn't be her fault.

It was Jane's turn to ignore Barbra as she continued to take cautious steps away from the bed. For the past three days she had secretly practiced walking around the room, ranging a little farther each time.

Watching, Barbra grudgingly admired the young woman's determination. It wouldn't be easy to fight back after all she'd gone through. For now though, she wanted the woman back in bed. She could practice walking on someone else's shift.

"Well, look who's up and walking." An orderly pushed open the door, carrying her breakfast tray. "Before you know it, you're going to be up and out of here."

Jane smiled gratefully. His cheerful attitude was welcome after Barbra's silent disapproval. "I sure hope so, Ken. I'm getting tired of lying around here." Since everyone was a stranger, one of them, or none of them, could be her attacker. After getting over her initial fear of everyone who entered her room, she began making friends with the staff. Everyone in the hospital was so nice to her. Nearly everyone, she amended, looking at Barbra's sour expression.

Picking up the warming cover to see what was on the tray, a soft groan escaped her lips. "Soft boiled eggs again." The wires holding her jaws closed had been removed the day before. Since then she'd had nothing to eat but soft food. "I hate hospital food," she muttered.

"You won't regain your strength if you don't eat, Jane Doe, and hospital food is all you've got for now." What little compassion Barbra possessed was all used up by the end of her shift.

"And I *hate* being called 'Jane Doe'," she gritted out,

glaring at Barbra.

"Well, until you tell us your name, that's all we have." The accusation made it sound like she wasn't telling them on purpose. "Pick out something you like, if you don't like the one we gave you. No one likes the name their parents stick them with." She certainly didn't. Barbra was so plain, so common. Without waiting for a reply, she breezed out of the room. She'd wasted enough time. Her relief would be in shortly, and she could go home.

She's right, Jane thought. I can choose any name I want. She refused to contemplate even another day as 'Jane Doe', let alone the rest of her life. The only alternative was to come up with something of her own choosing, she decided.

A quest for a name kept her thoughts off her other problems for the remainder of the day. Everyone who came into the room was asked the same question, "What's your favorite name?" The list was endless, Sarah, Amber, Heather, Megan. If she'd hoped one name would strike a chord in her stubborn memory, she was disappointed. None of the suggested names seemed to belong to her. She played each name over and over in her mind, trying to find one that was, if not familiar, at least comfortable to her.

She regained a little more strength each day while her memory remained stubbornly elusive. When she wasn't working on her physical rehabilitation, she searched through her empty memory looking for a part of her past, something that was familiar. There was nothing. She could walk and talk, feed herself and write. She had a good education, at least through high school and probably college. But what was she educated in?

Everyone commented on her Southern accent. She could quote facts about the south and picture scenes like in a movie. But she couldn't place those scenes in a specific state. In her mind's eye, she could see herself walking through lush, green fields and experience the fierce winds of a hurricane. Still, she didn't know where to call home.

Her hands balled into fists, tears of frustration burned

46

behind her eyes. "You've got to remember!" she told herself over and over. An urgent need pushed at her while something knocked at the back of her mind, waiting for her to unlock the door of her memory.

"Damn it!" she whispered fiercely as the images slowly faded, leaving only depressing blankness in their place.

She hounded all the doctors when they stopped by to see her, wanting to know when she would remember. The consensus was a resounding "I don't know."

"There doesn't seem to be any permanent brain damage," Doctor Collin Riley held up his hand to stop her protest. "I know you think amnesia is brain damage, but it really isn't in your case. It's more of a defense mechanism. All the tests are encouraging, and you have all your motor skills. When your body and mind are ready to remember, something familiar will trigger your memory."

"And what if there isn't anything familiar in Arizona?" she protested. "Sergeant Booker doesn't think I'm from around here." She looked forward to the handsome sergeant's daily visits.

Doctor Riley laughed. "No, that's definitely a Southern accent, not a Western drawl or even the non-accent most of us around here have." He paused for a moment before going on encouragingly. "You could be a recent transplant. Phoenix is full of those. Even I'm recently new to Phoenix. If that's the case, there's a reason you moved here. Something will trigger your memory."

"If I've lived here for a while, why can't I conjure up any images? I can't picture one single thing about Phoenix or Arizona."

He stared at her. "Are you beginning to remember things? What sort of things?" His intense blue eyes pinned her to the bed.

Jane gave a heavy sigh. "There's nothing specific. Impressions just come into my mind."

"What kind of impressions?" he pressed. "Is there something you can identify?"

47

She shook her head again. "It's just impressions. Feelings," she repeated. "I can almost feel the humidity of the summer, and I know everything is green. I like frozen yogurt, but not ice cream. I like to swim, hike, and walk on the beach. And I *hate* hospital food."

He laughed at that, a deep rumbling sound that made Jane feel slightly light headed. "I wouldn't call that last part a break-through," he chuckled. "Everyone hates hospital food, even the cooks complain about it. These impressions or feelings are a good sign though."

Alone again, Jane quickly dismissed Doctor Riley's idea of a "good sign". She wanted something concrete to grasp, not fleeting impressions.

When she wasn't searching for her past, she was pressing ahead in her search for a name. There were so many to choose from, but none felt like they belonged to her. Pacing her small room, she repeated the different names over in her mind, hoping one would jump out at her.

"Well, look at you!" Doctor Travis Dean stood in her doorway, a broad smile spreading across his handsome face. "Hard to believe just four days ago you were still in a coma." He came into the room, and sat down on the corner of her bed. "How are you feeling?"

"Frustrated!" The honest answer escaped before she could stop it. Struggling to remember who she was, struggling to regain her strength, struggling to find some kind of identity. All she did was struggle. Everything added to her frustration.

"Don't push yourself so hard. You can't expect too much right away." He understood her frustration, but considering all she'd gone through, she was doing remarkably well. "When your body is healed, your memory will follow."

"Can you guarantee that?" One finely arched brow lifted slightly. She was tired of people telling her that.

Doctor Dean reluctantly shook his head. "Not guaranteed, but I believe it will happen."

"And if it doesn't? What do I do then?" she asked. "I don't know who I am, or what I did before this happened. Someone has tried to kill me twice. Is he going to keep trying until he succeeds? Even if I get my memory back, will I be able to identify who did this to me?"

"You have to take one day at a time," he told her. A lot of things had been heaped on her plate in a short time.

"Easy for you to say," she muttered, looking at the unfamiliar landscape on the other side of the window.

The air conditioning kept the room cool, but heat radiated through the glass. Phoenix wasn't her home, she *knew* it. Everything was totally alien to her. In an effort to identify with something in Arizona, she pored over the newspaper and magazines hoping to conjure up some memory. Outside of the pictures she looked at, she had no mental images of the landscape. Surely, if this was her home, she would have some idea what it was like.

Her accent was proof she was from the south. But there were a lot of southern states. Which one was home for her, and why was she in Arizona? Why hadn't someone come forward to identify her? A photographer had come to the hospital, and her picture had been in all the local papers. She hoped someone would recognize her. At this point she held out little hope.

Turning away from the window, she shrugged aside the melancholy mood. "What's your favorite name, Doctor?"

"Ah yes, I've heard about your name game. What's wrong, you don't like the one you're using now?"

She grimaced slightly, "I'm afraid not. I don't think I'm the sort of person who constantly seeks the limelight, but 'Jane Doe' is a little too anonymous."

Doctor Dean stroked his chin thoughtfully. "Well, let's see, what would be a good name for you?" He paused for a minute, his eyes skimming over her hospital gown-clad body before going on. "I've always thought the Native Americans had the right idea, giving their children descriptive names like 'Walking Bear' or 'Blue Flower'. How would you like something like that?"

"I don't think either of those fit the real me," she joined in his joke. "But since I don't know the "real me," just about anything would describe me."

He studied her for another minute before offering a suggestion of his own. "Oh, I don't know. I think 'Flame' is rather appropriate considering all that red hair.

Jane couldn't stop the laugh that bubbled up in her throat. It felt good to have something to laugh about. "I'd rather have something a little less theatrical." She'd finally been able to take a shower and wash her hair revealing its true color. A nurse had also cut her hair so it was now short, and the bald patch wasn't so noticeable.

"Well, you'll find one that suits you. You couldn't do worse than most parents. When I was growing up there wasn't a single kid who liked the name his parents stuck him with. All the boys wanted something tough sounding or else really cool, and the girls all wanted something right out of Hollywood."

Leaving the room a few minutes later, he couldn't help but admire the inner strength she displayed. She had more guts than most people would in her situation. She was improving daily. Before long she'd be discharged. Where would she go then, he wondered? Since no one had come forward to identify her when she was first brought in, everyone assumed she had no family or friends in Arizona. Even the picture in the paper hadn't produced any information.

"So how's our star patient today?" Doctor Collin Riley interrupted his thoughts.

"Improving," Travis Dean didn't look up. "It won't be long before she'll be ready to leave." The two men were colleagues, but not friends.

For a minute Collin didn't comment. "Wonder what she'll do then?" He sounded as troubled by the question as Travis was a moment ago. Bracing his back against the counter, he crossed his arms over his broad chest. "Maybe there's something she can do around here. She seems bright enough. It wouldn't take her long to pick up on things." He drew a deep breath. "I know doctors aren't supposed to get personally involved with their patients, but this is one that warrants personal involvement."

Travis nodded agreement. "She's something, all right. What have you got in mind for her?"

Collin shrugged his broad shoulders. "There are never enough aides around here. She could do something like that."

"Good idea," Travis agreed. "But you'd better figure out a way to get Ben Weber to suggest it, not you."

Collin gave a crooked smile. "Got any suggestions how we can set that up?" Ben Weber was an excellent doctor, but his relationship with his staff wasn't always the greatest. He could be cold and impersonal to the other doctors and hospital staff. His kindness was reserved for his patients and their families. With a shrug, Travis turned away. "Something will come up."

CHAPTER SEVEN

A commotion in the hall first thing the following morning, brought nurses, doctors, and patients out to see what was happening. "I want to see her. You can't keep me from seeing her. She's my...wife." The man stammered before finishing his sentence.

"I'm sorry, sir, but we aren't allowing strangers in to see Jane without clearance from her doctor." Janice Able faced the agitated man. At five foot seven or eight, he was only a few inches taller than she. She looked over her shoulder at the nurse to send a silent message. Barbra didn't understand the message, or she chose to ignore her.

"Barbra," Janice snapped, "page Doctor Weber, now!" Frustrated at the woman's slow movements, she wanted to say more, but she had her hands full with the young man in front of her.

"I have to see that she's all right." His wild eyes moved from one person to the next as they stood around staring at the scene unfolding in front of them.

Patients stood in the hall to check out the disturbance. Janice had her back to Jane's room. If she had come into the hall to see what was happening, why hadn't this man recognized her?

When the elevator dinged to indicate someone was getting off, she breathed a sigh of relief to see Doctor Weber, along with several security officers, striding towards her.

"What's going on here? Who are you?" The doctor's authoritative voice broke in on the man's demands to see Jane Doe.

"I'm her fiancé," the man snapped. "You can't keep me from seeing her."

"I thought you said she was your wife," Janice spoke up.

"Oh, ah, we just got married. I'm not used to calling her my wife yet." Moving from one foot to the other in a nervous dance, his agitation increased when confronted by the men.

"Why don't you come to my office, and we'll discuss this." Doctor Weber reached out to take the man's arm. "What did you say your name is?"

"I don't want to go with you." He jerked his arm out of the doctor's grasp. "I want to see my wife."

"Just as soon as we have a talk," Doctor Weber's voice was calm. "What's her name? I'm sure she'll be happy to learn her real name." Without touching the man, he managed to move him towards the elevator. "She doesn't like being called Jane Doe." Before stepping into the elevator, he looked at Janice. Unlike Barbra, she understood the silent message that moved between them.

Once seated in the doctor's office, the man began wringing his hands. "Why are you doing this to me? I haven't done anything wrong."

"No one is saying you have. We just need to make sure that nothing more happens to this young woman. She's gone through a very traumatic time. Now, how about telling me her name?"

Before he could say anything, the office door flew open, slamming against the wall. Both men jumped in surprise, turning to see Sergeant Rex Booker in the doorway. He looked ready to strangle someone.

The young man cringed, sinking lower in his chair. "Who... who are you?" he stammered. "What are you going to do to me?"

"Who are you?" Booker growled.

"M...my name is Justin, Justin Caldwell. Who are you?" Sitting up straight, he tried to regain some of his composure.

"I'm Sergeant Booker with the Maricopa County Sheriff's Department. I'd like to hear what you have to say about our assault victim." He lowered his voice, making it all the more dangerous.

"It wasn't me; I didn't do anything to her."

"What's her name" So far he had avoided answering that question.

"Um, her name is…" He stalled some more before finally blurting out, "Betsy, Betsy Caldwell, she's my wife."

The sergeant's lip curled in a snarl, but he managed to control his temper. "Right, she's your wife. She's been in the hospital for quite some time. Where have you been? What's taken you so long to come forward?"

"Oh, I was away on business. I didn't know what happened to her." He couldn't maintain eye contact as he talked.

"What can you tell us about her? She doesn't remember anything about her former life."

This seemed to stump Justin. His light colored eyes moved between the detective and the doctor, trying to come up with a response. "Um, we just got married."

"You've already said that. How did you meet her? Where did she work? You don't sound like you're from the south."

"The south?" This confused him further. "No, I was born and raised here. What does the south have to do with anything?"

Rex ignored the question, repeating his. "How did you meet her? Where did she work?"

"Why are you doing this to me? I didn't do anything wrong. I just want to see her."

"Why won't you answer my questions? They're basic questions. If she's your wife, you should be able to answer them. Someone tried to kill her; I can't let anyone near her without checking them out first. Now, answer my questions." His voice was suddenly as sharp as a knife.

"I didn't do anything wrong." The young man slumped further down in the chair, still not answering the questions.

Letting the silence draw out, Rex pulled out his cell phone. He stepped away from the young man keeping his voice soft as he placed a call. It only took a few minutes to get the answer he was looking for. With a satisfied smile, he turned back to Justin. "Where do you live, Justin?"

When he didn't get an answer, Rex continued softly. "Are you a patient at the Northrup Psychiatric Hospital?"

"No," the young man wailed. "I'm not crazy."

"I didn't say you were crazy. Are you a patient at the hospital?" Justin nodded his head as tears seeped from the corners of his eyes. "Why did you say Jane Doe was your wife?"

"They told me to come get her. They said she could be mine," he whispered. "She doesn't have anyone so they said we could be together."

"Who said that?" The sharp question from both men startled Justin, and he let out another wail.

Ben Weber took control of the questioning as he sat down on the corner of his desk. "Who told you to come get her?" he asked softly.

"Them." Justin pointed to his head. "They tell me what to do all the time. They told me to come get her because someone wants to hurt her. They said I could protect her."

"That's not how it works, Justin," Ben said. "We need to find out who she is so we can protect her."

"I would never hurt her or anyone," he assured Ben. "I just wanted to help her."

"I know, but the police are protecting her. You need to go back to the hospital where they can help you."

When someone knocked on the office door, Rex opened it to allow an orderly from Northrup to come in. "Hello, Justin, it's time to come home now."

The young man stood up. Looking around, he seemed confused, but he allowed the orderly to lead him out of the room. "Is he going to be all right?" Rex turned to the older man.

"Northrup is a very good hospital. They'll take good care of him." He shook his head. How much more did Jane have to endure?

When the elevator doors closed on Doctor Weber and the man who had been making a fuss, Jane came out of her room. Her trembling legs barely held her up as she walked to the nurses' station. "Who was that man? He said I was his wife. Is that true?"

"Did you recognize him?" Janice Able asked her. She shook her head. "Doctor Weber will get to the bottom of this. I've called Detective Booker. He won't let anything happen to you."

Her heart gave a little tripping beat at the mention of Sergeant Booker. He stopped by daily to visit her. She tried to tell herself it was only because of the case. But she secretly wished it was more than that. Turning her mind from the good-looking detective, she looked at Janice Able. "Do you think that man is the one who tried to kill me?" She hated the tremble she heard in her voice matching the pounding of her heart in her chest.

Janice thought about that for a long moment, then gave her head a shake. "If he was the one who wanted to kill you, I don't think he would have come here announcing you were his wife. The man who tried to kill you is a coward, waiting to try something when no one is around. Doctor Weber will get it sorted out. Right now, you need to rest." She ushered her patient back to her room.

The stress of always trying to remember, always looking over her shoulder weighed heavily on her. *Why can't I remember? I need to remember before he comes after me again.* No matter how hard she tried, her memory remained stubbornly absent. Frustration ate at her.

~~~

Leaving the doctor's office, Rex Booker took the elevator to the next floor. He wanted to check on Jane Doe. As long as she'd been in a coma, he was able to think of her only as another victim, but now...he shook his head. Every time he looked into those turquoise-colored eyes, they drew him closer. He shook his head again trying to dislodge those thoughts. He didn't have any business thinking of her as anything more than a victim. Who was he kidding? There was something special about this woman.

He pushed open the door to her room. She stood at the window with her back to the door. Turning around, her eyes were large with fright until she saw him. "It's just me," he said softly. "Are you all right?"

Jane nodded her head. "Who was that man? Did he know me?" Her voice trembled.

"No, I'm sorry. He is a patient at a psychiatric hospital. The voices in his head told him to come here."

She gave a weary sigh. "Mentally ill people and murderous men are the only ones interested in me."

"Not the only ones," he corrected. "I care, the doctors and nurses here care," he quickly added, hoping he hadn't given away his feelings that were totally inappropriate. "We're going to find out who did this. It's just going to take time."

How much time do I have before he tries again, she questioned silently?

~~~

"Who was that man? Did he really know her?" The young man paced around the room.

"No, he didn't know her, you idiot. He's just some psycho looking for attention."

"But why would he say she was his wife?"

"Because he's a psycho, that's why," the older man snapped. "Now, shut up and go away. If you keep coming in here, someone is going to think something's up and want to know what's going on." When the young man tried to argue, he stood up, sending the younger man scurrying out of the room.

~~~

Ben Weber rolled his head around on his shoulders. It had been a long day. Once that young man's identity was figured out, and that he meant Jane no harm, things settled down. He was grateful the media hadn't gotten wind of what happened. He didn't need a swarm of reporters stalking the halls. Justin didn't need reporters hounding him either.

Pushing those thoughts aside, he looked over his patients' files. They were all doing well, especially Jane. A tired smile lifted the corners of his mouth. The woman had more spunk than most. That might be the only thing that saved her. Without plenty of determination and fight, she would have succumbed to her injuries.

She had all of her motor skills, she could walk and talk. Her lack of memory was the only lingering effect of the beating she'd endured. Muscle memory hadn't been affected. In a small experiment that afternoon, he had handed her a note pad and pen telling her to sign her name.

Without thinking, she'd done just that. There were plenty of swirls and squiggly lines, but not much else. "Maybe you're a doctor," he'd joked. "Your handwriting is as illegible as mine." A fleeting expression crossed her face, like something had tugged at her memory. Just as quickly it was gone.

With a frustrated sigh, she had examined the signature on the page. "That looks like an R or maybe a B. It could even be a D." She pointed at the first letter of the scribble. The rest were up for grabs. There was no separation between the first and last names. The experiment hadn't been very successful.

She is also intelligent, Ben told himself. While listening to the list of her injuries, she understood the medical terms; her only questions had been to clarify a point, proving she was well educated.

There was no medical reason for the amnesia to be permanent, he reminded himself. He was absolutely certain that when the time was right, she would remember everything. Only then would they catch the bastard who did this to her. For now, they would all have to trust that things happen for a reason even when they couldn't see that reason.

With nothing more they could medically do for her, she was ready to be discharged. He had been dragging his feet on this because she had nowhere to go, no family or friends to rely on. But the hospital administration was beginning to balk about keeping her as a patient. After much arguing on his part, he had managed to get them to agree to let her work here. At least, he would still be able to watch over her.

He knew the staff said he was overly protective of all of his patients, but this one more so. She was different. Maybe it was the circumstances, maybe not, but in this case he felt he was justified. Never before had someone tried to murder one of his patients right in his hospital.

He knew Rex Booker felt the same. He was doing all he could to find out who she is, and who tried to kill her. He wouldn't stop until he had all the answers. He also knew it was more than just the case for Rex, he thought with a tired smile. The man was falling in love with their pretty patient and victim.

~~~

"You have to do something before she remembers who she really is." He was beginning to sound like a broken record. The young man had ducked into the office without bothering to knock, pacing around the small space. "She's going to remember what happened. Once she's out of the hospital, you'll never be able to get at her."

His boss stood up so quick his chair toppled over, crashing to the floor. "I've told you to stop coming in here. I don't need people questioning me about you." It had been only a few hours since he chased the man out, only to have him back again with the same refrain.

"Can't you just tell them we're friends?"

He gave a bark of laughter. "No one would believe that. I don't associate with orderlies." His tone was full of scorn. "If you had done the job right in the first place, none of this would be necessary now, so stop whining." He conveniently forgot he had started this particular ball rolling.

The younger man swallowed the fear that threatened to choke him. "There isn't a guard outside her room anymore. Can't you do something? What happens when she remembers what you did to her? What we did to her," he quickly amended when his boss took a threatening step towards him.

"By that time, I'll be long gone. All I need is a little more time, one more deal." He stared over the younger man's head, his mind somewhere else.

The young man watched him for several moments before breaking the silence. "What about me?" His family was in Arizona. He didn't want to spend the rest of his life on the run.

The big man looked like he didn't understand the question.

Then his expression cleared, a smile spread across his handsome face. "Well, you can do anything you want. You'll be rich, too. Isn't that what you wanted?" He turned his back to the room, staring moodily out the window. She'd been nothing but trouble from the moment he laid eyes on her.

The little weasel was right about one thing. He had to do something. That was the problem though. He didn't know what. He couldn't make another attempt on her life here in the hospital. Once she was released, it might be easier to get at her. She wouldn't have the good Doctor Weber looking out for her. *Too bad they hadn't turned her over to that psycho today,* he thought. That would have solved all of his problems. At least some of them. He looked at the reflection of the young man in the window. He needed to do something about her and that idiot. As yet, he hadn't figured out what.

"Are you thinking of a way to get rid of her?" He couldn't stand the silence any longer. "Maybe you could blame that psycho guy."

Ignoring that comment, his boss turned, taking a menacing step towards him. He scurried out of the room, fear etched on his thin face. "What was I thinking getting hooked up with him?" he muttered. "No amount of money is worth it."

Inside the office, a flurry of papers hit the floor as the man swept the desk clean in a fit of anger. "What was I thinking involving that idiot in my plan?" His words echoed the younger man's thoughts.

CHAPTER EIGHT

Sleep eluded her, and she stood at the window staring out at the dark parking lot. Heat lightning streaked across the sky. Even at eleven o'clock at night she could feel the heat radiating through the glass. She had given up trying to picture something of Arizona beyond the parking lot.

She would be leaving the hospital at the end of the week. Where was she supposed to go? So far, no one had recognized the picture Rex, Sergeant Booker, she corrected, had placed in the paper. If she was from Phoenix, why hadn't anyone recognized her?

Someone out there wanted her dead. She didn't know who or why. She knew Sergeant Booker would do his best to keep her safe, but he couldn't be with her twenty-four hours a day.

A soft smile played around her lips. She wouldn't mind it if he could be.

She quickly chided herself for the fanciful thoughts. Until she knew who she was, she had no business entertaining romantic notions about anyone. *What if I'm married?* A shiver passed through her at the thought. If that was so, why hadn't her husband reported her missing?

The man who came today claiming to be her husband was a patient in a mental hospital. That didn't mean she wasn't married to someone else. What if her husband was the one who tried to kill her? Her thoughts continued to go in circles.

The door opened slowly, and Courtney peeked into the room. "I saw the light under the door, and thought you might like some company."

With a smile, Jane welcomed her into the room. "Walking up and down the halls a few times each day doesn't do much to wear me out. Consequently, I don't get tired enough to sleep." She gave a frustrated sigh.

"Then your physical therapist isn't doing his job if he can't keep you physically active enough to wear you out," Courtney chuckled. "Maybe you should talk to him about that."

Jane lifted her shoulders in a shrug. "He can only work with me so many hours a day. He has other patients who are worse off than me to help. You're a little early for your shift, aren't you?" Tired of talking about herself, she changed the subject.

Courtney nodded. "Barbra isn't riding with me now, so I come in a few minutes early." She didn't like getting to work just minutes before her shift was to start, but Barbra was never on time.

Jane knew the women were roommates, but she couldn't picture them as friends. They were so different. Courtney cared for her patients; Barbra was just putting in her time.

"I hear they're going to spring you soon. I'm going to miss you." Courtney's voice tightened in her throat. She was always happy when her patients recovered, but there were special ones she wished she could keep in touch with. Jane was one of those special patients.

Laughing, Jane said, "Not for long. Just as soon as I get my strength back, I'll be working here. Doctor Weber arranged it."

"That's great!" Impulsively, she gave Jane a quick hug. "What are you going to do?"

"Just a nurse's aide," she shrugged. "But it's a start. Do you know where I can rent a room, cheap? I don't know how much an aide makes, but I'm sure it isn't enough for an apartment." The social worker assigned to her case had suggested several rooming houses close to the hospital. They sounded more like halfway houses for recovering addicts or convicts right out of prison. She shuddered at the idea.

"Why don't you come live with me?" Courtney asked impulsively. She wanted to help her.

"Are you serious?" Jane couldn't believe her good fortune. Courtney nodded her head. "Sure! It'll be great."

"What about Barbra?" Jane questioned cautiously. "Shouldn't you check with her first?"

For just a moment Courtney had forgotten about her roommate, now her heart sank. Would she carry her ridiculous grudge against Courtney so far as to refuse to let Jane move in with them? Courtney quickly dismissed the idea. If it meant someone else sharing the rent, Barbra would agree. "Don't be silly. She'll be as excited as I am." That was an exaggeration, but she was still confident Barbra would agree.

~~~

"What do you mean you said she could move in with us?" Courtney had waited until they got home the following morning before broaching the subject of Jane moving in with them. "How could you do that without checking with me first? Did you forget that I live here too?"

If I only could, Courtney thought. "That's a familiar line. I remember saying the same thing a few times. Without any results, I might add."

"So this is payback time?" Barbra's face was an angry shade of red.

"No, of course not." Although it wasn't a bad idea, Courtney decided. "I just thought it would be nice since she has nowhere else to go."

"Well, that's not my fault. We're not running a charity house here."

"I let you move in with me when you were looking for a place to stay. The least we can do is return the favor to someone else in need."

"I pay my fair share around here, and if I remember correctly you needed a roommate more than I needed an apartment. We don't need her to move in with us."

"Maybe not, but she needs a place to stay. It won't hurt either of us to share."

"She doesn't even have a job. How's she going to pay her share of the rent?"

"Doctor Weber arranged for her to have a job at the hospital just as soon as she's strong enough."

"Until that happens, who's going to pick up her share of the rent? It won't be me."

"I will." Courtney huffed. She had just paid off the last of the bills her ex-fiancé had saddled her with. She'd have enough to make up the difference until Jane could pay her share. This was one argument she wasn't going to let Barbra win. She wanted to help Jane.

"You're being mighty generous," Barbra's lips curled in a snarl. "Did you forget that there are only two bedrooms here? I'm not sharing *my* room with her." Her glare grew even darker. "Or were you planning on kicking me out? Isn't it enough that you stole my boyfriend? Now you want to take away my home."

Courtney rolled her eyes. This argument was getting a little old. "This has nothing to do with Ted, we're talking about Jane."

Barbra shook her head, letting her long blond hair float around her face. "I think it's all tied together. You've managed to take my boyfriend, now you're trying to kick me out of my own home. I'm telling you that is not going to happen. I'm not going anywhere."

"I didn't steal your boyfriend, and I'm not trying to kick you out. If you'd been home, instead of on a date with another guy when Ted stopped by the other night, you would have been here to see him. What did you expect me to do, shut the door in his face?"

"You could have told him I was out with a girlfriend," Barbra snapped.

Courtney shook her head. "I'm not going to lie for you. Besides, he already knew you weren't here. I've tried to tell you this already."

"If he knew I wasn't here, why did he come over? Did you call him?"

Courtney sighed. She was tired and didn't need this right now. "No, I didn't call him. Maybe he just got tired of being walked on. Believe me, I know the feeling." She glared at Barbra. "Ted is a nice guy, and you've been treating him like a doormat."

"No, you wouldn't lie to him," Barbra sneered, ignoring everything Courtney said beyond her first statement. "You'd rather seduce him into your bed. Did you get him there before dinner or were you hoping to do that when you got back?"

"I didn't sleep with him, and you know it!" Courtney snapped. In the last three days, this was becoming a familiar refrain, but Barbra was getting more vicious each time they rehashed it.

"Do I?" One pencil thin eyebrow lifted slightly. "If I hadn't come home when I did, who's to say what might have happened, and where the two of you might have ended up."

"We didn't do anything wrong." Courtney felt like a teenager again, trying to explain to her mother what she was doing with a boy on the living room couch.

Barbra sniffed disdainfully. "You both looked pretty guilty when I came in. Of course, if I had just been caught with my roommate's boyfriend, I'd feel pretty guilty myself."

Courtney doubted that, but kept the thought to herself. "If he was your boyfriend, why were you out with another guy?"

"He certainly isn't my boyfriend now." She ignored Courtney's question. "I won't put up with a man two-timing me!" With that, Barbra turned, flouncing into her room. The door slammed behind her.

"How did this go from Jane moving in with us to another argument about Ted?" Courtney gave a frustrated sigh. Barbra was a master at turning the tables on you. *What else did I expect*, she asked herself. Barbra accused Ted of two-timing her, but that was like the pot calling the kettle black. During the two months Barbra had been dating Ted, she had also been seeing other men.

"Even one of Barbra's temper tantrums isn't going to change my mind," Courtney said out loud. That poor girl had been on a run of bad luck, and needed a helping hand right now. If Barbra didn't like it, that was just too bad. The lease was still in Courtney's name, and she could have someone move in if she wanted.

But Barbra wasn't going to make life easy, Courtney acknowledged. She had taken a dislike to Jane even before she regained consciousness. Living under the same roof was going to be difficult. *I should have thought of that before opening my mouth,* Courtney told herself. But she really wanted to help Jane out of a tough situation. Besides, she liked Jane more than she liked Barbra.

Jane was only a part of the problem though. As long as she continued seeing Ted, Barbra would make their lives a living hell. "I'm not going to stop seeing him either," Courtney vowed. She gave him away by treating him so badly.

She replayed that evening two nights ago in her mind. Ted hadn't been surprised when she told him Barbra wasn't home. "Actually I was hoping to see you." His admission had left her stunned. Butterflies fluttered in her stomach. She had been half afraid he was going to question her about where Barbra was. She hadn't been sure what she would say. But that hadn't been the case.

She invited him in, offering to fix coffee. Instead, he'd suggested they go out for something to eat. During dinner she'd tried to steer the conversation around to Barbra, but Ted hadn't been interested. "Could we forget about her for tonight?" he'd asked. "I'd rather get to know you."

Stunned, she blurted out the first thing that came to mind. "Why? I thought you wanted to marry her?"

"Marry her?" His shocked expression had startled her, but not half as much as his laughter. "Not hardly," he'd finally managed around his laughter. "I've been trying since our first date to cool things, but she has a way of ignoring everything I say, and getting her own way."

Courtney could relate to that. Everything Barbra had said about them had been a pack of lies. Ted hadn't asked her to marry him, and the times Barbra said he was coming over to spend the day with her had been more lies. He was only there for a few minutes each time, if he was there at all.

Even now, her blood boiled thinking of all the times Barbra duped her. The woman thought nothing of using people to get what she wanted. *Well, not any more,* Courtney silently promised herself. Barbra was bright and flashy on the outside, but black as coal inside.

There are going to be some changes around here, Courtney

vowed. I'm going to keep seeing Ted, and Jane is going to move in. If Barbra doesn't like it, she can leave. Wishful thinking, Courtney told herself. That woman will stay here just for the fun of making all of our lives miserable.

~~~

Two days later Barbra proved that statement to be true. "I'm asking you nicely. I'd like to fix dinner here tonight. Please go somewhere for a few hours." Courtney tried to be reasonable, but it wasn't easy in the face of the other girl's stubbornness.

"So you can sleep with *my* boyfriend? I don't think so. You'll have to go somewhere else. Besides, there's a movie on TV I really want to watch." Barbra sat down on the sofa, ignoring the killer look on her roommate's face.

Courtney drew a deep breath, trying not to lose her temper. "How many times did I leave the apartment for an entire day because you said you wanted to be alone with your date? I'm just asking you to return the favor."

"Don't you mean I wanted to be alone with Ted?" Barbra asked nastily. "You left because you couldn't stand to see me with the guy you wanted."

"No," Courtney snapped. "I left because *you* lied to me. You said Ted was going to be here all day, and he wasn't. You said he asked you to marry him, and he never did."

Barbra shrugged nonchalantly. "Are you sure about that? We might even be married right now if it weren't for you." Her blasé manner belied her words.

"Not very likely! Ted didn't ask you to marry him, and he had no intention of ever asking you." Unease swirled through Courtney though. Ted said he never asked Barbra to marry him, but she insisted he had. She knew Barbra was a habitual liar, so there was no reason to believe her. Could she believe Ted? Was her relationship with him doomed to be full of doubt because of Barbra?

"So he says now," Barbra continued to taunt. "But you'll never know for sure who to believe, him or me." She didn't bother to look at Courtney, fueling the other girl's temper and doubts even further.

"Oh, I know who to believe," Courtney laughed harshly. "You wouldn't know the truth if it jumped up and bit you on the butt."

"That may be so, but I'm still not leaving." She didn't bother to deny the accusation. To end the conversation, she picked up the remote control, turning on the television.

Courtney's hands curled into claws as she took a step toward Barbra's back, but the doorbell stopped her from going further. With a frustrated growl, she yanked open the door.

"Hi, Teddy," Barbra purred, looking over her shoulder. "Come on in." She chuckled at the murderous look her roommate sent her way.

Ignoring Barbra's invitation, Courtney picked her purse up off the table beside the door. On her way out, she slammed the door behind her. The childish act helped to vent her anger only slightly.

"The queen of manipulation at it again I see." Ted tried to make a joke out of it. "What'd she do now?"

"I asked her to leave for a few hours so we could have a nice dinner together, just the two of us before Jane moves in tomorrow. Of course she refused, even after all the times I left so she could be alone with..."

"I never slept with her," Ted interrupted gently; "I never spent the day with her either. I only stopped by for a few minutes between jobs." Barbra's many lies were going to be the biggest stumbling block in his relationship with Courtney.

Reaching Ted's truck, she leaned against the fender, forcing herself to relax. "I know that now, and I'm sorry. I didn't mean to take it out on you. Barbra just makes me crazy."

He pulled her against his hard chest, kissing the top of her silky head. "The lease is in your name, kick her out."

"I can't tell you how many times I've thought of doing just that," she released a weary sigh. "Until recently I couldn't afford to do that though. My lease is up in a few months. I'm already looking for a cheaper apartment. I was going to tell

Barbra about that, but now I'm not so sure. Let her figure it out by herself." Even as she said it, her conscience kicked at her. She couldn't be that mean, not even to Barbra. She huffed out a sigh. "Until I can move, I'm stuck with her. Besides, Jane is moving in tomorrow. She's counting on me. Maybe between the two of us we can ignore Barbra."

The woman has a good heart, he thought. That and so much more of what I want in a woman. Now he had to convince her of that. Not for the first time he wished he'd met Courtney before asking Barbra out. It hadn't taken long for him to realize he was dating the wrong roommate. But Barbra had a sixth sense when it came to men. She knew his interest had shifted, and had fed him a pack of lies about Courtney and her ex-fiancé. There had been no truth to the story that Courtney was still hung up on the jerk.

He only had himself to blame for letting his relationship with Barbra linger long after he knew nothing would ever come of it. Besides, he'd been hoping to see more of Courtney. That hadn't happened until now though. Barbra always made sure her roommate wasn't around when he was there.

Not for the first time, he gave himself a mental head slap. Until recently, he hadn't realized what Barbra had been pulling, the lies she'd been telling. Those lies had sent them both off in the wrong direction. He hoped now he could correct that. He just had to convince Courtney to forget the things Barbra had told her about him. It would take an act of God to pry Barbra out of the apartment right now though. She was having too much fun torturing Courtney.

"Well, I can be just as stubborn." A steely glint hardened Courtney's soft brown eyes. "When Jane moves in tomorrow, it will be two against one."

"What does Barbra think of having another roommate?" The woman did nothing out of the goodness of her heart.

Courtney released a long sigh. "Not much. As it is, I had to reduce her rent to one third even though Jane can't pay anything until she begins working at the hospital. Barbra isn't about to let anyone get something for nothing."

Barbra was a pro at getting something for nothing. He didn't think she had room to complain, but people like that were usually the first to think they were being taken advantage of.

Opening the passenger door on his truck, helping her inside, he asked. "What's this new roommate like? She's the woman who was found in the desert, right?" He was done talking about Barbra. She had occupied enough of their time already.

Courtney smiled. "Yes. When she was brought in no one expected her to pull through. The police are still looking for the person who attacked her." She gave a little laugh. "I think the detective on her case has a crush on her. He comes to the hospital to see her every day."

"But she still doesn't know who she is?" he asked. He loved hearing Courtney's voice and wanted to keep her talking.

"No, but hopefully it won't be much longer before her memory comes back. She's come a long way since she came out of the coma. With prayers and a lot of dedication from Doctor Weber and the rest of the medical team, she's going to be just fine."

"Who's Doctor Weber?" Barbra never talked about the hospital or the people she worked with. He always suspected it was because she didn't think he was smart enough to understand.

"Chief of Neurology," Courtney explained. "He's taken care of Jane since she was brought in. He refused to let the hospital administration move her to a county facility when she was stabilized after all the surgeries. He's seen to her care right along."

"Maybe he's got a crush on her, too," Ted suggested only half in jest. "I hear doctors sometimes fall for their patients, not just the other way around."

Courtney laughed out loud. "I don't think that's the case here. He's old enough to be her father."

"There's no fool like an old fool," Ted quoted, making Courtney laugh again.

She shook her head. "That wouldn't make Janice Able very happy. I think there is something going on between the two of them."

Ted sighed comically. "Who is Janice Able? I can't keep all these people straight."

"Janice Able is head nurse," Courtney explained. "The rumor mill has it that she's been in love with Doctor Weber for as long as anyone can remember. Only problem is, Doctor Weber is so involved with his patients he doesn't notice."

"That place is worse than a soap opera," Ted laughed. "You don't need the ones on TV. Don't you know better than to listen to what any rumor mill has to say?" He was only half joking.

His statement gave Courtney pause, her line of thought following his. "Hmmm, now that you mention it, I'd never heard anything about Doctor Weber and Janice until Barbra started working for her." She shook her head at her own gullibility. "The woman twists the truth to fit her own perspective."

~~~

Barbra stood at the window watching Ted and Courtney. "She's probably whining that I wouldn't leave so they could have the apartment to themselves," she sneered. "Well, that's too damn bad. If she wants to jump in bed with *my* boyfriend, she's going to have to go somewhere else to do it." Barbra conveniently forgot that she had been seeing other men while dating Ted.

"Ted was mine until I didn't want him any longer," she mumbled angrily, still watching the couple in the parking lot. "But Courtney just couldn't keep her hands off." Letting the blinds drop back into place as the big truck pulled out of the parking lot, Barbra turned away from the window, her eyes filled with hate. "Nobody takes something of mine without paying for it," she vowed. "If it's the last thing I do, I'll make them pay."

PART TWO
CHAPTER NINE

I would be leaving the hospital the following day, and I still hadn't settled on a name of my own. Nothing seemed right. Frustration pushed at me as I haunted the halls to regain my strength. Until I could begin working at the hospital, I would be living off Courtney's charity. Even though I don't know who I am, I know in my soul that accepting charity isn't something I take lightly.

My steps led me to the small chapel as it had each day. I didn't even know what beliefs I held, but the room called to me all the same. A peace settled over me each time I entered the chapel. Sinking down in the front pew, I bowed my head. "I know you're listening, God," I whispered. "I need your help. I need to know who I am." Lifting my head, I sat there for several minutes letting the silence surround me.

"Hello." A tall man I hadn't seen before stopped beside the pew. "I hope I didn't disturb you." My heart skittered in my chest. Until I knew who tried to kill me, strangers still frightened me. Sensing my fear, he took a step back. "I'm sorry that I frightened you. I'm the chaplain here at the hospital. My name is Theodore Winston." He offered his hand for me to shake.

I hesitated for a brief moment before placing my hand in his much larger one. As his hand cupped mine, that feeling of peace settled over me again. He was in his late sixties, with gray hair and a friendly smile.

"I've seen you here every day this week. How are you doing?" He sat down in the pew across the aisle, not wanting to crowd me. Like so many people in the hospital, he knew who I was, but only as that hated name, Jane Doe.

"I'll be a lot better when I remember who I am. I don't want to be Jane Doe forever." *I also wanted to know who tried to kill me*, but I kept that thought to myself.

"Something is calling you to this place, so I'd guess you know the Bible. Maybe we can find a name there that will suit you until you remember your own. Can you recall a particular story?"

For a long moment I thought about his statement. Did I know the Bible? I nodded my head. "Deborah was a strong woman. She led the Israelites. I want to be strong like that." I wasn't sure where the knowledge came from, but I knew it was true.

Chaplain Winston beamed at me. "She certainly did. She was a very strong woman, and I believe you are as well. You'll do the name proud."

A frown wrinkled my forehead. "People in the Bible didn't have last names. I don't want to be Deborah Doe," An involuntary shudder shook me.

He thought for a moment, then smiled at me. "I would be honored if you would use my last name until you can remember your own."

Deborah Winston, I rolled the name around in my mind. Giving a nod, I smiled at him. "Thank you. Deborah Winston has a nice ring to it."

I kept repeating the name over and over as I made my way back to my room. I wanted it to feel natural when asked what my name was. For the remainder of day I told everyone who would listen what my new name was. The key phrase there happened to be 'everyone who would listen.'

"That isn't your name, and I refuse to call you that." Barbra busied herself at the nurse's station when I walked up. Since Courtney asked me to move in with them, Barbra's attitude had turned even more disagreeable.

"Jane Doe isn't my name either, but you have no problem calling me that. Besides, you're the one who told me to choose a name I liked. I like this one." She sniffed disdainfully, but didn't comment.

Turning away from the unfriendly woman, I wasn't going to let her spoil my happy mood. I was getting out of the hospital, I would no longer have to answer to that non-name, and I had a job and a place to live. No one could dampen my mood.

How wrong that turned out to be. Who knew there were so many people in a hospital with very little compassion?

"Hello, Jane, I'm Nancy Brewster. I work in the finance department." She didn't bother looking at me, and her smile didn't quite reach her eyes.

"I'm no longer going by that name," I informed her quickly. "My name is Deborah Winston until I recover my memory." She shrugged, unconcerned with my statement. It didn't look like this interview was going to go very well.

"You're going to be released tomorrow. We need to arrange some sort of payment plan for your bill." My stomach sank to my toes. I'd been in the hospital for nearly two months. The charges had to be astronomical by this time.

"I'll be working here once I get my strength back. Can I arrange to have money from my pay check applied to my bill?" I couldn't make my voice work above a whisper.

"Do you have any idea what your bill amounts to? Your entire pay check won't make a dent in what you owe this hospital and the doctors who work here. Are you sure you don't have insurance, maybe with an employer?"

"I don't know who I am, so how am I supposed to know if I was employed somewhere?" Reminding myself that Deborah in the Bible had been a strong woman and I was going to be like her helped to give me the strength of will to stare her down. "I will pay as much as I possibly can every payday. As long as I make some kind of payment, you can't turn my account over to collections." I wasn't sure where that information came from, but I was fairly certain it was correct.

Before she could argue further, Doctor Weber pushed the heavy door open. The smile that lit up his lined face didn't last long when he spotted the woman with all her papers standing beside my bed. "Is there something you need from my patient, Ms. Brewster?" His tone was cold, almost glacial.

She moved away from him as he stalked into the room. "Um, I just had a few last minute items to take care of before she's discharged. It can wait until later."

"It can wait permanently." His craggy eyebrows lowered over his eyes. "The matter has been taken care of with your supervisor." He walked back to the door, opened it and waited for her to leave.

"What do you mean the matter has been taken care of? I owe the hospital thousands of dollars, probably hundreds of thousands. She was just trying to set up a way for me to repay what I owe."

"There are many generous people in this state, even the country. When people heard what happened to you, donations came pouring in."

"I can't let people do that!" Tears of shame burned behind my eyes.

"Why not? People helping people is what it's all about."

More charity, I thought. I didn't want to be a charity case. When I started to argue further, he held up his hand. "Have you ever heard the term 'Pay it forward'? When you're able, you can help someone else in need. Until then, let people help you. Don't think of it as charity." He might as well have read my mind.

How can I help someone else when I can't even help myself? I wondered. The thought swirled around in my mind. I needed to figure out what happened to me, and why before I would be able to help others.

~~~

It was noon the following day before the paperwork was finished allowing me to check out. For the first time in current memory, I was leaving the hospital. It was frightening to leave the only place I remembered.

People had been coming into my room since early morning to wish me good luck and say good-bye. They weren't exactly friends, but they were the closest thing I had to friends. It would be another week before I could begin working at the hospital. Maybe then some of those people would become friends.

The patch on my head that had been shaved because of the

surgery was growing out, but it still had a long way to go to catch up with the rest of my hair, even with the haircut the nurse had given me. At least it wasn't as noticeable now.

Courtney had taken the day off so she could help get me to her apartment. I was still apprehensive about living with Barbra. The woman was so filled with hate it poured off her in waves. But I had few choices where I would live. It was either with Courtney and Barbra, or a shelter somewhere. I shuddered at the thought.

As Courtney pushed the wheelchair out of the room, patients and staff lined the long hall. Even Rex Booker was there to see me off. He had continued to stop by every evening when he left work. I tried telling myself that he was just there to see if I remembered anything about my past, but in my heart I hoped it was more than that. I didn't want to be just another case to him. I was going to miss the handsome sergeant. My heart ached a little at the thought of never seeing him again. Maybe he'd still drop by the apartment, at least until the case was solved or it went cold.

Leaving the artificial chill of the hospital, the heat of the August afternoon hit me like a physical blow. "It's like breathing fire," I gasped, afraid I'd seared my lungs. "This is as bad as the soup-like air at home."

Everyone stopped moving. "You remember where you're from?" Rex Booker was the first one to recover his voice, shock registered on his face.

Until that moment, I didn't realize what I'd said. Now excitement bubbled up in my veins. Did I know where I'd lived before? I tried to bring something to the front of my mind. The harder I tried to remember, the more elusive it became. There was nothing but the same blank wall as before.

Giving a frustrated sigh, I shook my head. "I know the humidity is very high in the south making it hard to breathe sometimes, especially if you have asthma. That's probably what I meant." My shoulders drooped. We'd already established that I was from the south, we just didn't know where in the south. This wasn't exactly a revelation.

Barbra was sitting in the living room, her feet propped up on the coffee table when Courtney and I arrived a short time later. She didn't bother to look up from the television show she was watching.

"You'll be sharing my room," Courtney said.

"Damn straight," Barbra interrupted without looking at either of us. "I'm not sharing my room with anyone."

"Ignore her," Courtney instructed, glaring at the other woman. "Our room is down the hall."

My heart sunk a little. This wasn't going to be a happy arrangement. I wasn't sure what I had done to make her hate me so much. Now my heart skittered in my chest. Was she the one who had tried to kill me right there in the hospital? I still didn't know the complete story on what happened. Even if she isn't a killer, I felt certain I would have to keep an eye on her. She was filled with hate, and I was her current target.

The apartment was more luxurious than I expected. I wasn't sure what my share of the rent would be, but it would only be for a few months, I reminded myself. Courtney had already been planning on moving to another place with a cheaper rent. She said I could move in with her there as well. This time without Barbra, I added silently. The woman wasn't very nice.

"Would you like to lie down for a little while?" Courtney asked. "You don't want to overdo it on your first day out of the hospital." She pushed open the door to her bedroom. The biggest bed I'd ever seen sat in the middle of the room.

"Um, I hope you don't mind sharing my bed. It's all I have. I didn't think you'd want to sleep on the couch, especially with..." She nodded her head towards the living room where Barbra sat watching television.

"This is fine. It won't be for that much longer." I looked at her hopefully.

"Right, but for now, that's our little secret," she said quietly. "We can get you a bed of your own when we move." The room was almost big enough to hold another bed, but that would have to wait until I started working. Courtney's kind heart gave me hope that even if I don't remember my past, things would work out okay.

Sinking down on the bed, an involuntary sigh escaped my lips. I thought I'd regained most of my strength, but after being bedridden for so long I tired easily. Combine that with the extreme heat and the exertion of leaving the hospital, I felt like I'd been run through a wringer. I needed to work at getting stronger, or I'd never make it through a full day at the hospital. I was hoping to begin work the following week. Within minutes, my eyes drifted shut. The next time I opened them the sun was beginning to go down outside.

Barbra was still sitting on the couch staring at the television when I entered the living room. I wondered if she'd moved at all while I was sleeping. She turned her head to look at me, giving a disdainful sniff, but kept her thoughts to herself.

"How are you feeling, Deborah," Courtney asked from the kitchen. Something smelled wonderful. "Are you hungry?"

"I think I could eat just about anything as long as it isn't hospital food."

"That's rather ungrateful, considering you were there on someone else's dime," Barbra snapped.

"That's enough," Courtney said. There was steel in her tone.

"Well, she was. People had been donating money by the bucket full. If it didn't cover all of the hospital charges, I heard that Doctor Weber picked up the rest."

I gasped. "Why would he do that?"

"Because you're so special," Barbra sniped. Her lips curled up in a snarl. "If he treated all of his patients the way he's treated you, he'd be in the poor house along with his patients. It's no wonder Janice Able doesn't stand a chance with him. She isn't one of his patients." I didn't know what she was talking about, but didn't get the chance to ask.

Courtney stomped into the room, her hands fisted on her hips. "That's enough out of you. There's a television in your room, why don't you watch it in there?"

"You can't kick me out of the room just because she's here. Besides, it's my television, and I'll watch it if I want. At least I'm paying my share of the rent."

"And the lease for this apartment is in my name. If you enjoy living here, I suggest you try being civil for a change."

Barbra stood up, glaring daggers at Courtney. "I knew it would come down to this. First you steal my boyfriend, now you want to kick me out of my home. Well, that's not going to work. I've already contacted legal services at the hospital. As long as I'm paying my share of the rent, you can't kick me out."

"That isn't exactly the truth. I've done a little checking as well. I have to give you thirty days' notice. Consider yourself notified. My lease is up in three months. We'll all be moving at that time."

Barbra gasped. "Were you planning on telling me as you were moving out? Some friend you are."

Courtney laughed. "We've never been friends, and I'm through being a doormat for you to wipe your feet on. You might want to try being nice for a change. Maybe then you could get and keep a boyfriend for a change."

Without warning, Barbra threw the remote control she'd been holding at Courtney, hitting her on the cheek. Without stopping to see what damage she'd done, she stormed into her room, slamming the door behind her.

"I'm so sorry. This is my fault." Grabbing a towel, I rushed to Courtney's side. Blood was running down her face from a small cut. "Let's get ice on that." I led her over to the couch where Barbra had been sitting for so long there was a permanent indentation.

"This isn't your fault, it's hers." She pointed towards the room where Barbra had disappeared. She sighed. "Maybe a little of mine, too," she admitted. "I've put up with everything she dished out for so long because I was desperate for a roommate to help with the rent. Now she thinks she can continue treating me like her slave. I should have put my foot down right from the start."

I lifted the towel to take a look at the cut on her face. It had already stopped bleeding. "How bad is it? I'm not going to need stitches, am I?"

I shook my head. "No, I'll put a butterfly suture on it. I don't think it will even leave a scar."

"Oh, darn," she chuckled. "I was hoping to lay some guilt on her."

"You think she's capable of feeling guilty?" I lifted an eyebrow.

"Probably not, I doubt she even has a conscience." Within minutes, I had closed the small cut, and Courtney went to look in the mirror. "Where did you learn to do something like that? A doctor couldn't do a better job."

I shrugged. I just did what needed to be done; anyone could do it. I didn't think it was anything special.

"Maybe you have some medical training?"

Something skittered through my mind, but once again it was gone so fast I couldn't grasp onto it. "I have no idea," I sighed. "Maybe I heard the doctors and nurses talking while I was unconscious and learned some things that way." I wasn't even sure if that was a possibility, but I didn't have a better explanation.

When my stomach growled, we both laughed. "Let's forget about Miss Crabby Pants and eat. I'm starved." Courtney headed for the kitchen. She made a detour to the door when the doorbell rang.

"Well, hello Sergeant Booker. What are you doing here? Is something wrong?" I could hear the frown and fear in her voice.

"No, does something have to be wrong for me pay a visit? And please, call me Rex." He looked past her, his gray eyes falling on me, his full lips curving up in a smile. My heart seemed to skip a beat, while butterflies fluttered in my stomach. The man was beyond sexy.

She stepped back to let him in, and started to close the door when a strange man stepped into the doorway. "May I come in, too?"

My heart jumped into my throat now nearly choking me, it was beating so hard. I must have let out a gasp, because three pair of eyes turned to me.

Rex Booker was by my side instantly, moving me behind him. He turned to the man. "Who are you?" His hand rested on the gun at his hip.

"It's all right, Deborah, Rex." Courtney held out her hands in a calming gesture. "This is Ted, my boyfriend."

"My *ex*-boyfriend." All eyes turned to Barbra. No one had noticed that she'd left her bedroom when the doorbell rang. "Hi, Teddy," she purred.

He frowned, giving her a curt nod, before taking a close look at Courtney. "What happened to your face?" A bruise was already beginning to form around the small cut.

"Um, a little misunderstanding." She glared at Barbra. "It's no big deal. Deborah took care of it." Barbra snickered at that, but didn't say anything. "Who's hungry? I think I made enough for four." She made a point to exclude Barbra, but the woman didn't take the hint.

My heart rate was beginning to settle into a normal range. I'd heard about Ted, but didn't know he had been Barbra's boyfriend first. No wonder she was so hostile. I was willing to give Courtney the benefit of the doubt though. Being Barbra's boyfriend couldn't have been easy for him, or any fun.

"I just came to check up on Deborah," Rex said. "I didn't mean to intrude." He seemed reluctant to leave, and didn't move towards the door.

"No, I insist you stay," Courtney said. "There's plenty for the four of us." Again she made a point of excluding Barbra. She gave me a wink as she headed back to the kitchen. I wasn't sure what she was up to, but I hoped he'd stay all the same.

The others moved towards the table, but Sergeant Booker, Rex, held me back. "Are you okay with him here?" he asked quietly. "We can go somewhere else to eat."

"No, I'm fine." My hands were still shaking, and I buried them in the pockets of my pants so he wouldn't notice.

"Want to tell me about that cut on Courtney's face?" He lifted one eyebrow in question.

"Um, no, not really." My stomach growled then, and we both laughed.

"Later," he said. "I have a feeling it's something I'd like to hear about."

Barbra settled herself at the head of the table like she was queen, or something, earning her a glare from Courtney, and a frown from Ted. She ignored them both. This was going to be a very long few months before the lease was up here, and we moved.

CHAPTER TEN

Even with a long nap, my energy was beginning to wane, but I didn't want the evening to end. How much longer before Rex was too busy with other cases to come see me? It was hard to remember that there might be a husband out there somewhere looking for me. But if that was the case, why hadn't he come forward, my mind argued back? Why hadn't any family come forward? The questions were always the same. Until I could remember, there were no answers.

Barbra had planted herself on the couch, instilling herself in every conversation. The woman was beyond nervy. It made for a very uncomfortable evening, but she wasn't moving.

When I yawned for the third time, Rex stood up. "I think it's about time for us to leave." He gave Ted a meaningful look.

"No, everyone can stay here. I don't want to break up the…" My voice trailed off. It wasn't exactly a party with Barbra glaring at Courtney and Ted every time he touched her. Which he did often. Maybe he did it just to irritate Barbra.

Ted stood up. "You're right, Rex. We all have to work tomorrow." He pulled Courtney to her feet. "I'll see you tomorrow? I want to hear what happened here." His whisper was loud enough for everyone to hear him as he touched the bandage on her cheek. He turned a dark glare on Barbra.

Rex took my hand, pulling me to my feet as well. "You get some sleep tonight, and I'll see you tomorrow." His voice dropped to a sexy whisper. "Maybe you'll feel up to going out to eat with me then." Before I could think of an answer, he placed a light kiss on my lips and was out the door.

"That's so sweet," Barbra sneered. She'd used up all the nice she had during dinner. She was back to being her spiteful self. "You know he's just interested in you as a victim. When the case goes cold, he'll move on to the next case, one that he can solve. He won't even look back."

Her words echoed my own thoughts and fears. I really

didn't want him to stop coming over. Instead of rising to the bait, I turned away. I was beyond tired.

By the time I woke up the following morning, Courtney had already left for work. She left a note on the dresser for me. *"Take it easy today. You can start exercising tomorrow. Don't let Barbra get you down. C"*

I wasn't sure what she meant by the last. Both roommates would be gone all day giving me time to find my way around the apartment and complex.

Some of the nurses had taken up a collection and presented me with new clothes as I was leaving the hospital. I had two new outfits, underclothes, and two sets of scrubs for when I started work. They had even thrown in some hand-me-downs. It was embarrassing to take so much charity, but I had no other option at this point. I promised myself that I would repay them, or as Doctor Weber suggested, Pay It Forward by helping some other unfortunate person.

After a long shower and dressed in my new clothes, I wandered to the kitchen to see what I could eat. A pot of coffee was already made and waiting for me. I had discovered in the hospital that I did indeed drink coffee.

I was finishing a piece of toast when the doorbell rang. My heart fluttered as I tiptoed to the door. I didn't know who would come over at this time of day. As a precaution, I peeked through the security peep hole. Surprised, I opened the door. "Doctor Edmonds? What are you doing here? Is something wrong?"

"Oh, come on, there isn't any reason to be so formal. Call me Jerry. Everybody does when we aren't at the hospital." His smile was as big as the man himself.

"Why are you here?" I asked again. "Is there something wrong?" Did some of the many tests they'd run on me come back negative? My heart did a stutter-step at the thought of more problems.

He gave a hearty laugh. "Why does something have to be wrong? I just wanted to check up on our famous patient on her first morning out of the hospital. I thought I'd see if I could help you with your PT. You need to keep up with that, you know." He'd worked with the physical therapist in the hospital setting up the exercises I needed to do to regain my strength. "How's your arm feeling?"

"It's fine." I wiggled my fingers and moved my arm up and down to show him that I wasn't having any trouble.

I cast a furtive glance at the clock. It was only nine o'clock in the morning. I'd been out of the hospital less than twenty-four hours. Did he really expect me to be doing PT already? "I promise I'll keep up with the exercises. I thought I was through with PT when I left the hospital."

He chuckled. "Exercises are PT. After what you went through, you'll need to keep up the therapy for a long time. You lost a lot of muscle mass, and need to keep working to get it back. I'm here to see that you do just that." He chuckled, as he stepped into the room, forcing me to back up. His well-muscled body was proof that he practiced what he preached.

"But I don't have insurance or money. I can't afford to pay you."

He lifted his broad shoulders in a careless shrug. "I'm not asking for payment. You were my patient while you were in the hospital. I don't want all that hard work to go to waste."

"Jerry, what the hell are you doing here?"

I let out a strangled shriek when someone spoke from behind me. Whirling around, I stared at Barbra for several beats until I found my voice. "Barbra, you nearly scared me to death."

"Well, that would never do, after all that we did to keep you alive and kicking," she replied with a sneer. She returned her attention to the doctor. "I asked what you're doing here, Jerry." It wasn't like her to be so rude to one of the doctors, so what was up? Had she tried to date him and he rejected her? That could be the only explanation for her actions now.

"Just checking on my patient. She needs to keep up with her physical therapy." He had a hard time keeping his eyes on her face. She was clad in the shortest nightgown I'd ever seen. Or maybe it was just the top of a pair of baby doll pajamas.

The bodice was form fitting, and barely there. I wasn't sure she had anything on underneath. Whatever the case, she shouldn't be parading around dressed like that in front of someone she barely knew.

"Well, she can't do it here," she snapped, stretching her arms over her head. The short nighty climbed even higher on her thighs. "Go away."

Her rudeness was embarrassing, but he didn't notice or care. For a minute I thought his eyes were going to pop out of his head at the show she was putting on. Finally, he got control, and looked at me instead of her. "Th...that's fine with me. There's a nice swimming pool in this complex. Water aerobics are a great way to exercise and gain strength without putting too much strain on the muscles."

"No, I can't do that." I shook my head to emphasize my point, my short hair moving around my face.

"Can't swim?" He asked. "Not to worry, we won't go in the deep end."

"Um, no, that's not it. I don't have a swim suit," I said softly.

"Oh." He looked at Barbra for help.

"Don't look at me. She's not using *anything* of mine, especially my bathing suit. Now, go away." She made shooing motions with her hands. "You don't belong here." She could have meant the last for me as well as him.

A murderous look crossed his usually docile features, and I took a step back. Finally he gave a shrug, before turning to me. "Do what you can on your own. I'll check on you later when you're free." He was out the door before I could say anything.

"You didn't need to be so rude. He was trying to be nice."

"Don't let his visit go to your head. He ran out of nurses to ask out so I guess he's going to start with the patients. He'll only ask you out once before he moves on to someone else." Picking up the remote control and flipping through the channels, she ignored me.

"I'm not going to go out with him." Her pronouncement

sounded like it came from personal experience. That could explain why she acted the way she did. I pushed that thought aside for now. "What are you doing home? I thought you had to go to work today." I stepped in front of the television, forcing her to look at me.

"I called in sick."

"Why? What's wrong with you?" She didn't look like she was sick.

"What's wrong with me?" she snapped. "I'm sick of people trampling all over my feelings." She was one to talk. She wasn't even nice to the patients under her care part of the time. I kept that thought to myself. "I don't like strangers in my home when I'm not here. I wasn't even consulted about you moving in here. I don't know who you are. For all I know, you could be a thief or worse, someone looking for an easy score."

For a minute I was too stunned to say anything before I got some starch in my backbone, reminding myself to be strong like Deborah in the Bible. "So you think I'm faking the amnesia so I can rob you blind. Did I also fake the beating and everything else?" She gave a careless shrug, but didn't say anything. "Are you planning on staying home until I begin working at the hospital? I wonder how long the administration will put up with that."

That seemed to give her a little pause, but she lifted her shoulders in another shrug without commenting. She just waved her hand indicating she wanted me to move aside so she could watch her show. Now I knew what Courtney meant about not letting Barbra get me down.

I spent the day in Courtney's room, doing the exercises the therapist had given me. At one point I tried to go for a walk, but the heat was unbearable. After fifteen minutes, sweat was running down my face, dripping off my nose and the tips of my short hair. I gave it up as a lost cause and returned to the apartment. It was going to take time to get accustomed to the intense heat, if that could ever happen.

My attempt to get something for lunch was quickly shot

down. "Do you remember me saying that I wasn't giving you anything of mine? The food in the refrigerator belongs to me. If you're hungry, there's a Jack-in-the-Box on the corner." A wicked smile lifted the corners of her mouth when I put the cup of yogurt back in the refrigerator, and returned to the bedroom. I had no money for food even if I had a way to get to the store. Maybe she was hoping I would starve to death.

If she was going to stay home every day until I was able to go to work, things were going to get very tense. The only time she moved from the couch for the remainder of the day was to go to the bathroom or get something to eat. I needed to discover what the rules were around here. Even a shelter would be better than living under Barbra's thumb until we could move.

She was still in her nighty when Courtney came home, and I was feeling a bit of cabin fever from staying in my room all day. I was also very hungry. At least in the hospital there had been people I could talk to. I was also fed three times a day, not necessarily the best food, but at least it was more than I had here.

"Why aren't you dressed, Barbra? What have you done all day?" She looked at me as I came out of the bedroom. "What's going on?"

Barbra shrugged. "Whatever do you mean? Nothing is going on." She was acting all innocent, but she wasn't a very good actress.

"I mean what have you done all day? You're still in your nighty."

"Well, maybe I was entertaining my boyfriend. Oh I mean my ex-boyfriend. He's your boyfriend now. I didn't want an audience so she was nice enough to stay in your bedroom." It was a pack of lies, and we all knew it.

"Doctor Edmonds said he came over here to help Deborah with some PT, but you wouldn't let him do it here. What's wrong with you?"

The doorbell rang before Barbra said anything. Courtney glared at her. "Go get some clothes on." She stepped to the door, but waited for Barbra to move.

"Why should I? If it's Ted, he's seen me like this before. In fact, he's seen me in less than this." She lifted the edge of the nighty.

I could tell the taunt had hit its mark, but Courtney did her best to ignore it. "And what if it's not Ted? Maybe it's Rex to see Deborah."

"Even better, he's one handsome man. Go ahead, open the door."

Taking the dare, Courtney opened the door without checking the peep hole first. "Oh, Doctor Riley, hello." She stepped back in surprise. "Is something wrong at the hospital?"

He chuckled as he stepped inside. "No, of course not. I just came to check up on our patient." He turned to me. "How was your first day out of the hospital?"

"Um, okay, I guess." I turned to look at Barbra, but she was no longer sitting on the couch. She had managed to disappear into her bedroom. When she reappeared minutes later, fully dressed, yet just as provocatively as before, I decided the woman was a quick-change artist.

"Why, Doctor Riley, welcome to our home," she cooed. "And Doctor Dean." A big smile spread across her face. In the time she was out of the room, our guests had multiplied. "Are we having a party?" She clapped her hands childishly. "I just love a party." Gone was the harridan that had forbidden me to eat any of her food all day. In her place was someone so sweet I wondered if we would all end up with tooth decay from all the sugar she was dishing out.

Did doctors in Arizona make a habit of visiting former patients? I didn't think this was something that happened on a regular basis. Why were they really here?

Courtney stared at her roommate, her mouth open in surprise. She clamped her jaws shut. "No, we're not having a party," she stated between clenched teeth before turning her back on Barbra. "Come in, Doctors. Have a seat." She started to shut the door, but we weren't through with company yet.

Rex and Ted got off the elevator together.

This was a little overwhelming for me. Although I knew each of these men, I was still uncomfortable around so many people at once. Knowing and trusting them were two different things. *But why wouldn't I trust the doctors who had worked to make me well?* I questioned. And Ted had nothing to do with me.

"What's going on?" Rex looked at the two doctors. "Did something happen today?" He came over to me, taking my hands, his light-colored eyes boring into mine. "Are you okay? Are you sick? Did something happen today?" His voice was filled with worry.

Before I could answer, Doctor Dean spoke up. "We just came to see how Jane, I mean Deborah made out on her first day away from the hospital." He stepped towards the door. "I guess we should be going." He sent a pointed look at the other doctor. Both men seemed a little embarrassed now.

"Oh, please don't go," Barbra chimed in. "Stay for dinner. I'm sure Courtney has a wonderful meal planned. She's such a good cook." She was willing to let them eat her food, just not me.

Courtney sent her a murderous look, but refrained from saying anything. The tension in the room had built to a physical presence.

Both doctors declined the invitation, and hurried to the door. "I'm glad to see you're doing okay." Doctor Riley looked at me. "I'm sure we'll see you around the hospital when you start working." At the door, Doctor Dean's eyes swept over Barbra's curves highlighted by the tight-fitting sundress. She didn't miss his smile of approval.

Once the door closed behind the doctors, Barbra glared at Courtney and me, her fists braced on her slim hips. "Well, you weren't very welcoming. The least you could have done was to offer them a drink, instead of almost pushing them out the door."

Pulling me aside, Rex ignored her. "Are you all right?" His voice was a soft whisper against my skin as he leaned over me.

My stomach answered for me when a hungry growl rumbled loud enough for everyone to hear. "I'm fine, just hungry." I sent a dark frown in Barbra's direction.

"Didn't you eat today?" Courtney asked. "There's plenty of food here." Her puzzled frown moved between Barbra and me.

I simply shrugged. There was enough animosity between the two women; I didn't need to add more by telling her what Barbra had done.

"Let me take you out for dinner," Rex spoke into the uneasy silence.

"I second that," Ted said, "if you don't mind us joining you, that is." He took Courtney's hand.

"Sounds good, let's go." Rex looked at me, lifting one eyebrow in question. I gave a small nod. I wasn't sure about going to a crowded restaurant, but it would be better than staying here with Barbra for another minute. The next three months were going to feel like a lifetime.

"Well, what about me?" Barbra whined. "I'm hungry, too."

"You said yourself that there's plenty of food. Fix something."

"You know I can't cook," she whined again when Courtney hurried to the bedroom to change out of her hospital scrubs. She was back almost as fast as Barbra had been when she saw the doctor at the door. As the door closed behind us, something crashed against the other side. Rex whirled around, taking a step back to the apartment.

"Ignore her," Courtney sighed. "She's having a temper tantrum."

"You can't let her get away with that," he advised. "Has she done this in the past?"

"No, but that's only because I've bent over backwards to avoid a confrontation. I'm through giving in to her. I only have three months left on my lease. After that I won't have to put up with her."

"You still shouldn't let her destroy your things."

Courtney chuckled. "My ex-fiancé took everything but the bills when he moved out. Whatever she just threw at the door belonged to her." She looked at me. "I made sure the door to our room was locked when I walked out. She can't get in there."

I shrugged. "I don't have anything for her to destroy." For once I was glad I had nothing to my name.

Rex shook his head. It went against his cop nature to let her get away with destroying property, even if it was her own.

Deciding we would take his SUV instead of going in two cars, Rex looked over the seat back at Courtney. "You want to tell me why those doctors came over? I've had a lot of dealings with doctors and victims. I've never known any of them to check up on a patient after they left the hospital." He reached across the console, taking my cold hand in his much larger one.

She shrugged. "Your guess is as good as mine. Deborah was our patient for a long time. Maybe they're having separation anxiety." She chuckled at the idea. "They're both fairly new to the hospital. The only doctor I've ever seen follow up with a patient after they're released is Doctor Weber. He's always been very hands-on. Doctor Edmonds stopped by this morning to check up on her as well."

"I don't like it when people start acting out of character," he muttered. "It usually means they're up to something." He backed the big truck out of the parking space. "What would you like to eat?" He trained his warm gaze on me. "Any suggestions where you'd like to go eat?"

My stomach rumbled loudly at the mention of food. "As long as it isn't hospital food, I don't care where we eat." The others laughed, but I could feel the questioning look Rex sent my way. At least he didn't voice his questions in front of the others. I knew Courtney was going to have some questions for me once we were alone.

Everyone agreed on a local steak house that was close by, which was fine with me. By now, my stomach felt like it was nibbling on my backbone, I was so hungry.

"Would you like steak and lobster?" Rex asked softly once we were seated.

"No, thank you. I'm allergic to shell fish." I answered absently as I studied the menu. When the import of my words sunk in, I looked up in surprise. Three pairs of eyes were staring at me.

A slow smile spread across Rex's handsome face. "Something else we now know about you."

"But what good does that piece of information do? A lot of people are allergic to shell fish, and there isn't a national database of people with that allergy, is there? I still don't know who I am."

"Maybe not, but it does mean that things are beginning to come back to you. It's a start." I wasn't so sure about that. It could be another example of muscle memory, or something of the sort.

"We also need to put that in your medical chart," Courtney said. "We'll get you an epi pen as well. Do you know how to use one of them?"

Before I could answer, the waiter stopped at our table to take our orders. I was just as glad. The sooner we ordered, the sooner the food would come. Other than shell fish, I was certain I liked just about any other kind of food. I ordered a steak and baked potato with a salad. When a tray of warm bread was placed in the center of the table, it took all the willpower I could muster to keep from grabbing a piece and shove it in my mouth.

If Barbra stayed home tomorrow, I promised myself that I wouldn't be cowed by her overbearing attitude. I'd eat whether she approved or not.

After inhaling the first piece of warm bread the waiter brought to the table, I tried to slow down. I didn't want to fill up on bread and not be able to eat the steak I'd ordered. Then again, I thought, maybe I should take some leftovers with me. That way Barbra couldn't accuse me of eating her food. A determined smile crept across my face. I wasn't going to let her intimidate me, I reminded myself.

While I concentrated on my food, I let their conversation flow around me. Remembering Courtney's question, I tried to recall if I had ever used an epi pen. I had no memory of actually using one, but I was certain I knew how to use it.

Finishing the last bite of steak, I sat back with a contented sigh. "Are you finally full?" Rex asked with a grin. "I don't recall anyone ever enjoying their food quite as much as you just did."

My face heated up with embarrassment. "I'm sorry." I wasn't sure why I was apologizing. "Did I do something wrong?" Maybe along with the rest of my memory, I'd also forgotten my manners.

"No, honey." Rex took my hand that suddenly felt icy cold. "You were just enjoying that steak like you haven't eaten for a week." He frowned at me. "You did eat today, right?"

"Um, sure, of course I did." I couldn't look him in the eye.

"What did Barbra do?" Courtney asked the question. "Did she tell you that you couldn't eat anything?" Apparently she knew her roommate very well.

"Look, it's okay. I'd rather not go into it. It won't happen again."

"Damn right it won't," Rex muttered. His fingers tightened possessively around mine. "That woman needs to learn she isn't in charge of the world."

My stomach gave an uncomfortable roll. Some of the fun of the evening evaporated.

Back at the apartment, I reached for the door handle to get out, but Rex took my hand, keeping me in the seat. "Just a minute, Hon." He was getting very free with the endearments. Not that I minded, but I needed to remind myself that there might be a husband or boyfriend out there somewhere looking for me.

When Courtney and Ted got out, I figured Rex was giving them time to be alone before I followed them to the door. It was a certainty that they wouldn't get any alone time in the apartment with Barbra there.

Pulling me across the bench seat, Rex draped his arm across my shoulder. "Why were you so hungry? You want to tell me what happened today?"

"Um, no?" It came out more as a question than an answer.

He chuckled. "Okay, I'll rephrase that. Tell me why you were so hungry tonight."

"I'd rather not." I avoided looking at him.

"Why? What did she do?" He was in full cop mode, and wasn't going to let me weasel out of answering.

"Look, there's enough trouble between Courtney and Barbra without me telling what that...that woman did." I couldn't think of an appropriate name to call her.

"You won't be telling Courtney, you'll be telling me. So tell. What did she do?"

With a heavy sigh, I repeated what Barbra told me about eating her food. "She's very possessive about anything she considers hers."

"That extends to food?" He shook his head. "I suppose that also includes Ted, if I'm not mistaken."

"I didn't say that! I never said anything about Ted and Barbra."

"Honey, you didn't have to say anything." He chuckled. "Her actions speak louder than words." Lacing his fingers through mine as we went inside the building, we waited for the elevator. Once the doors slid shut behind us, he dipped his head to claim my lips in a soft kiss.

As we stepped off the elevator, Ted stormed out of the apartment, slamming the door. "Watch your back, Deborah, or that bitch will stab you for sure."

"Wow!" "Not a chance." Rex and I spoke at the same time. Ted didn't bother with the elevator. We could hear his footsteps pounding down the stairs long after he disappeared from sight.

Rex pulled me into his arms. "I don't want you staying here if she's dangerous."

"She isn't homicidal," I told him. At least I hope she isn't, I added silently. I was too comfortable with his arms around me to even think of pulling away.

"Maybe not, but she isn't a very nice person." I couldn't argue with that, but I had few choices where I would stay until I could start working. Lowering his head, and gently touching his lips against mine, I let myself relax. Although he didn't deepen the kiss, I was feeling a little breathless when he raised his head.

"Maybe we shouldn't be doing this," I whispered reluctantly. "What if it turns out I'm married?" I didn't want that to be true.

"He gave up his rights when he didn't come forward to identify you. Your picture has been all over the news here in Arizona. I've contacted police departments throughout the south hoping a missing person's report had been filed. So far there hasn't been anything. Whoever did this to you doesn't want you to be found."

"So I don't even have family somewhere?" It was a lonely feeling that no one cared enough to miss me.

~~~

Was it a mistake to go see her today? He paced around the small room, second guessing his actions. Doctors don't make house calls any longer. Drawing attention to himself isn't what he should be doing. He'd been hoping to make friends with the woman, maybe even ask her out. Toying with her, messing with her mind might have been amusing. But that stupid detective had already claimed her for himself. A growl escaped his lips. What was he supposed to do about that?

CHAPTER ELEVEN

Barbra went to work the next morning, only because she was afraid of losing her job. "Stay out of my room," she snapped. "I'll know if you've been in there." She stormed out, slamming the door behind her.

Courtney was already gone so I had no way to find out what had put the bee under Barbra's bonnet so early in the morning. I still didn't know what Barbra had done to Ted the night before to make him storm out of the apartment. Whatever it was, I knew it wouldn't be good.

There was no lock on the refrigerator and no one to stop me from eating, so I fixed scrambled eggs and toast for breakfast. If Doctor Edmonds came over for PT, there was no reason he couldn't stay and help me through the exercises. Maybe when I started working, I would get a bathing suit and work out in the pool. Without thinking about it, I knew I could swim. I could feel the pull of the waves as I swam in the ocean.

Every day there was a procession of people from the hospital stopping by to see how I was progressing. I was never alone for very long, but the three doctors who had come over the first day weren't among them. The questions were always the same: "How are you?" "What are you doing?" "Have you remembered your name?" I quickly ran out of small talk.

Rex Booker stopped by as well to make sure there were no more attempts on my life. At least that's what I told myself, although the warm kisses we shared told me otherwise.

By mid-week, staying in the apartment was getting boring, even with all the company popping in at odd times throughout the day. It was too hot to go outside, and without a car or money I couldn't go anywhere. I needed a distraction.

At the sound of the doorbell, I sighed wondering who it would be now. "Chaplain Winston, what a wonderful surprise." Of all the people who had stopped by he was the most welcome. I had enjoyed our conversations while I was in

97

the hospital. "Please, come in. How are you?" I was chattering like a magpie.

"I'm doing very well, and I can see how you are. You look wonderful. What have you been up to that has you looking so great?"

"With nothing else to do, I've been doing the exercises they gave me at the hospital so I can regain my strength."

"Well, whatever you're doing, I'd say it's working. There's color in your cheeks, and I think you've even put on some weight. You were mighty thin when I first met you. I'd say you've always been in good shape or you wouldn't have survived your ordeal. It won't take long before you're back to your old self."

I had no idea what my old self was like, but that wasn't what he meant. Once again I searched through my blank memory trying to recall working out. The exercises the therapist had me doing at the hospital were all foreign to me. What other types of exercises would I have done to keep in shape?

Finally, I shook my head. Even vague images escaped me. "I have no idea what I was like before this happened," I sighed unhappily.

He patted my hand. "Maybe you're trying too hard. When God is ready for you to remember, you will." Unfortunately, I didn't have his faith, or his patience. I wanted to remember now.

Alone again, I decided to search out the fitness room furnished by the apartment complex for the tenants. I wasn't sure what it would prove, but I went all the same. A number of big machines were scattered around the room.

Without thinking about what I was doing, I stepped up on one. Immediately, I knew I'd used a similar machine in my forgotten past. For several minutes I was engrossed in the feel of my muscles stretching out, warming up to the exercise.

It felt good, but I tired quickly. I was certain I had used this kind of machine and others like it, but after being inactive for nearly two months, I needed to take things slow. I couldn't overdo, or I could delay any progress I'd made so far.

Stepping off the machine, I went over to the treadmill. It was so hot outside that just walking to the fitness center had sweat running down my face and between my breasts. Using the treadmill would be ideal to help build up my stamina. There were also free weights and several other machines that I was certain I had used before, but I couldn't name.

What did this prove? I asked myself as I walked back to the apartment. This little piece of information wouldn't lead me to who I am.

"Hello, Jane." I let out a shriek at the voice directly behind me. I'd been so lost in my thoughts I hadn't seen the man leaning against the car. "I'm sorry; I didn't mean to scare you. And I keep forgetting your new name. You were Jane Doe for so long; I keep forgetting to call you Deborah now." Doctor Dean pushed himself away from the car, a warm smile tilting his lips up.

"What are you doing here in the middle of the day? Shouldn't you be at the hospital?" The fright he'd given me caused my voice to be sharp. I took a cautious step back as he came towards me.

"Well, your roommate said you were getting bored staying at home all day."

"Courtney said that?" I wasn't sure if I believed him.

He chuckled. "No, your other roommate; she seemed concerned about you."

It was my turn to laugh. Barbra wasn't concerned about anyone but herself. I kept that unkind thought to myself. If he wanted to believe she was a nice person, who was I to disillusion him? Still, I couldn't believe she would send him over to see me. It wouldn't make her happy to know one of the doctors she coveted was interested in someone other than her.

"Can I take you to lunch?" His unexpected question startled me, breaking in on my thoughts, but I didn't have to think about an answer.

"No, I've already eaten." I answered a little too quickly. "But, thank you for asking," I added hastily. I wasn't sure why

I told that lie, but maybe it was self-preservation. His offer made me uncomfortable. What did I really know about any of the doctors at the hospital? Besides, he didn't look sorry for startling me. Maybe he and Barbra were cut from the same cloth. They might make a good pair.

"Well, maybe another time. I'm glad to see you're getting around so well. Barbra said you were cooped up in the apartment all day, and she wasn't sure how you occupied your time."

She was probably worried that I'd found a way to get in her bedroom. That sounded more like Barbra. She made a point of putting a big piece of tape between the door and the jamb each morning, so she would know if I went into her room. Like that would stop anyone from actually getting into her room. I shook my head at the idea.

"I'm doing fine. I'm hoping to be able to start working at the hospital next week."

"That sounds great. I'll be seeing you then."

I watched as he pulled out of the parking lot before going on to the apartment. Although he and Doctor Riley had come over my first day here, neither of them had come around again. It seemed a little strange that he came over now.

~~~

Watching her caused his blood to boil, but for now there was little he could do. There were too many people parading through her life right now. Another attempt to get rid of her would prove too dangerous. He wasn't taking any chances of getting caught. For now, he had to bide his time, and wait for the perfect opportunity. Until then, that little weasel was beginning to lose what little nerve he had. It's time to rid myself of that irritant, he thought. Then he could concentrate on getting rid of 'Deborah Winston'.

~~~

Doctor Weber finally pronounced me well enough to begin working at the hospital just a week after being released. Butterflies fluttered in my stomach as I walked up the steps to the hospital. Rex had insisted on bringing me on my first day.

I could feel him watching from his car. I felt like a little girl on my first day of school with daddy dropping me off. His kiss was imprinted on my mind and my lips, causing my heart to beat a little faster. There'd been nothing fatherly about that kiss.

I still didn't know if there could be a future for us since I didn't know what was on the other side of my blank memory. I just knew my feelings for the handsome detective were growing stronger every day, and I wanted to see where it would lead me.

Doctor Weber said to report to Human Resources, and they would show me around. I couldn't remember applying for a job, but common sense told me there would be a lot of forms to fill out. I wasn't sure how they were going to get around the fact that I didn't have a Social Security Number.

Two hours later, I finally finished with those forms, most of which required answers I couldn't supply. The rest of the morning I followed behind other aides learning what my duties would be.

"Honey, I'm so glad you're better." Donna Martin was a small woman in her late fifties. She'd worked at the hospital for ten years, and knew all the ins and outs of being a nurse's aide. "We were all worried about you, that's for sure."

"I'm fine now," I mumbled for lack of something better to say. I could feel a slight blush creeping over face. The entire staff knew me, greeting me with a cheerful welcome and wishing me well. This minor celebrity status was embarrassing.

"It must be terrible not to know who you are," she commented. I nodded my head at that, but didn't say anything.

By noon, my energy was beginning to lag. I had been on my feet for several hours, and they were beginning to hurt. I needed to get a pair of Crocs like the other aides and nurses wore. That was one more thing that would have to wait.

~~~

"You've got to do something about her. You can't let her work at the hospital," the young man whined. It was becoming

101

a litany for him. "What if working here brings back her memory?"

"What do you expect me to do about it?" One eye brow went up slightly. "When Weber says jump, even Human Resources asks how high." The little weasel was right though. Something had to be done. There was just one problem. She was never alone, at home or at the hospital. That damn detective has become her personal body guard.

I also need to do something about you, he thought, looking at his young companion. You're more trouble than you're worth. Maybe I can take care of both problems at the same time. The anticipation was almost as good as the actual deed.

He did agree with the little bastard about one thing though. It could prove dangerous to have that bitch working here. In a familiar setting, doing familiar things, her memory could return, and that would be disastrous, for all concerned.

"Do you have a plan?" the small man whispered, afraid to intrude on his boss's thoughts, but more afraid of not knowing what was going to happen.

Oh yeah, I have a plan, the big man continued to keep his thoughts to himself, keeping his companion in suspense. But you aren't going to like it. Turning slowly, he trained his steely gaze on the younger man, causing any other complaints to freeze on his tongue. "You're going to have to get your hands dirty," he finally said. "Think you can finish the job this time?" His sneer was openly challengingly.

"Y...yes," the young man stammered. "I don't want to go to prison."

"That's more like it." The young man started to relax at the deceptively pleasant tone. "Your life depends on how you handle this little crisis." He watched the young man gulp in air, his eyes wide with fear. Standing up, he came around the desk, placing a beefy hand on the smaller man's shoulder. "This time I'll be right beside you to help out." And to make sure the job gets done correctly, he added silently. He might have to risk letting her work here for a few days before he could finalize his plan, but in the end it would be well worth it.

Sitting in the hospital cafeteria the next day, his brooding gaze moved over the tables without seeing the people sitting there. Something had to be done about that damn girl, and soon. His assurances to the little weasel that everything was under control notwithstanding, he wanted to get on with his life. He couldn't do that as long as she was still a threat. He should have taken care of her himself, he acknowledged, but the little weasel had always followed his orders. Until that night, he corrected. Now his life was in a holding pattern, and it was beginning to wear thin.

He needed to come up with a plan that would point all fingers at the little weasel. If they died together, he would be in the clear. Figuring out how to accomplish that was the problem.

He cursed 'Deborah Winston' again. He wouldn't be in this mess, or even in this hospital, if she had just died like she was supposed to. The odds had been in his favor, had been right from the inception of his plan. Everything had been moving along on schedule, right up to the minute she walked into the hospital pharmacy. From that moment on his plans, and his life, had gone to hell.

Giving his head a fierce shake, he blinked his eyes to clear his vision of the apparition that had just materialized in the doorway of the cafeteria. When he opened his eyes again, she was still there. She was real; his mind hadn't conjured her up. As she approached Ben Weber seated at a table across the room, he escaped through another door. He wouldn't be able to conceal his murderous thoughts if he stuck around.

~~~

"Well, hello, Deborah," Doctor Weber smiled at me as I approached his table. "How is your first day going?" He stood up, pulling out a chair for me to join him.

I could feel a number of people watching us, surprise and shock written on their faces. I knew what people said about him. He wasn't very friendly with the other staff members. He only had time for his patients. But I wasn't just one of his staff. I had been a patient. I hoped he wouldn't revert to giving me the same cold shoulder he gave to so many others. I needed someone in the hospital I could rely on.

I gave a shrug, unsure how to categorize my day so far. "Did someone in HR give you a hard time?" He misinterpreted my hesitation, and was ready to go to battle for me.

"No, nothing like that. Everyone has been very nice to me." I hadn't seen Barbra, so that much was true. "It's just..." I searched for the right word.

"You don't like your job?" He kept guessing at what I was having trouble putting into words.

"It's not that, exactly. It's just mundane, routine. I feel..." Again I stumbled to a halt trying to figure out what I was trying to say. Coming up empty, I shrugged. "I don't know. I feel like I should be doing something more." That didn't make sense, but I didn't know what else to say.

"More in what way?" he asked, a frown drawing his bushy eyebrows together. "Is there something you're beginning to remember?"

I sighed. "I wish I could say yes, but I don't remember anything specific. It feels like I'm just going through the motions, that I've done something similar before, and I should be doing something else, something more." That was only part of it, but I didn't know how to explain any better.

A broad smile split his face. "You are beginning to remember, even if you don't think so. Right now though, you look tired. Maybe I shouldn't have let you begin working so soon after leaving the hospital." He began to worry again.

"Oh, no, please, I need to have something to do." I reached out to lay my hand on his arm. "Sitting in the apartment with nothing to do gave me way too much time to think. Pushing myself to remember when there was nothing there was driving me crazy. I'll just rest here for a little while, and I'll be fine." I was afraid he'd change his mind and send me home, but he finally nodded his head.

"Get yourself something to eat before you go back to the floor."

"Hospital food?" I spoke without thinking. I could hear the horrified note in my voice. "I brought a sandwich from home." I held up a small brown sack.

Standing up, he gave a chuckle. "Well, take your time. There's no hurry. No one is going to be upset if you take a few extra minutes for lunch." He gave my shoulder a pat as he walked off, his thoughts already shifting to his patients.

I could already hear Barbra's rampage if she thought for a minute that I was getting special treatment from the Chief of Neurology. That wouldn't sit well with her.

CHAPTER TWELVE

"**Y**ou always manage to set the hospital on its ear," Barbra sneered at me as I walked in the door. She got off work at the same time as Courtney and me, yet she managed to beat us home. She had already changed out of her uniform, and was sitting on the couch with her feet up waiting to be served dinner like she was royalty.

"What are you talking about?" Courtney asked on a sigh.

Barbra glared at me before answering. "She has the entire hospital buzzing. I'm surprised Janice Able hasn't come after her with a scalpel."

"Why? What did I do wrong?"

"You had lunch with *her man*, that's what." She gave a snickering laugh as she emphasized those words. "You better hope they don't place you on her floor, or she'll have you doing every dirty job there is to be done."

"I didn't have lunch with anyone."

"No?" One finely arched brow lifted slightly. "Everyone was talking about you and Doctor Weber in the cafeteria."

"I sat with him for just a minute before he went back to work," I tried to explain.

"Try explaining that to Janice Able," Barbra snickered.

I looked at Courtney for confirmation that what I did was so bad. She patted my shoulder as she walked past me. "Don't listen to her. She's just jealous. Besides, that isn't exactly the way I heard things. The hospital may be buzzing, but not in the way she's suggesting. Everyone thinks this is a good thing. Maybe Doctor Weber will warm up to the staff instead of just his patients."

Barbra's permanent glower darkened. "That's not likely to happen. Besides, Janice isn't a very forgiving woman. If she thinks that Jane here is encroaching on her territory, she'll…"

"The name is Deborah," I interrupted forcefully. I was tired of her continuing to call me by that hated name.

"That isn't even your name." Scorn filled her voice. "I don't know how the hospital administration let that pass."

"Well, Jane isn't my name either," I insisted.

She shrugged, going back to her original rant. "Janice is going to be in a real snit over your little faux pas with *her man*." She kept referring to Doctor Weber as Janice Able's man. Maybe I'd missed something of hospital gossip. "Because of Doctor Weber's influence they had to hire you. Janice is going to be ready to hand you your head if you aren't careful."

"She has always been very nice to me," I stated, remembering the time I had spent on her floor before I left the hospital.

Barbra's laugh grated on my nerves. "That's before you had lunch…"

"I know," I interrupted, "with her man." I finished her sentence. "I didn't know that they were…dating?" I finished lamely.

Barbra laughed again. "Probably the big man doesn't know it himself. Janice has been pining after him for as far back as anyone at the hospital can remember." She made it sound like forever. Barbra hadn't worked at the hospital very long, so how did she know this piece of gossip?

"He barely looks at her, or anyone else on staff for that matter. He only has eyes for his patients. Still, you need to be careful," she insisted. "You never know how a woman scorned will react to someone she considers her rival."

"Oh, for heaven's sake, Barbra, you make her sound like a homicidal maniac." Courtney looked at me. "Ignore her, she doesn't know what she's talking about. Janice is a nice lady." She walked past Barbra, heading to our bedroom.

"By the way, where are your shadows?" Barbra abruptly changed the subject when she couldn't get a rise out of either of us.

"Huh?" Courtney and I stared at her, unsure what she was talking about now.

Barbra chuckled. "Oh, come on, you know I'm talking

about Teddy and that hunky detective. They follow the two of you around like lost little puppy dogs hoping you'll toss them a bone of affection." She snickered at the double meaning of her words. "I wonder what's going to happen when your true identity turns out to be something less than the stellar person everyone has made you out to be. It might even mean that detective's job."

"If you're hinting that I'm some sort of criminal, you're wrong. My fingerprints aren't in any criminal data base." It was something I'd asked Rex when I first met him. I was tired and not in the mood to continue sparring with her. All I wanted to do was sit down with my feet up. But Barbra had command of the couch, and she'd made it clear she didn't share.

"What's for dinner?" she called as the bedroom door closed behind Courtney. "I'm hungry."

"When did I become your personal chef? I don't recall applying for that position." Courtney went back into the living room.

"You've always done the cooking." Barbra gave a careless shrug.

"That's only because you burned up several of my good pans with your inept attempts at cooking. Or did you do that on purpose?" She lifted one eyebrow. "From now on, things will be changing around here. If you're hungry, fix it yourself, with your own cookware; or go out to eat. Deborah and I won't touch anything of yours, and you won't touch anything of ours. Understood?"

"She doesn't have anything," Barbra sneered.

Courtney shrugged. "The rule still stands. The three of us have to co-exist in this apartment for the next three months. What you do after that will be up to you. In the meantime, everything of mine is off limits. Now, I'm going to change clothes. Our 'shadows'," she made air quotes around the word, "are going to pick us up in a few minutes. I'm cooking dinner at Ted's house." She turned to me. "Come on, Deborah, we don't want to keep the guys waiting."

"I haven't heard from Rex since this morning," I whispered once we were behind closed doors. "I don't think he'll be over tonight. You go on with Ted. I'll stay out of her way. I'm going to bed early."

Courtney shook her head. "Nope, you're coming with me. I'm not leaving you here at her mercy. She'll have you waiting on her just to prove she can."

I tried to object, but it was useless. She wasn't leaving me alone with Barbra. When the doorbell rang, she hurried out of the room. Leaving either man alone with Barbra was a risky proposition, but I figured both of them could hold their own, even against Barbra.

Barbra stayed seated on the couch. If the person at the door wasn't for her, she wasn't going to put herself out to open it. But it wasn't Rex or Ted.

"Oh, um, hi Doctor Dean," Courtney stammered, surprised to see him. She stepped back, allowing him to enter.

"I didn't get a chance to see how things went on Deborah's first day on the job, and thought I'd stop by on my way home." He gave each of us a beaming smile.

Barbra had jumped up the instant she realized who was at the door. She ignored the fact that he had come over to see me, not her. "As you can see, she's doing just fine. In fact, she's getting ready for her date with that detective."

His eyes swept over me. Like it had last week, my heart hammered harder. I didn't know why he had this effect on me. He never acted hostile towards me.

"Well, I'm glad things are going so well for you." He turned his attention to Barbra. Even when she wasn't going anywhere, she dressed proactively, and his eyes moved hungrily over her body. "If you don't have plans, would you like to have dinner with me? I don't like eating alone." That was a silly question.

"Why, that sounds wonderful." She jumped at the offer. "I'll just change out of this old dress into something more appropriate." She didn't move towards her room though.

"You look fine just the way you are." His dark eyes moved

down her body again. She was always dressed to show off her augmented curves. I doubted she even owned a pair of sweats.

"Why thank you, Doctor," she preened, running her hands down her sides. "I'll just put on a pair of shoes." She was back in a flash, and they were out the door as Ted got off the elevator. "Bye Teddy," she cooed seductively, linking her arm through Doctor Dean's. "Your date is waiting inside." As the elevator door closed, she looked like the cat that swallowed the canary.

"What was that all about?" Ted closed the door as he entered the apartment.

Courtney chuckled. "She wanted to make sure you knew a doctor had finally asked her out."

"Better him than me." He gave an exaggerated shudder. "That woman is a piranha. Are we going out for dinner?" He was finished talking about Barbra.

"No, since she'll probably be gone for the better part of the night, I can fix dinner here. Rex should be here in time to eat." She looked at me for confirmation.

I lifted my shoulders. "I don't know what his plans are."

Ted chuckled. "The man will be here no matter how late it gets."

"What makes you think that?" I was confused.

"Because he's so far in love with you he wouldn't miss an evening if his life depended on it."

Butterflies suddenly attacked my stomach. I didn't have any right being in love with anyone, or have them in love with me. "But he doesn't even know who I am yet. I don't know who I am."

"I don't think that matters to him in the least." Ted's prediction proved true a few minutes later when the doorbell rang. "Go ahead and answer it," he chuckled. "It'll be for you."

Checking the security peep hole first, I opened the door. Rex looked tired, but his smile still warmed my heart. "Hi there, pretty lady." His voice was husky. He leaned down to place a soft kiss on my lips. "How'd your first day at the hospital go?"

"It was…" I stumbled with my answer as I had when Doctor Weber asked the same question. Finally, I shrugged. "It was okay."

"Just okay? You don't like the job?" One eyebrow lifted slightly. "Did anyone give you a hard time?" His gaze wandered around the room like he was looking for someone. "Is she still giving you trouble?" He didn't need to explain who he was talking about.

"No, of course not." It was the truth as long as I ignored the barbs she shot in my direction.

He leaned close to me again, his voice a stage whisper now. "Is she lurking in the shadows waiting to pounce on any unsuspecting male? I have my gun, just in case."

"You're safe for tonight." I laughed, giving his arm a pat. "We all lucked out. Doctor Dean asked her out to dinner." I felt bad talking about her behind her back. It was something she did all the time, and I didn't want to be like her.

"Okay, we're coming in," Ted called out from the kitchen before he and Courtney came into the living room. "No more necking." The two men had met every evening since I moved in with Courtney, and they were always friendly. Maybe they would become friends, not just friendly.

Shaking hands with Ted, Rex placed a kiss on Courtney's cheek before sitting down on the couch Barbra had claimed as her throne. Within minutes the men were deep in conversation, swapping work related stories.

"Come on, Deborah; let's let the men talk shop. You can help me with dinner."

"Oh, I'm sorry." Rex stood up. "I didn't come over so you could feed me. I was going to see if Deborah wanted to go out for dinner."

"Nonsense, I enjoy cooking for people who appreciate my efforts."

Ted chuckled. "Translation: She enjoys cooking for anyone but Barbra."

"That's true, but I didn't mean it like that." She was quiet

111

for a minute. "Come to think of it, maybe I did. I've never heard her say thank you to anyone about anything." She was just realizing that fact.

"I'm willing to bet the doc gets a thank you in some form tonight." His meaning was clear, and I could feel a blush creeping up my face.

Courtney and I disappeared into the kitchen without any further discussion on whether we were staying. I had helped her with dinner every evening no matter where we ate, and learned that not only did I know how to cook, I enjoyed it.

"Do you really think Barbra would sleep with Doctor Dean just because he took her out for dinner?" Maybe I was being naive. It probably happened more than anyone wanted to admit.

Courtney nodded her head, her bobbed haircut swaying with the motion. "She would in a heartbeat if she thought it would get her what she wants most in life."

"What is that?" I didn't know the other woman well enough to judge what she wanted out of life.

"Her biggest desire is to marry a doctor and live the good life. She's never hidden the fact that she became a nurse for that reason, and that reason only."

I shook my head. "Doctors and nurses should care about their patients, not how much money they'll make off them. Medical school is expensive and it takes years to pay off student loans, but you shouldn't go into medicine for a big pay check."

Courtney looked over her shoulder at me, a frown drawing her eyebrows together. "It sounds like you're talking from experience. Maybe you have some form of medical training."

Was that why everything I did today seemed so familiar? I tried to picture something beyond what I had done so far, but there was nothing there. I just felt like I should be doing more, but more of what? I didn't know. Finally I shook my head. "I have no idea if I have training of any kind including medical training. Things just feel familiar when I do them."

"It'll come to you when you're ready. Don't push

yourself."

Everyone kept telling me that, but I wanted to remember. I wanted to know who wanted me dead bad enough to try killing me. Twice.

After dinner, the guys helped clear the table, and load the dishwasher. The one night Barbra ate dinner with us, she hadn't lifted a finger to help before or after dinner. It was nice that the guys didn't take us for granted.

Within minutes of sitting down after dinner, I began to nod off. It was only seven-thirty, and I wasn't ready for Rex to leave yet. The soothing hum of their voices flowed gently around me, relaxing me further.

When I felt someone touch my hair, I jerked up bumping my head against Rex's chin. "Oh, I'm sorry. What time is it?" I blinked my eyes, looking around the room.

He chuckled softly. "It's ten-fifteen. The news is almost over. I think it's time for you to go to bed." Courtney was standing at the door with Ted saying a lengthy good night.

"I'm sorry I fell asleep. You shouldn't have let me sleep like that."

"I'm not sorry." He placed another kiss in my hair. "I kind of like having your head on my shoulder. It is time for me to go home though." He lowered his head, claiming my lips in a passionate kiss, his tongue dueling with mine. It was several minutes later before he drew back. We were both breathing heavily. "I think I need to go now." He chuckled, standing up and pulling me with him. "I'll see you in the morning."

"You don't need to be my chauffeur. I can go in with Courtney."

"I kind of like seeing you before I go to the office."

"Oh, in that case..." I let my sentence trail off. I didn't have an argument for that. I could feel my face heating up. Unwilling to disturb Courtney and Ted, Rex nibbled at my neck while we waited until Ted opened the door. It took another ten minutes for the men to finally make it out the door.

"I think I'm in love." Courtney sighed. "No, I don't think I am; I know I am." She floated across the room to our bedroom.

I chuckled, but I silently agreed with her. No matter how ill-advised it was, I knew I was falling in love with Rex. What would I do if it turned out I had a husband somewhere? For the next hour that thought haunted me until exhaustion finally drew my eyes closed.

CHAPTER THIRTEEN

Instead of heading right to the floor I'd been assigned to, I made a quick stop at the chapel, hoping Chaplain Winston would be there. The cross at the front of the room was back-lit, and soft lights lined the walls, but the room was empty. Chaplain Winston wasn't around. Maybe he didn't start working at seven in the morning. Or maybe he only came in when there was a crisis. I didn't know enough about the workings of this hospital to guess.

Sinking down on the front pew, I looked up. "Will I ever remember who I am?" I whispered. "Am I going to spend the rest of my life looking over my shoulder for a killer?"

There was no thunderous answer, just a peaceful feeling sweeping over me. I wasn't in this alone. I sat there for several minutes absorbing the silence and peace. Maybe my second day on the job would be more fulfilling than the first one.

Doctor Edmonds was lounging against the wall as I left the chapel. "I've heard a lot of good things about you," He never seemed to be in a rush like the other doctors always were. "I'm glad you're keeping up with your exercises." His penetrating gaze moved over me, causing a shiver to move down my spine.

"It's in my best interest to do that: isn't it, Doctor Edmonds?" My voice sounded stilted even to my own ears. What was it about the man that made me uncomfortable? When he stepped into my personal space, I took a step back. I didn't want him getting close enough to touch me.

"Oh, come on. There's no need for such formality now that you're no longer my patient. I told you to call me Jerry. Everyone does." He chuckled. He finally answered my question as he pushed himself away from the wall. "You'd be surprised how many patients don't want to follow the proper regimen, even when it means it will help them get better. Well, I'll be seeing you around." There was a swagger in his step as he walked off.

For a long moment, I watched him before heading in the opposite direction. I was glad I wouldn't be working with him any longer. I put all thoughts of him aside as I hurried to my floor. Maybe I would be able to connect with some of the patients today.

By noon that hadn't happened. I'd given six patients sponge baths, emptied countless bed pans, and delivered the horrible breakfast trays. The feeling that I should be doing more for these people persisted. I just didn't know what that would be. I released a weary sigh as I headed to the cafeteria to eat the sandwich I'd brought. Even a peanut butter and pickle sandwich was preferable to hospital food. Fixing my lunch that morning, I put together an unlikely combination, but it sounded good. I hoped I wasn't wrong.

Surveying the cafeteria, I was hoping to see Doctor Weber. Would it cause trouble with Nurse Janice Able like Barbra suggested if I sat with him again? It was a moot point, the doctor wasn't here today.

"Well, hello there, Deborah. It's good to see you're doing so well. Everyone is singing your praises." Doctor Dean stopped beside me. "Can I buy you lunch?"

I held up the brown paper bag I'd brought with me. "Thanks, but I brought mine." I hurried to a table in the back of the room. It might not cause trouble if I ate with Doctor Weber, but it would definitely cause trouble if I had lunch with Doctor Dean. Barbra would be ready to cut my heart out with a dull knife if she thought I was poaching on her territory. I wasn't sure what he saw in the self-centered woman.

I shook my head. She'd only had one date with the man, but that wouldn't matter to her. She was probably planning the wedding already. She hadn't been home when I finally fell off to sleep the night before. Had they spent the night together?

~~~

"I've never had a new aide learn the ropes as fast as you have." Donna complimented me for the third time that day. "Are you sure you haven't worked in a hospital before?"

I wished people would stop asking about my past. As far

Suzanne Floyd

as I was concerned, I didn't have one. I lifted my shoulders. There really wasn't anything I could say.

"Oh, well, it doesn't matter. I'm just glad to have you on my staff. You should go to school to get your nursing degree." Before I could say anything, she hurried off to attend to some other chore.

Within a matter of days I was doing more than emptying bed pans and passing out meal trays with the horrible food. "I need you to run down to the pharmacy and pick up these meds." Donna handed me a slip of paper with the pharmacy order. My heart skipped a beat, and my hands were suddenly sweaty. They were shaking when I reached out to take the piece of paper.

"Are you okay, Deborah?" Donna frowned at me. "You look like you've seen a ghost. We aren't working you too hard, are you? Do you need to lie down? We don't want you having a relapse."

I drew a deep breath, trying to slow my racing heart. "N...no, I'm fine," I stuttered. "It's just a little headache." I rubbed at the scar from the surgery. I couldn't explain what had just happened. Turning away, I could feel her frowning gaze on my back as I headed for the stairway.

The elevator would have been faster, but I needed a minute alone to calm my abruptly frazzled nerves. I didn't know what had caused that reaction, but I didn't need anyone questioning what had just happened. If they thought I couldn't handle the workload, they would fire me, and I needed this job.

On the first floor, I stopped outside the pharmacy. Once again my heart rate skyrocketed. With sheer force of will, I reached out to open the door. What was behind the frosted glass panel that was so frightening?

A counter ran the width of the small room. A man in his forties with silver blonde hair was busy filling orders. "May I help you?" He looked up at me, a smile crossed his face, lighting up his blue eyes. "You're Jane Doe, or I should say Deborah Winston. I heard that you're working here at the hospital now. How are you doing?"

117

My eyes traveled around the room lined with shelves of drugs. There was nothing scary, so why was I afraid? I rubbed the scar on my head that had begun to throb again. "I'm fine, thank you. I came to pick up an order." The paper shook when I held out the form Donna had given me.

"Yes, I have that right here. By the way, my name is David Davies." He chuckled. "My mom wasn't very imaginative. I'm one of the hospital pharmacists" He reached out to shake my hand.

I forced myself to reach out and take his hand. He looked friendly and harmless. Why was I reacting like he was a blood-sucking monster?

"It's nice to finally meet you face to face. Welcome aboard." He turned back to his work. "I'll be seeing you." He spoke over his shoulder. The words sounded like a threat.

Leaving the claustrophobic room, I felt like I had escaped with my life. Shutting the door behind me, I leaned against the wall to keep from falling down. *What is the matter with you?* I silently asked myself. The man was being nice, and I acted like he was going to jump over the counter to attack me.

"Are you sure you're all right?" Donna frowned at me a few minutes later. "You're awfully pale."

"No, I'm fine, really." I gave a sigh of relief when the call button over a patient's door pinged. "I'll go check on Mr. Butler."

By the end of the day the episode was all but forgotten by everyone but me. There had been nothing dangerous or frightening about the pharmacy, so why had I reacted that way? I had no answers.

~~~

Barbra wasn't in her usual foul mood when we came home that night. Instead of sitting in her usual place on the couch, she was in a flurry of activity rushing around picking up her things that she'd left scattered around the living room. It was either so late when she came home the night before that she left a trail of clothes strewn across the floor on her way to bed. Or she hadn't come home until this morning, and had to scramble in order to get to work on time. My money was on the latter.

"You need to be a little more careful about leaving your things lying around," she admonished Courtney and me. "We don't want to give Travis, or anyone," she hastily corrected, "to get the idea that a bunch of slobs live here."

"Just one slob lives here," Courtney countered. "I put my things away where they belong."

"And I don't have anything to leave lying around," I added. Once again I was grateful I didn't have anything.

"Whatever," she brushed our comments aside. "We need to be tidier. He'll be here soon." She stopped what she was doing, giving Courtney that ingratiating smile she used when she wanted something. "I thought it would be nice if we all had dinner together tonight. That way we can get better acquainted. I'm sure he…they" she amended again "would enjoy a home cooked meal." She belatedly included Ted and Rex in her statement.

"I'm sure *he* would," Courtney agreed. "Ted and Rex have been getting home cooked meals every night. What are you planning on fixing for Doctor Dean?"

"Me?" Barbra squeaked. "I can't cook, you know that."

"You should have thought of that before inviting Doctor Dean over for dinner. I'm not sticking around to be your chef."

"But I told him you were teaching me to cook."

Courtney choked at that statement. "You've never shown any interest in learning to cook. Besides, you should have checked with me first."

"You mean like you checked with me before inviting *her* to move in with us?" Barbra snapped, sending a killer look in my direction.

"You had a choice then just like I have now."

"And exactly what choice did I have? You'd already told *her* she could move in."

"You could have moved out," Courtney chuckled. She sauntered to the bedroom, a smug smile playing around her lips. An angry, frustrated shriek came from the living room as Courtney shut the door behind us.

"Is she going to start throwing things again?" I whispered. I didn't know what to expect from the very angry woman.

"She'll be breaking her own things if she does, and she'll have to clean up the mess all by herself. The only thing I had after my ex walked out was this bed, my cookware, my clothes, and a pile of bills. He even took the dishes. When I tried to sell the engagement ring he'd given me, I found out it wasn't even real. The lying cheat didn't even buy a real diamond ring. Everything in the apartment belongs to Barbra. Now, let's get out of our scrubs, and get ready for our dates."

"But I don't have a date. I haven't heard from Rex all day. I'm sure he has other things to do besides babysit me."

Courtney laughed. "Is that what you call it? It didn't look like he was babysitting last night."

My face heated up, and I turned away hoping she wouldn't notice. "I haven't heard from him today," I said again. There was no way he could reach me at work. "I'm sure he's busy with his friends." She chuckled, but didn't contradict me.

The doorbell rang a few minutes later, and we could hear Barbra's purring voice when she answered the door. I assumed Doctor Dean had arrived.

I wished I was a fly on the wall. It would be interesting to see what excuse she gave for not having dinner here. I was certain she wouldn't admit she couldn't cook. What man wanted a woman who couldn't even fix a decent meal? Well, maybe a very rich man, I decided, but I didn't think the doctor qualified quite yet. He was probably still paying off student loans.

"Come on; let's go see how she wiggles out of not having dinner here tonight," Courtney's words mirrored my thoughts.

"You go ahead, I'm not quite ready. I'll be out in a minute." I was hoping Barbra would leave soon. I couldn't expect Rex to spend every evening with me, but I didn't want Barbra to think he was standing me up either. She would be merciless if that was the case.

"Don't take too long. The guys will be here soon. We need to be ready so Barbra can't suggest we all stay here for dinner. I'm done cooking for her." She gave an exaggerated shudder at the memory.

"I won't be long. Maybe she'll be gone by then." Courtney shut the bedroom door, but not before I could hear the purring tone in Barbra's voice as she talked to Doctor Dean. Was the man so blind that he couldn't see what she was after? Not my problem, I told myself. He's a big man, and can take care of himself.

When the doorbell rang a few minutes later, I was still sitting on the bed. Maybe Ted and Courtney could escape before Barbra tried to coerce her into cooking dinner for them.

When the door opened, I looked up in surprise. "You'd better finish getting dressed," Courtney whispered with a laugh. "Your babysitter is here, and he looks anxious to see his charge."

My stomach fluttered. After the kisses we'd shared the night before, I knew what Rex felt for me wasn't simply a responsibility to find a killer. But I didn't have the right to be falling in love with him until I knew who I was. There was always the thought in the back of my mind that maybe I already had a husband. There was also the possibility that he was the one who tried to kill me.

At least Barbra won't think he'd stood me up, I thought as I slipped on a pair of shoes. But that had nothing to do with the excitement bubbling up inside me. No matter how hard I tried to tell myself I didn't care if he didn't come over, I knew it for the lie it was. If I could be certain there wasn't a husband and a killer out there somewhere, I wouldn't care if I never knew who I was as long as Rex was in my life.

Courtney had called Ted to warn him about Barbra's little dinner scheme, and he was at the door as I left the bedroom. "Hi, babe, you ready for dinner?" He didn't bother to come in the apartment. "I made reservations. We don't want to be late." He looked at Rex. "I'm glad you made it in time. Shall we go?"

Rex didn't miss a beat. "Yeah, I wasn't sure if I'd get away in time to pick Deborah up, or if I'd have to meet you at the restaurant." He turned to me. "Ready, sweetheart? You look beautiful tonight as always." He placed a light kiss on my lips. We were out the door before Barbra could object.

Once the elevator doors closed behind us, we burst out laughing. The look on Barbra's face had been priceless. I wished I'd had my cell phone to take her picture.

The thought was momentarily sobering. In my former life I must have had a cell phone. Where was it? What would happen if I tried calling the number? Most people had some sort of personalized message on their phone. If I could automatically dial the right number, maybe it would give my real name. Would muscle memory take over, and I would push the right numbers the way it had when I signed my name? But that experiment hadn't produced any helpful information.

"Would someone like to clue me in on what just happened?" The laughing question brought me back to the present. I tucked thoughts of cell phones away until I was alone.

"Thanks for playing along," Courtney said after explaining about Barbra's dinner plan. "I didn't think any of us wanted to spend an evening with her." Both men winced at the thought, and we laughed again.

It was only six o'clock, and the temperature was still very warm when we stepped outside. Without much discussion it was decided we would all go to Ted's house. Courtney and I could fix dinner there instead of going to a restaurant. Cooking seemed to come naturally to me, but no specific memories surfaced. Pushing that thought aside, I enjoyed what I was doing.

"I'm glad the men are becoming friends," Courtney whispered as she peeked into the living room where the men were deep in conversation. "Sometimes friendships break up because the spouses don't get along. I don't want that to happen to us."

The men were still discussing jobs when we had the food

ready. "My sister and brother-in-law bought one of those old houses downtown for a song," Rex said while helping carry the food to the table. "They spent a fortune fixing it up, but I've got to admit it's gorgeous."

"I've done a couple of those houses myself," Ted stated proudly. "The new tract homes can't compare with those built fifty years ago, but they require a lot of work. Where's your sister live? Maybe I've seen the house. I like to keep track of what my competition is doing."

When Rex gave him the address, Ted smiled. "Joanne and Mike Billings," he said. "Theirs was one of mine."

"Really?" Rex was impressed. "You did a great job. I've always enjoyed doing things like that, but the job doesn't leave me much time." He gave a sigh. "I bought an older house with the intent of fixing it up myself. So far, that hasn't happened. Maybe you could come over sometime and give me an estimate on what it would take." The men talked about different building projects throughout dinner.

After only my second day at work, I still tired easily. By nine o'clock, I was ready to call it a night, but I didn't want to ruin the evening for Courtney and Ted. When I felt my head nod towards Rex's muscled shoulder, I jerked upright. I needed to move around in order to keep awake.

"I think we're going to call it a night, folks." Rex stood up, pulling me up with him. "I'll take Deborah home." We'd come in his car, so we didn't need to disturb the other couple. "Maybe tomorrow night we can do this at my place. You can see what I'm up against." He joked with Ted about the remodel he wanted to do.

"I hope I don't disturb Barbra when I go in the apartment." I twisted my fingers together. It wouldn't be a pretty sight if I intruded on something intimate.

"I'll go in with you," Rex offered, guessing where my thoughts were headed. "If she starts something, I'll be there to stop it. I still haven't heard the full story about what caused that cut on Courtney's cheek." He lifted one eyebrow in question. I shrugged, but didn't comment. I wasn't sure what he would do to Barbra if I told him the truth.

Pulling in to the parking lot at the apartment complex, I tried to pick out Doctor Dean's car. I didn't remember what kind of car he drove the day he stopped by the apartment, so I wasn't sure if he was still here. Maybe they'd gone out like they had the night before.

I made a production of unlocking the door, making as much racket as I possibly could without bringing the neighbors out to see what was going on. "Thank you for dinner," I spoke in an over-loud voice once I had the door open a narrow crack.

Rex reached over my head, giving the door a push. "It was a fun night." His gaze moved around the empty living room. "You're safe. She isn't here."

"Shhh, they might be in there." I nodded my head towards Barbra's bedroom.

He lifted one eyebrow. "She's sleeping with him already? I thought they just started dating." He chuckled. "Sorry, stupid question. I keep forgetting who we're dealing with."

He bent his head, placing a soft kiss on my lips. "You get some sleep now. I'll see you tomorrow." He backed out the door, then took a step back in the room, pulling me against his hard chest. This kiss was possessive and full of pent up passion. When he raised his head, my arms had made their way around his neck, holding him close. "Now, go to bed, and dream of me." This time he closed the door. "Lock this," he said through the solid panel.

"Wow," I whispered. I pushed myself away from the wall where I had sagged when he released me. "I need a cold shower before I can go to sleep."

I headed to the kitchen for a glass of water, and stopped, staring at the destruction I found. It looked like a tornado had swept through the room. My heart thudded against my ribs. Had someone broken in? What were they looking for in the kitchen? There were several blobs of something thick and red and lumpy on the floor. It didn't look like blood, but I couldn't tell what it was.

I needed to get Rex to come back. For a second time tonight I regretted the fact that I didn't have a cell phone. There wasn't a land line in the apartment. Looking around the living room, I tried to decide what to do. I stopped, staring at the neat room, nothing was out of place. Only the kitchen had been destroyed.

Turning back to the kitchen, I took a second look at the mess. Several pots were scattered around the counter, gooey spaghetti was stuck to the sides and burned to the bottom of one pan. An empty jar of spaghetti sauce was tipped over beside another pan with burned sauce stuck to the bottom of that one as well. It looked like small pieces of spaghetti were sticking to the wall in front of the stove.

This was Barbra's attempt at making dinner? How hard was it to boil spaghetti and heat up a jar of ready-made sauce? It would be a miracle if Doctor Dean ever asked her out again after this. But if he'd left, where was Barbra? She wouldn't just go to her room in tears. She would be waiting up for Courtney to return so she could accuse her of causing the man of her dreams to run away.

I looked at the closed bedroom door. Were they in there? I gave my head a shake. I wasn't going to check that out. Tomorrow we'd find out what happened.

For a brief moment I considered cleaning up the mess, but quickly discarded that idea. She made the mess, she could clean it up. I hoped Courtney would decide the same thing. It was too early for Barbra to come home, if they had actually gone out. Wherever she was, I didn't want to be the one to confront her about this mess.

~~~

The next day I decided to try out my cell phone experiment. Picking up the phone at the nurses' station, I tried not to think about what I was doing, and let my fingers move over the buttons. The phone on the other end rang once before an automated message came on. The number had been disconnected.

Disappointed, I replaced the receiver. Either the person

who tried to kill me had covered all his bases, and canceled the number. Or the cell phone carrier had shut off my phone for non-payment. It had been several months since the attack. I had no idea which carrier had provided my service, or how to find out that information.

CHAPTER FOURTEEN

"When are you going to do something about her?" the younger man groused again as he paced around the small room. *"She's going to remember what happened to her. I don't want to go to prison."*

The bigger man huffed out a breath. *"You aren't going to go to prison."*

"How can you say that? If she remembers what we did to her, she'll tell her cop boyfriend. Then he'll arrest us." Tears sparkled in his eyes.

"You aren't going to go to prison," the big man repeated. *"Now stop sniveling, and let me think."* Getting at her wasn't as easy as he thought it would be. She was never alone no matter where she was. That damn cop was with her every night. Taking him out along with the bitch would be a major mistake. Cop killers were hunted down and killed without a trial.

She might not realize what she knew, but everything she did was flawless and automatic. How long before she realized she'd done all this before? How long before the old man realized the same thing?

He jerked around when a movement across the room caught his eye. The little weasel cowered in the corner. He'd forgotten all about him. He needed to get rid of him before he spilled the beans.

An evil smile tilted the corners of his mouth. *"Come on; let's go out for a drink. It's been a long day, and I'm tired of being cooped up in here."*

"You want to have a drink with me? You said we couldn't be friends?"

He chuckled, forcing himself to relax. *"Well, we don't have to be friends to have a drink together. Besides, we're partners of sorts, right? Let's go."* He walked out knowing the younger man would follow.

~~~

The pharmacy still haunted me to the point that I went out of my way to avoid walking past the room. I used the stairs to go to the third floor where I worked instead of taking the elevator. That way I didn't have to pass the cursed room that caused my heart to pound and my head to hurt. There didn't seem to be any reason for this to happen, but I avoided going near the pharmacy unless I was sent to pick up meds. *Not only am I frightened of strangers, now I'm frightened of a room*, I thought with disgust.

The pharmacist with the repetitive name, David Davies, was always friendly, going out of his way to speak to me whenever he saw me. "I've heard a lot of good things about you." He smiled at me. I'd made the unforeseen mistake of arriving for work at the same time he did.

"Thank you." I wondered exactly what he'd heard, and from whom. "Have a nice day." I hurried down the hall, hoping he wouldn't follow.

I'd made a habit of stopping at the chapel before starting work hoping to see Chaplain Winston. Even though I couldn't remember going to church in my forgotten life, I knew it was something I'd always done. I enjoyed the peace and serenity the small chapel here offered.

After the early morning battle between Courtney and Barbra I needed some peace and serenity. Courtney had come home shortly after I had the night before. When she saw the mess in the kitchen, she was ready to confront Barbra right then, but her room was empty. It shouldn't have been a big surprise. She wouldn't want a confrontation in front of the doctor. It must have been long after midnight when she came home, ensuring that Courtney would be asleep.

She might as well have saved herself the trouble. Courtney woke her up bright and early that morning. "What happened to the kitchen?" She stood over Barbra's bed with her hands braced on her hips. "You are planning on cleaning it up, right?"

Barbra struggled to sit up. "What? What are you talking about?" Playing dumb or innocent wasn't going to work.

"You know what I'm talking about. When are you going to clean up the kitchen?"

Barbra pushed herself out of bed, brushing past Courtney on her way to the bathroom. "If you hadn't run out on me the way you did, that wouldn't have happened."

"So the mess you made is my fault. Is that what you're saying?"

"Of course; I told you I had invited Travis over for dinner, and you know I can't cook. When I tried to fix something, everything went wrong." Tears began to sparkle in her blue eyes. "It's your fault."

Courtney's laugh surprised both Barbra and me. "Well, you can blame me all you want, but you'll be the one to clean up the mess or it will stay that way. Those are your pans, not mine. If you ever want to use them again, you'll need to clean the gunk out of them. You might also consider taking some cooking lessons. I don't think Doctor Dean will be willing to take you out every night."

Looking over her shoulder as she turned away, she gave one parting shot. "Until that mess is cleaned up, Deborah and I will be eating at Ted's."

"You never treated me like this before *she* moved in here." Barbra glared at me. If she couldn't blame Courtney for her cooking fiasco, she tried blaming me. I turned away. I wasn't going to let her guilt me into cleaning up her mess either.

As always happened, the peacefulness of the chapel seeped through me, quieting my fears and anxieties. After a few minutes, I peeked down the hall. No one was lurking about. The door to the pharmacy was shut; the frosted window was illuminated indicating that David Davies was inside. I headed for the stairway in the opposite direction.

For the remainder of the week there was a definite chill in the air whenever Courtney and Barbra were in the same room. Barbra took her time cleaning up the kitchen, and Courtney didn't lift a finger to help her. When she informed Barbra that she had given the apartment management notice that she would be moving at the end of her lease, the chill turned into a deep freeze.

~~~

"What's taking them so long?" The big man paced around his apartment. It had been two days. What were they waiting for? Hadn't anyone even missed the little weasel? He chuckled at that. He was so insignificant no one missed him. Even so, you'd think by now someone would have gone looking for him. Until he was found, he had to play it cool.

~~~

The hospital was buzzing with the news about one of the orderlies. After failing to come to work for three days, his supervisor sent someone to check on him. They found him dead in his apartment of an apparent overdose. When Doctor Weber summoned me to his office I wondered what was wrong. But he wasn't the one waiting for me.

Staring at Rex for a moment, nerves jittered in my stomach. Unless something important had happened, he wouldn't be here in the middle of the day. "Have you heard about the orderly who committed suicide?" he asked softly. I nodded my head, wondering what that had to do with me. "Did you know him? His name was Bobby Morrow."

This time I shook my head. "I don't recall meeting him, but I could have. What's this about?"

Instead of answering my question, he placed a picture on the table in front of me. "Does he look familiar?"

A chill moved up my spine as some fleeting memory moved across the back of my mind. Just as fast as it appeared, it was gone again, not giving me a chance to grab hold of it.

"No, I don't think I've ever seen him here at the hospital, but I might have. A lot of people work here. What does his suicide have to do with me? Is he someone from my other life?" I gripped my fingers in my lap to keep them from shaking.

Rex drew a deep breath before answering. "He left a suicide note explaining what he'd done."

"And?" I prompted when he didn't go on. "What aren't you telling me?" Whatever he was holding back had to be bad.

"His note said he's the one who attacked you."

I gasped, taking a closer look at his picture. I willed myself to remember something, but again my stubborn memory remained blank. There was nothing to remember. "Did he explain why he did that? What did I do to him?"

"He said he met you in a bar. You were flirting with him, leading him to think that you wanted to sleep with him. You left the bar together. When you turned down his advances, he became angry and hit you. Once he started, he couldn't stop himself until he thought you were dead. He panicked and took you out to desert, and left you there."

I tried to picture myself sitting in some bar, but the image wouldn't come up. I sighed with frustration, lifting my shoulders in a shrug. "I don't recall ever being in a bar, but I don't recall anything else either so that doesn't mean anything."

I stared at the young man in the picture for several seconds. His thin face held no distinguishing marks, nothing that would make him stand out in a crowd. If I'd seen him around the hospital, he hadn't made an impression on me.

"So it's over just like that?" I snapped my fingers. "I don't have to worry that a killer is coming after me?" I should have felt relief, but I didn't. "I still don't know who I am. Did he tell what my name is?"

"Sorry, honey. He said he never knew your name." Rex shook his head. "He covered all the bases in that note. That's what makes it so suspicious. Most suicides leave more questions than answers. This is just too neat for me."

"You don't believe what he wrote?"

He shook his head. "It's just too neat," he said again. I wasn't sure where he was going with this. "He'd been working in Tucson until two weeks *after* your attack, so what was he doing in Phoenix picking someone up in a bar the night you were attacked? He'd never been in trouble of any kind, in fact he's never been known to go to a bar, let alone pick up a woman in one."

He shook his head. "Most suicide notes aren't this

detailed. It's just kind of curious. There's also the fact that there wasn't any alcohol or drugs in your system when you were found."

"But why would he kill himself if he didn't attack me?" I felt like I was going in circles. "Why would he say he attacked me if he didn't do it?"

"Those are very good questions. I'd like the answers before I buy into this whole suicide thing."

"You think someone killed him to make him look guilty?" Horror filled my voice. Would this nightmare never end?

He hesitated so long my stomach began to hurt. He finally took my hand. "I'm sorry, honey. I don't buy this whole suicide scenario."

"How are you going to find out the truth since he's already dead?"

"Phoenix has one of the best forensic scientists around. If there's any evidence to be found, Cassie Gonzales is the one to find it."

He drew in a heavy breath. "If I'm right on this, we still have a killer out there. We can't tip our hand on what we're thinking though. We don't want him to go underground. We need to have the real killer think we've stopped looking for him. You can't say anything to anyone about our thoughts on this, not Courtney, and especially not Barbra. She'd blab to anyone who would listen."

I gave a sniff. "She's barely talking to Courtney, and I'm invisible as far as she's concerned. Her nose is so far out of joint since Courtney gave notice that she'll be moving out at the end of her lease. Doctor Dean hasn't invited her to move in with him either. She hasn't been looking for another apartment, so she's probably wondering where she's going to live.

~~~

"How are you, Deborah?" Chaplain Winston stopped by my table at lunch. "May I join you?"

"Of course," I smiled up at him. "I've been stopping by the chapel each morning hoping to see you. I guess you don't start working at seven in the morning." I laughed.

He chuckled. "No, I don't have regular hours; I'm more on call. This has been a particularly trying day for everyone here at the hospital. Did you know young Bobby?"

I shook my head. "I don't think so. There are so many people working here, I can't say for certain. Did you know him?" I wished I could tell him that Rex didn't believe he had killed himself, but I had to make like I believed the suicide story. I didn't know if the police would release the contents of the note. I hope not.

"He came to see me once or twice. I'm afraid he was a very troubled young man. He never said what was troubling him, but something was eating away at him. He jumped at every little sound, always looking over his shoulder." He shook his head. "I wish I could have helped him more. I tried to tell him he needed to place his trust in Jesus; that He would be there for him in his time of need. I'm just not sure he believed that." He gave a heavy sigh.

"Have you been able to remember anything from your past?" He changed the subject.

I shook my head. "No, but I'm trying hard to take the advice you gave him. Some things come easily to me like I've done them before, but I can't remember where or when. Doctor Weber says my memory will return when my brain is ready to handle it. I hope he's right." I sighed.

"He's a good doctor and a good man. He wouldn't tell you something just to make you feel better. He must really believe that." He stood up. "Come to the chapel whenever you want. Maybe next time, I'll be there." He left, letting me finish my lunch.

~~~

The news was finally out. "One down, one to go," he told himself as he left the hospital. A self-satisfied smile tilted the corners of his mouth upwards. The next one won't be so easy, but it will be more enjoyable.

~~~

"I don't know what's going on around that hospital,"

Barbra started complaining as soon as Courtney and I came through the door that evening. She was sitting in her usual place on the couch. She always managed to beat us home. "We've had more trouble since you darkened the hospital door than we've ever had before." She glared at me. "Bad luck must follow you around like a big black cloud, and it's rubbing off on anyone who gets close to you. I hope it doesn't extend to me."

"I'm sorry about what happened to that young man, but I didn't even know him. I certainly wasn't close to him. How do you figure this is my fault?"

She stood up, ignoring my question as she headed for her bedroom. "I need to change. I have a date tonight." Doctor Dean's visits were a nightly occurrence now. Although there was never any show of affection between them at the hospital, Barbra made sure everyone knew that she was dating a doctor. Since that first fiasco, he hadn't expected her to cook him a meal again. Either he didn't care that she couldn't cook or he enjoyed her other attributes enough to overlook that fact. She had finally cleaned the kitchen, but only so Doctor Dean wouldn't continue to see the same mess every time he came over.

"As long as she's going out," Courtney said cheerfully, "we can have dinner here. I'll be glad when we don't have to arrange our evenings around her." Although they went out every night, there was still a lot of tension in the air whenever we were all together.

"I'm not sure if Rex will be over tonight." I said that every night even though he was always there. That night, he might really be busy. I sat down on the side of the bed. "He might be busy with…a case." I finished my sentence with a lame excuse. I needed to remember not to call what happened to the young orderly murder instead of suicide.

"I'm sure he'll call if he can't make it. He has my cell phone number." She stripped off her scrubs, and headed for the shower.

When the doorbell rang, Barbra hurried out of her room to

answer the door the same time as I came into the living room. "I'll take care of this. It's for me anyway." She glared at me.

For a brief moment, I was taken aback, staring at her. Finally gathering my wits, I took a step towards the door. "You aren't the only one to have a date tonight. It might be Ted or Rex."

"I don't care. I said I'll get this. Just go back to your room."

"I'm not two years old, Barbra. You can't send me to my room and expect me to obey." I walked over to the couch, sitting down in her usual spot. Her hands curled into fists. If she could get them around my throat, I felt certain she would enjoy strangling me. She drew a deep breath as she opened the door.

"Hi, Teddy," she purred seductively. "Your date is running a little late, as usual. Come in and have a seat." I looked over my shoulder. She had taken his hand, running her fingers suggestively over his palm. She chuckled when he jerked his hand out of her grasp.

She turned away just as the doorbell rang again. "Don't bother getting up," she instructed me. "This will be for me."

"Or it could be for me," I said just to see the hackles rise on her neck. "But you can answer it anyway. I'm a little tired tonight." I winked at Ted, letting him know I was yanking Barbra's chain. I used the same condescending tone that she used on those she considered beneath her. Basically, that meant everyone, but Doctor Dean.

"Hi Travis, sweetie. Come in." Her voice was as smooth as honey. Standing on tiptoe, she placed a passionate kiss on his lips. When she pulled back, she gave Ted a smug smile, like she expected him to be jealous. He wasn't even looking at her. "It will only take me a minute to finish getting ready." She was fully dressed; I didn't know how much more she needed to do.

"Take your time; I'm not in a hurry." Doctor Dean sank down on the opposite end of the couch. "How are you doing? Any memories popping up yet?" He ignored Ted.

I gave my head a shake. "Nothing yet." People were wearing that subject out. When my memory returned, if it ever did, I would let the entire world know.

Barbra gave me another hard glare behind the doctor's back; she didn't want him showing attention to anyone but her. She quickly grabbed her purse out of her room. "I want to tell you again how sorry I am about the kitchen fiasco the other night," she said with a little pout.

It had been more than a week since that happened, but she was still milking it. "If my mother hadn't died when I was little, she would have taught me to cook. Courtney promised to give me some pointers, but she's been much too busy with her new boyfriend." She practically pulled him off the couch to hustle him out the door.

Courtney stepped out of her room to catch this last exchange. Her mouth dropped open, too astonished to contradict Barbra until it was too late. "I did no such thing. She had no interest in learning to cook."

"Forget about her. She's never going to change," Ted said with a shake of his head.

"Her mother isn't dead either."

When the doorbell rang again, it could only be Rex. He was the only one missing from our foursome. He placed a soft kiss on my lips, wrapping his arm around my shoulder. "Where are we eating tonight?" He sounded tired.

CHAPTER FIFTEEN

The next day my mind was still occupied with the death of Bobby Morrow. He didn't look much older than twenty or twenty-one. If Rex was right, someone had tried to make murder look like suicide. Whoever killed him was the same person who had tried to kill me. This wasn't over by a long shot.

A suicide garnered very little coverage from the media, an overdose even less. It broke my heart how quickly he was forgotten by the press, and by the people he worked with at the hospital. The police hadn't released the contents of the suicide note, not even to Bobby Morrow's family. My heart went out to them. They were being led to believe he had killed himself for some unknown reason. The note would have made headlines if the contents were revealed. Disclosing the suspicions of the police would have tipped off the real killer, and they didn't want that to happen.

With my mind distracted, I entered Mrs. Taylor's room. The woman was in her seventies, and had been admitted the day before complaining of stomach pains. So far, they hadn't been able to pinpoint the problem.

"How are you feeling this morning, Mrs. Taylor?" I was too preoccupied to notice she didn't answer. I didn't notice that her breakfast had barely been touched either. "Doesn't it ever cool off here?" I asked as I came back into the room. I always tried to carry on a conversation with the patients as I helped them. "It's the middle of September; I can't believe the temperature is still over one hundred."

Mrs. Taylor had been a regular chatterbox when she'd been admitted, but not so much today. Her silence finally captured my attention. "Oh, my gosh!" Her normally ruddy complexion was pasty gray; her breathing was rapid and shallow.

I pushed the emergency call button that would signal the operator of the emergency. The Code Red went out over the intercom indicating a patient was in cardiac arrest almost immediately. Turning back to Mrs. Taylor, my heart skipped a beat. Her shallow breathing had stopped, her complexion was now ashen. "I need a crash cart in here STAT! Where the hell is everyone?" Without waiting for a response, I lowered the head of the bed, removing the pillow under her head to begin CPR.

Seconds seemed like hours before the room filled with people and equipment. I reluctantly moved aside, allowing the doctors to take over. As they worked on Mrs. Taylor, I mentally went over each procedure being done, willing them to work faster so the woman wouldn't die.

When she began breathing on her own, I slipped out of the room. Stepping into the stairwell, I collapsed against the wall. Mrs. Taylor was going to be all right. Tears of relief welled up in my eyes. "It was my fault she almost died," I whispered. "I should have noticed sooner that she was in trouble." Guilt weighed down on me.

Pulling myself together, I opened the door. It was time to face the music. It wouldn't take long for the doctors to figure out that I had almost let the poor woman die because I was so preoccupied with my own problems. Doctors were still in with Mrs. Taylor when I walked past her room, but I could see she was now conscious. Machines beeped quietly, monitoring her heart rate.

"Deborah!" Doctor Dean stepped into the hall as I walked by the room.

My heart sank. It was time to own up to my mistake. Feeling like a prisoner facing the firing squad, I turned to face him. At least he wasn't going to accuse me in front of Mrs. Taylor. "I'm sorry, Doctor Dean," I didn't give him a chance to say anything. "I don't know what else to say. There isn't any excuse for what I did."

His eyebrows formed a straight line over his dark eyes. "What do you mean? I thought you were the one who gave her CPR." I nodded my head, but couldn't look at him. "If you hadn't been in there, Mrs. Taylor wouldn't be with us now.

You saved her life."

I couldn't let him think I was a hero. "No, if I hadn't been distracted, I would have noticed sooner that she was in trouble."

Before he could say anything more, orderlies wheeled Mrs. Taylor out of her room taking her to the Cardiac Care Unit. The older woman reached out for my hand. "Thank you." Her voice was still weak, but color was already returning to her face.

I didn't know how to respond so I simply nodded. She would eventually learn that I wasn't the hero she thought I was. Now wasn't the time though. She needed to be moved to CCU.

"She's damn lucky you were with her," the doctor said.

"No! It's my fault she almost died." Tears stung my eyes again.

His thick brows drew together in a frown. "What are you talking about? You did give her CPR, right?"

"Yes, of course I did, but I should have been paying more attention."

Taking my arm in a firm grip, he led me down the hall. I thought he was going to drag me to the police. What would Rex do if he had to arrest me? Instead, he led me into an empty room, away from listening ears. "What weren't you paying attention to, and how did it nearly cost Mrs. Taylor her life?" He stood with his arms crossed over his broad chest, a fierce frown riding his dark features.

"I was distracted when I went into her room. I didn't notice she was having trouble breathing. I didn't see how bad her coloring was until it was almost too late. Even a first year med student would have known she was having a heart attack."

"I rather doubt that." His smile seemed a little forced. "I've seen some of those first year students do some pretty dumb things. Even interns and residents don't always respond appropriately in an emergency. That's why there is always an attending doctor with them. You did all the right things. Why do you think you should know as much as a first year med student?" His tone was confused.

The question stopped me in my tracks. Why *did* I think I should know as much as a med student? I'd only been working at the hospital for two weeks. Finally I shook my head. "I don't know. I just know I should have been paying closer attention to her. She was my patient."

"The fact that you reacted so quickly saved her life." He patted my shoulder. "Stop beating yourself up for something that isn't your fault." He quickly dismissed my worries.

The rest of the afternoon I replayed the scene in Mrs. Taylor's room over and over in my head along with the conversation with Doctor Dean. I couldn't let go of the conviction that I should have done more, known more. But why did I think that? Everyone congratulated me on taking such quick action to save her life, making me feel even guiltier. I wasn't a hero.

~~~

She might not consciously remember who and what she was, but that doesn't mean her body doesn't know what to do. He paced across the living room of his apartment. She moved instinctively and quickly to save that woman's life. How long before someone recognizes the fact that she has medical training and starts asking the right questions? Would that be the key to unlocking her memory?

He slammed his fist against the wall in frustration. Even the best medical experts couldn't predict what would trigger the memory of an amnesiac. He was at the mercy of whatever gods there happened to be.

His whole plan was coming apart at the seams all because of her. In fact, his entire life was unraveling before his eyes. "Damn that bitch!" he swore out loud.

Right now everyone was concerned about the old woman. No one was paying attention to the fact that an aide knew the correct codes, or what needed to be done to save the old woman. He couldn't count on the collective forgetfulness to last forever. As long as she continued to work at the hospital the chances of her stepping into another emergency were always there. It wouldn't take many times before the old man realized she wasn't your average nurse's aide. He could feel his luck running out like sand in an hour glass.

That damn sergeant was sticking to her like glue. He had to figure out a way to pry her away from the detective so he could end this once and for all. At least he was rid of the little bastard, he thought with a grim smile.

Ever since she walked into the drug room more than three months ago, his problems had snowballed, one on top of another. Just when he had one solved, another cropped up to thwart him.

Somehow he had to keep her from remembering until he was ready to leave on his own terms. He mentally calculated how much was in his account in the Cayman Islands. There was almost enough to maintain the life style he intended for himself, now that he didn't have to share any of it with that little weasel. Of course, that had never been a part of his plan. He'd never intended to share his profits with anyone. The little weasel had always been expendable.

Now he had to find a solution to his most pressing problem. Simply disappearing was not an option. He refused to spend the rest of his life looking over his shoulder, waiting for someone to recognize him. She had to be taken care of, permanently.

If she had just minded her own damn business months ago, things would have been fine, for both of them. "Damn nosey bitch," he muttered. He refused to call her by name. She was just another obstacle, nothing more, nothing less. One he wouldn't have to put up with much longer. He'd put his life and his plans on hold long enough. If he was ever going to get out of here, he had to start doing business again. It wouldn't be hard to connect with the network he'd had in place in Tucson.

He had always considered violence a crude way to accomplish things. But he was going to enjoy removing her from his life. Recalling the first time his fists slammed into her

141

face, a rush of pleasure shot through him. The aborted attempts on her life were foreplay. The climax would finally come when he killed her. And this time he would watch as the life drained out of her. Nothing would be left to chance again.

CHAPTER SIXTEEN

"**W**hat the hell were you thinking today?" Barbra stormed at me the minute I stepped into the apartment.

I wasn't sure why she was so upset, but I knew what she was talking about. I had nothing to say though. I wasn't going to give her any ammunition to use against me. Taking my silence for guilt, Barbra continued to vent her anger. "You've got the entire hospital worried about what's going to happen. They're all waiting for the other shoe to drop."

Now I was confused. Yes, people were talking about what happened today, but I hadn't heard that they were worried about what I did. Releasing a weary sigh, I set my purse down on the table. "OK, Barbra, why is everyone worried?"

"Don't you realize the hospital could be sued because of you?"

"Give it a rest, Barbra," Courtney jumped to my defense. "She didn't do anything wrong."

"No? She performed a medical procedure on a patient. That should worry all of us."

Courtney shook her head. "Aides are allowed to do CPR in emergencies, and I think what happened could be classified as an emergency."

"Sure trained aides are allowed to do that, but she hasn't been trained. That woman could have died because of what she did."

"She *didn't* die because of what Deborah did." She was defending me like I wasn't in the room with them. "Mrs. Taylor was having a heart attack. What did you expect her to do, sit on her hands until someone else got there to help?"

"Someone with training, yes," Barbra snapped.

"You don't think I should have done CPR?" I cut into their argument. "Mrs. Taylor was having a heart attack!" I repeated Courtney's argument for emphasis. "What was I supposed to do, let her die?" Ignoring the first warning signs of a heart attack had been bad enough; I couldn't let her die while I waited for help to arrive. It had seemed like a lifetime before the doctors and nurses finally got there.

"You couldn't know she was having a heart attack," she snapped scornfully. "You don't have any medical training. You were supposed to call for a doctor or nurse. You're *just* a nurse's aide. That means you *aid* the nurses, not try to do their jobs."

"I did call the nurses. I wasn't trying to do their jobs either, but I had to do something until help came." This conversation was ridiculous.

"She's right, Barbra." Courtney stepped back into the conversation. "Mrs. Taylor would have died if Deborah hadn't started CPR. If you'd stop trying to find fault with Deborah, you'd see she did the right thing."

"She couldn't know the woman was having a heart attack," Barbra insisted. Once again they were talking about me as though I wasn't standing right there beside them. "She doesn't have any medical training. She's an aide because Doctor Weber pushed for it. Wait until Mrs. Taylor's family finds out what she did. I'll bet there will be a big lawsuit against the hospital. We could all lose our jobs if the hospital is closed down."

"It doesn't take..."

My patience finally exhausted, I interrupted Courtney. "I'm not a complete idiot, Barbra! I knew she had stopped breathing. If someone wants to sue me, they're welcome to try." I glared at Barbra, daring her to argue further. Our angry stares were locked in silent warfare for several more seconds. Finally Barbra tossed back her head in a haughty gesture, and flounced out of the room without another word.

"Don't let her get to you," Courtney tried to ease the tension still hanging heavy in the room. "Even though she won't admit it, she knows you did the right thing. She just doesn't like someone else getting all the attention, especially from the doctors."

"I don't want their attention. I just want my life back, whatever that was before all this started."

~~~

It was finally mid-September, but the temperatures still crept into the hundreds during the day. Being cooped up inside all the time was beginning to wear on me. I didn't consider it being outside when all I did was go from the apartment to the car, then from the car to the hospital, only to reverse the process in the evening. I wanted to be doing something outside, but I wasn't sure what. Ever since I came out of the coma it had been too hot to do much outside though. Maybe in my former life I'd been some sort of outdoors person.

The night time temperatures had cooled off some, but even at that I had to wait until the sun went down before it was cool enough to go for a walk. Rex was still convinced the killer was out there, and he didn't want me going out alone.

It had been two months since the last attempt on my life, and more than a month since the death of young Bobby Morrow. Rex still believed that had been murder set up to look like suicide, but even the forensic team hadn't been able to come up with conclusive evidence to prove that. He had taken an overdose of pills. There was nothing to indicate he had been forced to take them.

"If you must go walking alone, please don't go after dark," Rex stated firmly. "You need to be able to see your surroundings."

"I also need to be able to breathe without searing my lungs," I shot back. "Does the term 'helicopter mom' ring a bell?" I tried for a teasing tone.

"I'm not trying to be your mom, and I'm not hovering over you. I care about you. I don't want anything to happen to you."

I placed my hand on his cheek. "I know, but you can't be with me twenty-four hours a day. I need to be able to look out for myself. I have the stun gun you gave me, and I promise I won't go anywhere without it. I also have a can of wasp spray."

"Wasp spray?" He frowned at me. "Are you expecting a swarm of wasps to attack you?"

145

"No, but I read that wasp spray is better than pepper spray in ridding yourself of an attacker. It shoots farther than pepper spray, and the can is much larger." That was my one objection to carrying something like that. It didn't fit into my bag. I kept the thought to myself.

Running his fingers through his thick hair, he finally nodded his head. "All right, I'll try not to hover any more than this." He pulled me against his hard body, his lips mere centimeters from mine. "You have to know I'm in love with you. When this is all over, I have an important question to ask you." He closed the small distance between us, claiming my lips in a passion-filled kiss.

That night, I took him at his word and went for a walk by myself. The sun wasn't quite gone, but it was down enough that I could breathe without worrying about burning my lungs.

As I started across the street heading for a small neighborhood park, the roar of a powerful engine startled me. Turning towards the noise, I was like a deer caught in the oncoming headlights of the car rushing towards me, frozen in place and unable to move. Someone screamed, and it took a second to realize I was the one screaming.

At the last possible moment fear released me, and I managed to jump out of the way. I could feel the rush of air as the big vehicle moved past me. The side mirror clipped my shoulder knocking me off my feet. A sharp pain jabbed my hip as I landed on a sharp rock in the gravel at the side of the road. My side ached where I had hit the ground. If I didn't have a few broken ribs, I would have some deep bruises. They would hurt almost as bad as though they were broken.

"Miss, are you all right?" I wasn't sure how long I'd laid there before people began coming out to see what the ruckus was all about.

"I...don't know," I stammered. "I guess so." The skin on my arms and legs felt like it had been peeled off by the gravel, and my hip ached.

"I've called 911," the stranger said as he helped me sit up. I took stock of any injuries beyond the obvious scrapes and bruises. Nothing seemed to be broken.

I wished he hadn't called the police. Rex would know what happened within minutes. He'd never let me out of his sight after this.

~~~

"That bitch has more lives than a damn cat, and she's twice as hard to kill," he groused as he sped past her lying on the side of the road. "How did she manage to avoid getting hit?" Had he clipped her enough to throw her? Could he be so lucky that she hit her head when she landed?

He shook his head. He wasn't leaving anything to chance this time. He had to make sure she was finally dead. He started to make a U-turn to take another run at her when the street seemed to fill with people coming to her aid.

His beefy fist pounded on the steering wheel, curses turned the air in the car blue. He straightened out the car on the road, moving away before someone spotted him. He couldn't take the chance that he would be identified.

~~~

Rex arrived seconds behind the paramedics. He jumped out of his car before the engine died. Gingerly taking my hands, his intense gaze moved down my body looking for injuries that couldn't be seen. "Are you all right? What happened? Who did this?" He didn't give me a chance to answer his questions. Instead, he gently placed his lips against mine in a heart wrenching kiss. When he pulled back, he rested his forehead against mine. "What happened?" he asked, only slightly more calm this time.

I still wasn't sure what had happened, other than the car was speeding. "Maybe the driver was blinded by the sun, and didn't see me?" My voice rose at the end, turning my statement into a question.

People gave differing accounts of what they saw. No one could agree on exactly what happened. Even the color of the vehicle was under debate. It was a blur to me, but each time I closed my eyes I could see the speeding car bearing down on me.

The paramedics patched me up and weren't happy when I declined a ride to the hospital. "Nothing's broken." I insisted. "I can walk." I moved my arms and legs to demonstrate that nothing was broken.

"You won't know that for sure without X-rays," the young paramedic argued. "You landed pretty hard on that hip."

"I promise I won't do any exercises for a few days, and if it still hurts I'll have it checked out." I'd spent too much of my life recently as a patient. I wasn't going there again.

For the remainder of the evening Rex treated me like an invalid. "I knew I shouldn't have left you alone," he muttered to himself. "I would have shot that SOB if I'd been there." He had me propped up on the couch with pillows behind my back and a glass of wine at my elbow. "It will help you relax," he insisted.

"If I wasn't alone, he wouldn't have come after me," I interrupted his muttering. "I don't even know if the driver was the same person who attacked me before."

I finally managed to convince Rex to go home. I was going to bed where I assured him I would be safe. He was getting ready to leave when Barbra and Doctor Dean came home from their date. It was earlier than usual for them, and Barbra was clearly unhappy to find me sitting on the couch, her couch. "Why are you out there?" she snapped. She made no effort to hide her displeasure. "You should be in bed."

"But mommy, I'm not tired." I whined like a little child being told she had to go to bed.

"I'm not your mommy!" she snapped.

"Then stop acting like I'm two years old, and you can send me to bed."

Rex changed his mind about leaving, and stuck around just in case Barbra got any nastier. He'd finally gotten the full story about the cut on Courtney's face right after I moved in with them. He'd wanted to arrest her for assault, but Courtney wouldn't cooperate.

"You need to buy a lottery ticket." Doctor Dean smiled at me after hearing what happened.

"Why?" I frowned, unsure what a lottery ticket had to do with what had just happened. I ignored Barbra's glare. She didn't like him talking to another woman, especially me.

He chuckled. "It's a sure bet you'd win."

I still didn't understand what he was talking about. "Why would I win the lottery?"

"Because you're the luckiest person I've ever met." He gave a callous laugh.

"Excuse me?" My mouth dropped open. "How do you figure I'm lucky?"

"I don't know of very many people who have survived three attempts on their life. Like I said, you should buy a lottery ticket."

Rex balled his fingers into a fist, itching to plant one on the smug doctor's face. Someone needed to defuse the situation, but I was too astonished to think of anything to say.

"Think about it," he continued, unaware of the murderous look on Rex's face. "You weren't expected to live when you were brought to the hospital. You've made it this far without any side effects. I'd say that's pretty lucky." He turned away, wrapping his arm around Barbra's waist, nuzzling her neck.

I breathed a sigh of relief when Courtney opened the door. "What's going on?" Her question was for anyone, but she glared at Barbra. The tension in the room ramped up several notches.

"Don't give me that glare," Barbra snapped. "I didn't do anything to her."

Travis shrugged. "I was just telling Deborah how lucky she is. For some reason they got all bent out of shape." He turned to his date, pulling her towards the door. "I have to be at the hospital early tomorrow." They stepped out in the hall to say their goodnights in private. Before the door closed behind them, he looked at Rex. "You've got one lucky girlfriend there, man. Talk her into buying a lottery ticket." He was stuck on that theme.

"What is that about a lottery ticket?" Courtney frowned at us.

She gave her head a shake when I explained his reason for insisting I buy a lottery ticket. "And the man thinks you're lucky because you've survived three attempts on your life? He's as big an idiot as his girlfriend. Those two deserve each other.

"Did you get checked out at the hospital?" she asked, changing the subject. "Were you able to see who was driving the car?"

I shrugged, trying to downplay what happened as a simple accident. "The driver probably didn't see me," I said, explaining what happened. "The sun was just going down. Maybe I was in the shadows, or the setting sun blinded him." I didn't want to believe this was another attempt on my life.

Clearly the others didn't buy into that theory. "You had a flashlight with you, right?" Courtney asked.

At that moment I couldn't recall if I had turned it on. There had still been enough light that I could see where I was going. "It was an accident," I insisted. But if Rex was right, it could have been the same person who had tried to kill me before. He was still out there and still wanted me dead. A shiver passed through me at the thought.

Barbra came back in the room, still unhappy that we were all there. "I suppose this means that you'll be the center of attention at the hospital tomorrow." She glared at me. "You certainly enjoy the limelight."

"That's right; I planned all of this so I could get some well-deserved attention. But just for you, I won't tell anyone what happened, if you won't. Would that make you happy? I do think I'll get that lottery ticket though. Maybe I'll win a million dollars, and I'll have Doctor Dean to thank for the suggestion. You'll be rid of me for good then."

"I don't suppose you'd share it with him even though it was his idea. You'd hoard it all for yourself." She huffed off, slamming the bedroom door behind her.

"Wow, that woman is a real piece of work." Rex shook his head. Turning the subject back to the matter at hand, he looked at me. "I wish you had family you could go to until we had this sorted out. I don't like the idea of you being here for this mad man to be able to get at."

"If I had family, I would know who I am, and would be able to tell you who tried to kill me and why. But I'm stuck with the hand I was dealt." I wasn't any happier about this than he was.

"What do you know about that guy?" He looked at the door where Travis Dean had exited.

Courtney lifting her shoulders in a shrug. "Nothing. He hasn't been at the hospital very long. Why?"

"Just wondering, that's all." Rex sent a meaningful look in my direction. Convinced a killer was still stalking me, he was looking at everyone who came near me.

The next morning I was sore, but I wasn't going to call in sick. That would mean I would have to give an explanation. I wasn't going to tell anyone about the accident. I was hoping Doctor Dean would keep it to himself as well.

Barbra came out of her room as Courtney and I were ready to leave. "Remember not to say anything about your little mishap last night." She gave me a phony smile. "It's our little secret."

"Are you afraid she'll get some attention that you want?" Courtney asked with an equally phony smile. "It wasn't exactly a 'little mishap'. Someone tried to run her down."

"That's not the way she told it last night. She probably crossed the street in front of the speeding car." I knew that wasn't what happened, that I had looked before starting across the street. But I didn't contradict her. If it made her happy to think that, I was willing to let it go.

Courtney fumed as we walked outside. "She is the most selfish, self-centered person I've ever had the displeasure of knowing. She knows you didn't walk in front of that car."

"It's all right. I don't care what she thinks. We only have one more month and we'll be rid of her as our roommate." We were both counting the days. Our new apartment was closer to the hospital, and the rent was much cheaper. It wouldn't be long before Ted popped the question, asking her to marry him.

Then I would have to find an apartment of my own, but at least I wouldn't have to put up with Barbra.

Barbra hadn't been looking for another apartment. Whatever her plans were, they included Travis Dean. I knew she was hoping he would ask her to move in with him. If she played the 'poor little me' card, I was sure he would do just that. At least as long as it was a benefit to him. They seemed to be cut from the same cloth. They deserved each other.

CHAPTER SEVENTEEN

I didn't need to worry about Doctor Dean telling anyone about what happened the night before. Apparently it had slipped his mind when I saw him at the hospital. He acted like he didn't even recognize me.

As had become my custom, I stopped at the chapel before going up to my floor. Leaving there a few minutes later, I let out a startled squeal when someone came up behind me. "You're limping. What did you do?" Jerry Edmonds came out of nowhere. For a man his size, he moved with the stealth of a mountain lion. Was he just as dangerous?

Whirling around to look up at him, I nearly lost my balance in the process. He reached out, taking my arm to keep me from falling down. "What did you do?" He asked again, unaware or ignoring my wince as he gripped one of the many scrapes on my arm. "Are you overdoing your exercises?"

"That must be it." I jumped on that as an excuse. "I must have pulled a muscle."

"Come down to my office, and let me take a look. I'll check to see if you did any harm to yourself." Still holding my arm, he turned away without giving me a chance to object.

Stubbornly, I dug in my heels, pulling my arm out of his grasp. "That's not necessary. I'm fine. I'll just take it easy for a couple of days." I had bruises up and down one leg and arm. I didn't need him or anyone else to see them.

He looked a little disappointed, but didn't push the issue. "Whatever, just remember you can do a lot of damage by pushing yourself." He walked off with a swagger to his step. He didn't act like any of the other doctors I saw every day. Something was off with the man, but I couldn't put my finger on what it was. Shivers moved up my spine every time the man came around.

When he was out of sight, I headed for the stairs. Taking the elevator would be easier on my sore hip, but walking past the pharmacy was still off limits for me. The only time I went near the place was when work required it. Maybe someday I would figure out what that was about.

For the rest of the day I tried to avoid him and anyone else who might take an interest in why I was limping. It wasn't an easy task. The hospital was like a small town where everyone knew the business of everyone else.

"Hello, Deborah. Are you all right?" Chaplain Winston stopped me in the hall. A frown drew his bushy brows together.

"Yes, I'm fine." I was grateful that the hospital was so cool. That allowed me to wear a long sleeved tee shirt underneath the scrub shirt to cover up the scrapes down my arm, thus avoiding a lot more of questions. My hands were another matter.

"Were you in a fight?" He looked pointedly at my knuckles. There was no way I could hide the scrapes there.

"No, of course not," I tried to laugh off his concern. He let the silence stretch out, waiting for me to explain further. I finally gave a heavy sigh, looking around to make sure no one else would be able to eavesdrop on our conversation.

"I fell last night. It's no big deal, and I don't want anyone to make more of it than it was. Please don't say anything." It was the simplest explanation I could give without outright lying to him.

"How did you fall? How bad were you hurt?" His questions were exactly what I was trying to avoid.

"Just a few scrapes and sore muscles. Really, I'm fine." The power of suggestion is very strong. Every time someone told me that I looked tired, or sore, or sick, I felt even worse. I knew they were only concerned for me, but I wished they wouldn't keep telling me that.

"When you're ready to talk about it, you know where I am." A little disappointed in me, he patted my hand. "Take it easy today; you don't want to overdo it."

Doctor Weber was always busy with his many patients, but even he had heard about my limp. Stopping by the table while I was eating my sandwich, his faded eyes moved over my face. "You look tired today, Deborah. Are they working you too hard? We don't want you hurting yourself."

I laughed. "Thank you, but I'm fine. I wish I could be doing more." I tucked my hands in my lap so he couldn't see the scrapes.

"The fact that you saved that patient's life is doing more," he insisted. It had been a week since that incident. I had hoped my part had been forgotten. Barbra still insisted the hospital could be sued because of me. "I've heard only good things about your work here," he went on, "but if it's wearing you out, you should take it easy. We don't want you to have a relapse."

"I think I'm beyond that stage in my recovery. I never said thank you for everything you did for me." I wanted to change the direction of the conversation. "I know you went above and beyond what any other doctor would do for a patient, especially one they didn't know and had no family."

"That's exactly why you needed someone in your corner pulling for you." He brushed my gratitude aside. Looking off as though looking at some unseen object, he said softly, "Lately too many doctors are going into the profession for the wrong reasons." I wasn't sure if he had a specific doctor in mind. "Well, you take it easy today, and get some rest tonight." He hurried off, seemingly embarrassed, either by my gratitude or his assessment of the latest crop of doctors.

The day was finally over, but Barbra was waiting to pounce on me as soon as I entered the apartment. "You just couldn't keep to our little bargain, could you." It was an accusation, not a question.

I didn't bother to answer as I headed for the bedroom. My limp had gotten more pronounced as the day went on. I just wanted to sit down and put my feet up.

"You don't have anything to say for yourself?" she continued her harangue. "I heard even Doctor Weber is concerned about you again. I'm sure your detective told him about your little mishap."

"Lay off, Barbra," Courtney snapped. "If someone tried to

run you down, you'd be milking it instead of trying to ignore it."

"You have no idea what I would do. And no one tried to run her down. She's just being overly dramatic to get more attention."

Courtney started to argue, but I cut her off. "Stop it both of you." I glared at Barbra. "I don't care what you think happened, Barbra; I don't care what you think of me. Just shut up and leave me alone." I continued on to the bedroom.

Before I got there, someone rang the doorbell. I didn't stop to see who it was until Courtney opened the door. Rex waited impatiently to be allowed in. He placed a quick kiss on her cheek, ignoring Barbra as he came towards me.

"See what I mean," she snapped. "She has people coming out of the woodwork, dancing attendance on her."

"Shut up, Barbra." The three of us all spoke as one.

She staggered back like she'd been struck. "Well," she huffed. "Why don't you tell me how you really feel?"

"If I told you how I really feel, I'd have to ask God's forgiveness afterwards," Courtney stated.

A satisfied smirk lifted the corners of Rex's mouth, but he kept his thoughts to himself as he took my hand. "How did it go today? Did everybody want to know what happened to you?"

As much as I wanted to avoid this subject, I knew he wasn't going to let it go. "No, and I didn't tell anyone." I didn't bother looking at Barbra, but she knew what I was talking about. She huffed off to her room, slamming the door behind her.

She popped back out minutes later when the doorbell rang again. If it was Doctor Dean, she didn't want to give him the opportunity to talk to me. Disappointed when it was Ted, she flounced back into her room.

"Where are we eating tonight?" he asked. "I'm hungry." We spent as little time in our apartment as possible, cooking at Ted's and Rex's places to avoid Barbra. Courtney wasn't taking any chances with her inviting herself to our dinner.

156

Rex looked at the closed door where Barbra had disappeared. "Would it be okay if we stayed here?" His voice was soft. "Maybe we could include…" He nodded his head at the closed door.

There was shocked silence from the rest of us. He was up to something, but he wasn't letting us in on what.

"Um, sure, I guess" Courtney stammered warily. "I can fix something for all of us." She looked at me with a question in her eyes. All I could do was shrug. I had no idea why he would want to invite them.

When the doorbell rang again, there was little doubt who it would be this time. Instantly Barbra flew out of her room. "That will be for me."

"Oh, sweetie, you look so tired." Barbra pulled Travis into the room. "Come sit down." She led him to the couch, sitting him down in her usual spot. She began massaging his temples, making kissy sounds.

"I'm beat. Weber had us going all day without a break. I hope you don't mind if we don't go anywhere tonight. I'm afraid I'd fall asleep in my dinner plate if we went out." He was playing right into whatever Rex had planned.

For a second, her face filled with disappointment, but she swallowed it, not wanting to show her true nature. "That's all right, sweetie. We can have something delivered." She shot an angry look at the four of us. "We'll have a quiet dinner here, just the two of us." She sent each of us a pointed look, telling us to clear out, but that wasn't what Rex wanted.

He nudged my arm, tipping his head in her direction. "Um, Courtney and I were planning on cooking here tonight. There will be plenty if you'd like to join us." I almost choked on the words.

Barbra narrowed her eyes at us, suspecting something was up, but she didn't get the chance to argue. "Sounds great to me," Travis said, inserting himself into the conversation. "Babs said Courtney was going to give her cooking lessons. Maybe you could start tonight."

I didn't miss her cringe when he shortened her name, but

she didn't snap his head off like she did with everyone else who did the same thing. "That's so sweet of you to invite us," she managed to say through clenched teeth. She gave each of us a suspicious glare. She knew something was up.

When Travis laid his head down on the back of the couch and closed his eyes, she marched over to Courtney pushing her into the kitchen. "What's up with the invitation? Are you planning on putting poison in our food?" She kept her voice low.

"If I only could, but no," Courtney snapped back. "I'm just tired of being run out of my own home. Again. If cooking here means I have to feed you as well, I'll do it. For one night," she emphasized. She wasn't taking the chance that Barbra would do this on a regular basis as she had in the past. "You can help out. Count this as your one and only cooking lesson from me. You might just learn something in the process." She smirked as she said the last. As it turns out Barbra was more hindrance than help. I wasn't much help either as I tried to eavesdrop on what Rex was saying in the living room.

I wanted to know why he wanted to stay here with the other couple. Whatever it was, he was happy with the situation. With the three of us working in the kitchen, he sat down. His attention was riveted on the doctor.

"So Dean, I hear you're from Tucson," Rex started conversationally. Ted sat down on the end of the couch to watch the show. Like the rest of us, he knew Rex had something up his sleeve.

"Right," Dean lifted his head off the back of the couch, giving him a wary look. He looked away like he thought if he ignored Rex he would go away. The breakfast bar gave open access to the living room. I tried not to appear to be listening, but I wanted to know what Rex was up to.

"That young orderly at the hospital who killed himself was also from Tucson. Did you know him when you worked down there?"

The doctor chuckled at that. "In case you weren't aware of it, Tucson is a big city now, has been for a very long time. Just because that's where I had been living doesn't mean that I knew everyone in town."

"Oh, sure," Rex lifted his shoulders. "I didn't mean to suggest you would. I just thought that maybe you'd crossed paths with him sometime. It's kind of a coincidence that both of you worked there, and moved to Phoenix about the same time." He shrugged again.

"Why would you think I would automatically know him? He was an orderly, not a doctor." His tone was as superior as I'd ever heard from Barbra. They really were meant for each other.

"Sorry, I didn't mean to offend you." Rex didn't sound very sorry. Where he was going with this and what did he hope to discover? If his intent was to rile the doctor, he had accomplished that endeavor. Although he was trying hard to hide his displeasure, Travis was upset by the suggestion that he knew Bobby Morrow. Was it just because he thought the younger man was beneath him?

"What brought you up to Phoenix?" Rex wasn't going to let the conversation die. "Most people I know would rather live there instead of here."

"Bigger city, bigger opportunities," Dean stated. His voice was tight. "What's with the third degree?" He frowned at Rex.

"Just making conversation," Rex said with a shrug in his voice. "I thought it would be nice to get to know Deborah's friends a little better." I almost choked on that. There was no way the doctor could be classified as my friend.

Dean didn't look like he bought that statement either. "You know I'm not the only doctor who used to live in Tucson."

"Really? I wasn't aware of that."

"Collin Riley and Jerry Edmonds moved here about the same time I did. Are you asking them if they knew that orderly?"

Rex gave a small chuckle. "Well, I would, but I wasn't aware that they were friends of Deborah's. Like I said, I'm just trying to get to know you better.

"I wonder why so many doctors are leaving Tucson and moving to Phoenix." He directed the conversation back to his original topic. "I thought they had some great hospitals in Tucson."

"Doctor Weber draws doctors from all over the country; all over the world in fact. He's one of the country's top neurologists. Having trained and worked under him can give a big boost to a doctor's career."

"Oh, sure, I can see that." Rex nodded his head. "He's a great guy. He was great to Deborah. Not many doctors would waive their fee for a patient."

This wasn't the first time I'd heard what Doctor Weber had done for me. I wished there was some way I could repay him.

Travis Dean gave a disdainful sniff. "Not many doctors can afford to waive their fees. With malpractice premiums going higher every year, and the payments from insurance companies and the government going down, it's a wonder anyone even wants to be a doctor anymore. You can barely make a living at it now."

"Is that why you became a doctor, to get rich? I thought most doctors wanted to help people."

"That's not what I said," he snapped. "Of course I became a doctor to help people, but making a decent living in the process doesn't hurt. Would you still be a cop if you couldn't support your family?" His tone was full of disdain. Turning to look at Ted, he asked. "What do you do for a living?" He was finished with this topic.

The atmosphere was a little strained throughout dinner. Travis barely looked at Rex. As soon as he finished eating, he stood up, stretching and yawning. "I think I need to call it a night. Thanks for dinner, girls. It was delicious." His tone was slightly condescending, but he included Barbra in his compliment like she had done most of the work. I wondered how long it would be before he would expect her to duplicate the effort.

Taking Barbra's hand, he pulled her towards the door.

"Thanks again for dinner," he called over his shoulder. He wasn't taking the chance that Rex would corner him with more questions.

"Damn, she got out of helping clear the table and doing the dishes." Courtney shook her head.

"You want to tell us what that was all about?" Ted waited until Barbra and Travis were safely out the door before turning his question on Rex.

The look Rex returned was pure innocence. "What do you mean? I was just trying to get a feel for the guy." He shrugged. "We haven't exactly been friendly to him."

"And we've spent the last six weeks doing our best to avoid any contact with him or his self-centered girlfriend. Why the sudden interest in getting to know him?" Ted wasn't buying his lame excuse.

I wanted to ask if this had anything to do with Bobby Morrow's death, but I had to keep my questions to myself until we were alone. Media coverage had stopped with the suicide note. A suicide wasn't sensational enough for them. So far they hadn't gotten wind of the contents of the note, or the fact that the police didn't buy the suicide theory. Once that happened, they would be all over us, me, I corrected.

"Like I said, just trying to get a feel for the guy. He's as phony as his girlfriend." Rex shook his head in disgust.

"You don't think he's a real doctor?" I was shocked at the thought of someone pretending to be a doctor and getting away with it.

"Oh, sure he's a real doctor, just not a very good one. He's only in it for the money. He might want to make it to the level that Weber has attained, but he won't get there. That probably eats at him, too."

"If he doesn't become the rich man she's looking for, Barbra won't stick around," Courtney predicted. "She doesn't hide the fact that she only became a nurse so she could marry a rich doctor." We started clearing the table while we talked, filling the dishwasher with the dirty dishes.

"I think you dodged a close call there, my friend." Rex

slapped Ted on the back. "Just think, if you owned one of those mega contracting companies, she might have decided you qualified to be her husband."

We all laughed when Ted shuddered at the idea.

CHAPTER EIGHTEEN

The scrapes and bruises took longer to heal than the limp. Barbra still acted like I had planned the entire incident in order to gain attention while Travis Dean avoided Rex like the plague. That was fine with the rest of us. That meant we didn't have to worry about cooking another meal for them.

Barbra had made no effort to find another apartment, and time was running out. We heard nothing about Travis asking her to move in with him either. I wasn't sure what she was going to do, I just knew we weren't letting her move in with us.

Courtney rotated shifts with another nurse in the ICU, and was on nights again. When we were on different shifts, Rex insisted on taking me to the hospital each day. "You don't have to do this. I can take the bus to work." My objection sounded half-hearted even to my own ears.

"You wouldn't take away my one pleasure in the morning, would you?" He tried to pout, but it turned out comical instead, and I couldn't stop the laughter from bubbling up in my throat.

"How can I refuse when you put it that way?" He pulled me against his hard chest, lowering his head to take possession of my lips. I kept telling myself I had to put a stop to the romance that was building between us, but I hadn't done anything about it yet. My feelings for him were growing stronger every day.

When he lifted his head, we were both breathing heavily, ideas I had no right to contemplate were swimming through my mind. What if it turned out I was married? The question continued to plague me. I tried to tell myself that wasn't possible since no one had come forward to file a missing person's report. No one had recognized my picture in the paper either. Did I have so little worth in my former life that no one recognized me? The thought was depressing.

I pushed those thoughts aside as I slid out of the car. "I'll

163

see you tonight," he called out to me. I could feel his hot gaze on my back until I went inside.

I headed for the small chapel on the first floor before going up to the third floor. When Courtney had Sunday off, I went to church with her. When she was working, I spent as much time in the small chapel as I could.

Usually the small room was empty at this time of day, but two people were sitting in the front row, their heads close together in conversation. Thinking they were family members of a sick patient, I didn't want to disturb them.

Sitting down in the last row, I bowed my head. *Please God, help me remember my former life,* I silently prayed. *I need to know if it's okay to be in love with Rex Booker.* I waited for some sort of answer to my question, but nothing materialized out of thin air. Instead, a quiet calm washed over me. Was that God's answer, I wondered? Was He trying to tell me it was okay, that He approved?

Waiting several more minutes for some sort of revelation, I released a heavy sigh. I guess He was going to let me figure it out on my own. I finally stood up just as the couple in the front row also stood up. I gave a small gasp of surprise when I realized it was Doctor Weber and Janice Able. He had his arm around her waist; a small smile curved his lips. They seemed very cozy with each other. Barbra had called the doctor "Janice's man." Was there really something going on between them?

I quickly sat back down. Bowing my head, I hoped they wouldn't notice me. I silently willed them to leave the room without saying anything to me, but that wasn't to be. They stopped beside the pew where I was sitting. An expression of surprise registered on their faces.

"Hello, Deborah," Doctor Weber found his voice first. "How are you this morning?"

"Good morning, Doctor, Nurse Able. Um," I cleared my throat. "I'm doing fine, thank you. I'd better get up to the third floor. I don't want to be late." I tried to move past them, but they didn't move aside for me to step into the aisle.

"I've heard a lot of good things about you, Deborah." Janice Able spoke up. "I'm glad that you fit in here at the hospital. Everyone thinks you would make an excellent nurse." They no longer seemed uncomfortable at being caught together.

"Thank you, I like working here."

"Do you still feel like you should be doing more for your patients?" He would remember the statement I made my first day on the job. A smile curved his lips.

"Well, I do wish I could be more helpful." The feeling that there was more I should be doing wouldn't go away, but I kept that to myself. "I'm very grateful for everything that has been done for me. I hope to be able to repay everyone someday."

Giving her graying head a shake, Janice chuckled. "That isn't necessary. Everyone is glad to see you doing so well. You had us all worried when you were first brought in." She wasn't the shrew that Barbra described. "Maybe you'll be assigned to my floor someday. I would enjoy working with such a bright young woman dedicated to her job."

My face heated up at the compliment, but I didn't think working with Janice Able would be a good idea, since she was Barbra's supervisor. Living with the woman was hard enough; working with her would be impossible. As far as she was concerned, I couldn't do anything right.

For the next three mornings when I went to the chapel, Doctor Weber and Janice Able were there with their heads together, talking quietly. It looked like Barbra was right about them, but her nasty insinuation was way off the mark. They seemed very much in love. But why would they choose the chapel for a secret tryst? Anyone could walk in on them like I had. I couldn't see that they were doing anything wrong. I didn't know if either of them was married. Did Chaplain Winston know about their meetings, I wondered? What would he think of this arrangement?

Each morning I tried to sneak out quietly, but I thought they knew I was there anyway. I wouldn't say anything to anyone about seeing them though, especially Barbra. She would spread all sorts of dirty tales about them.

"Hello, Deborah. How are you this morning?" Before I could escape without them seeing me, they stopped beside the pew again. Doctor Weber smiled at me. They were holding hands today. Maybe they were going to bring their relationship out into the open. I was glad of that.

"I'm fine, how are you both doing?" I kept my eyes on their faces, not wanting to acknowledge the fact that they were holding hands.

"We're fine as well." A happy smile spread across Janice's face. "I suppose you've been wondering why we're here every morning."

"It's none of my business." I said quickly, hoping they would leave it at that. I should have known better. They both gave a small laugh, looking at each other.

"Would you believe I married this wonderful woman twenty-five years ago? For some silly reason, we've kept that fact a secret and very few people here at the hospital are aware of it." He shook his head. "I foolishly felt it would be a distraction if people knew our personal business. I was so busy being the big doctor I forgot about the important things in life. We have you to thank for making me see what is really important."

Janice patted his hand. "It wasn't entirely your fault, Ben. I shouldn't have agreed with you when this first started."

I didn't understand where they were going with this conversation, and what it had to do with me. "I'm grateful that she never got tired of the status quo and asked for a divorce," he continued, giving her hand a pat, "We have two sons, Ned is now twenty-three and Jon just turned twenty. They're grown up now, and I've been so busy being an important doctor that I've missed so much in their lives." Sadness drew his bushy brows together.

"We've finally decided to stop pretending we don't care about each other." Janice gave a contented sigh. "Anyway, we want to thank you for being discrete and not saying anything until we could decide how to handle things."

I didn't know why they were telling me all this. "What does this have to do with me?"

"After you came out of the coma and didn't remember your past life, it was like you were getting a chance to start your life over again," she said. "I decided I also wanted a do-over. It didn't matter if people knew we were married. That fact doesn't diminish who we each are. When I change shifts we have very little time to talk about things at home. We've always used the chapel as our meeting place." She smiled. "It always felt right to meet here, and we've been doing it for years."

I still didn't understand why they were telling me this.

"You have no memory of your past, but you shouldn't let that ruin the rest of your life," she said, as though reading my thoughts. "God has given you a wonderful man who loves you. We don't want to see you waste time simply because you don't know what was in the past. Grab hold of what God has given you now, and hold tight."

"But what if I'm married?" I whispered, almost afraid to say it out loud for fear that would make it true. "If that's the case, I don't have the right to be with anyone else."

"If you'd take an educated guess from an old man," Doctor Weber said, "there isn't a husband out there. I don't know the story of what happened to you, or why, but I can say with some confidence that if you were married, he would have come forward by now. Rex Booker is a good man, and he loves you very much. Grab hold of that, and hang on for all it's worth. Don't waste your life." He left unsaid, "like we did". He patted my hand as they walked away.

They'd given me a lot to think about, but I wasn't sure I could take their advice. It would break my heart to admit my love for Rex only to find out that nothing could ever come of it because I was already married. I needed time to consider what they said.

It turned out their way of handling things was to not make any sort of announcement. They just went about their lives as usual, but included each other while they were at work. While

Janice was working the night shift and Doctor Weber worked days, they would meet in the cafeteria to discuss any family issues instead of the chapel where few employees would see them. There was no overt display of affection, but it was obvious they were a couple. I thought it was rather sweet.

Of course, Barbra had to put her spin on things. "Everyone thinks they are so cute together. I think it's disgusting. They're the same age as my parents, maybe older." She shuddered at the thought of her parents in any kind of intimate situation.

"Just because they're in their fifties, doesn't mean they're dead," Courtney said. "Someday you're going to be their age. Don't you still want to have a love life?"

Barbra harrumphed, and walked off without saying anything more. Maybe she didn't want to think about being that old.

I was still thinking over what they had said to me. I wanted to know what had happened in my past, but should I let it ruin my future? As long as I couldn't remember, would the killer leave me alone? Was it fair to Rex to possibly put his life in jeopardy?

CHAPTER NINETEEN

Time is getting short, he thought as he paced around his apartment. It felt like the walls were closing in on him. Either he left with that one loose end hanging over his head, or he stuck around hoping for one more chance to take her out. There was always the possibility that she would regain her memory. If that happened while he was still here, his goose was cooked.

"That is not acceptable," he growled. "I'm not going to prison because that little weasel was too squeamish to finish the job I'd given him." He still wouldn't accept any blame for what happened.

If that damn detective hadn't swept her off her feet, I could have asked her out. He was so convinced of his own prowess with women that he knew he could have gotten close enough to charm her into going out with him. After that it would have been easy to finish her off without anyone being the wiser. But she was a lot harder to kill than the weasel had been, he admitted. He still refused to say either of their names. Using their names made them real, gave them life and importance. He wouldn't do that.

Letting her live was taking a big chance, but it was one he might have to take. Even if she regained her full memory, he would be hard to find once he disappeared. He would be a new man with a new name and a new life. His present identity would cease to exist like he fell off the face of the earth. If he was no longer around, she couldn't point her finger at him.

He slammed his fist into the wall. It would have taken just a few minutes more, and he would have been out of that pharmacy. She never would have seen him, and none of this would have happened. In the time he'd spent spinning his wheels in Phoenix, he could have had enough money to retire on without ever having to work again. She needed to pay for ruining his plans.

Accomplishing that was another matter. He growled in

frustration. The saying 'Three strikes and you're out,' kept running through his mind. He'd had three shots at killing her, yet she was still a thorn in his side.

"No," he spoke out loud, his outlook brightening. "The first time was on the weasel, not me. I still have one more to go." Third time's a charm, sounded so much better. The next time I get her in my sights, I'll finish her off, he told himself. An evil laugh erupted from his mouth. Until then, he would begin to fatten his getaway fund.

~~~

The news spread through the hospital in whispers and furtive looks. Over the weekend drugs had turned up missing from the hospital pharmacy. Just small amounts, but it was enough that it wasn't simply a matter of sloppy bookkeeping. People acted as though it was a common occurrence in any hospital. Still people were on edge, looking at their co-workers with suspicion, wondering who the thief was.

Each time the missing drugs were mentioned, dizziness swept over me, causing my head to hurt. Something tugged at my mind, but my memory remained stubbornly absent. The harder I tried to remember, the more elusive the memories were. Frustration added to my case of nerves.

"You are a bad luck omen for the hospital if I ever saw one," Barbra groused as soon as I walked in the door that evening. We were no longer on the same shift which meant we stayed out of each other's hair most of the time. Still she made a point of blaming me for every little thing that went wrong at the hospital.

"What have I done to displease your highness now?" I sighed wearily. I had gotten more of a backbone lately, and didn't let her intimidate me. That seemed to bother her as much as anything else about me.

"We've had more troubles at the hospital since you darkened our door than we've ever had."

"Really," I said sarcastically. "What kind of troubles have I brought down on the hospital?" I didn't know where she was headed with her accusation, but I was getting tired of her innuendos.

"How about attempted murder? Have you forgotten about that?"

"How could I forget that since I was the intended victim?" I snapped back. "How is that my fault?"

"Well, you had to do something horrible for someone to want you dead," she continued her tirade. "An orderly also committed suicide not too long ago."

"You're blaming me for that?" She was reaching for any incident she could conjure up. The police still considered Bobby Morrow's death a homicide, not suicide, but they were keeping that under wraps. But she was on a roll, and wasn't going to let my question sidetrack her.

"There is still the possibility of a lawsuit from that patient's family. You never should have performed a medical procedure on her."

"So you think I should have let her die?" I couldn't believe she thought that would have been preferable. I shook my head. She wouldn't admit that I had done something right. "You're beating a dead horse with that one, Barbra." I gave a small laugh, trying not to let her rile me. "I did nothing more than what anyone would have done in the same instance. Besides, you don't need a medical license to preform CPR. Anyone could have done that."

"Only if they've been properly trained, and you haven't been trained. That's the difference."

"Did I perform the procedure incorrectly? Did I harm Mrs. Taylor instead of help her?" I had taken several first aid courses at the hospital, CPR being one of them, passing each with flying colors. Each course was like I was reliving some part of my life that I couldn't remember.

"That's beside the point," she snapped. "You weren't trained to do CPR at the time. You had no business even touching a patient." We would be moving out in two weeks. I couldn't wait to get away from this woman.

"Now drugs are being stolen from right under our noses." She continued her rant, raising her voice as though I was deaf.

171

That same wave of dizziness swept over me, threatening to send me to the floor. I reached out for the wall to steady myself to keep from falling down. "Do you think I'm stealing those drugs?" I asked incredulously. My voice sounded hollow in my ears.

"You might not be the one taking the drugs, but you have to admit there has been a lot of bad luck surrounding the hospital since you arrived."

"Don't listen to her." Courtney had arrived in time to hear the end of Barbra's tirade. Barbra had me cornered just inside the door of the apartment, and I hadn't been able to move until Courtney pushed past Barbra. She pulled me away from the angry woman. "Ignore her. She enjoys stirring the pot. No one believes you are involved with those missing drugs." She glared at Barbra before heading to our room. "The guys will be here soon. Let's get ready for our dates." That meant Travis Dean would also be there.

My stomach rolled. Since the encounter Rex had with the man, he wasn't very nice to any of us, except Barbra of course. I couldn't imagine a marriage between them though. They were both so self-centered; I didn't know how they even got along.

"You know, the four of you are pretty kinky." Barbra's snide comment stopped us from going very far.

"What are you talking about now?" Courtney turned around to stare at her.

"Well, the four of you go everywhere together. I just thought you were attached at the hip. It has to get pretty kinky at times."

"We don't have to explain or justify what we do. Just because you jumped into bed with Travis," Courtney snapped, "doesn't mean we're doing the same thing."

Barbra snickered, "Holding out for a ring, are you? Good luck with that. You don't buy a pair of shoes without trying them on. Why would a man marry a woman before he knew if they were compatible in bed?" She snickered again, closing the door to her room.

"Why buy the cow when you can get the milk for free," Courtney yelled at the closed door in retaliation. "Moving day can't happen soon enough. I will be so glad to be rid of her."

In spite of what Barbra might think, the four of us didn't always go out together. We just left the apartment at the same time to get away from her. I was cooking for Rex at his house. I didn't know what Ted had planned for them. After this latest display, staying at the apartment was out of the question. Even though Travis Dean always took her out to eat, there was still the chance they would return early. I didn't want to run the chance of that happening. I'd had enough of Barbra to last a lifetime.

It was early when Rex brought me home that evening. Ted's truck was already there. Usually they weren't home this early. My heart did a little flip flop. I hoped that didn't mean they'd had a fight.

My fears were so far off the mark it was funny. Courtney grabbed me the minute we opened the door. "Guess what! Oh, you'll never guess. I'll just tell you." She led me in a happy dance. Ted was grinning from ear to ear about something. She finally let go of me long enough to hold up her left hand. A beautiful ring rested on her ring finger.

"He asked me to marry him," she squealed, starting her dance again. "I said yes! We're getting married." She pulled me into a bear hug.

Rex slapped Ted on the back. "Way to go, man! Congratulations!"

"Thanks, when are you going to pop the question?" I could feel my face turning red even before Rex answered.

"We have a few things to be worked out first." Rex looked at me with such longing, my face heated up even further.

"Well, hurry up. We can make it a double."

Courtney pulled a bottle of champagne out of the refrigerator that she had put in there to chill. It hadn't been there earlier, or Barbra would have swiped it for her and Travis to use.

"To the future bride and groom." I lifted up my glass in a

toast. "May God bless you with many happy years."

"May all your troubles be little ones," Rex added. We laughed at the double meaning.

Before we finished the bottle, the door opened for Barbra and Travis to come inside. "What's going on?" She looked at us like we'd done something wrong. "Why are you here?"

"Not even you can spoil my night." Courtney told her, holding up her hand to show off her engagement ring. "Ted and I are getting married."

For a long moment, Barbra was too stunned to react, but it didn't last long. "Well, I guess he didn't need to try on the shoes after all. Or maybe he already has." She turned to Travis. "I don't want to be here tonight." Without another word, she marched out the door. If Travis hadn't been fast enough, she would have slammed the door in his face.

"Wow! That's what I call sour grapes." Rex shook his head. "Why was she talking about trying on shoes?"

"Just an old saying, forget about it." Courtney brushed away the question. She looked at Ted, trying to judge his reaction to Barbra's angry display.

He took her in his arms, kissing her softly. "Don't let her get to you. Some people will never be happy no matter how much they have in this life. She's one of those people." He kissed her again. "Thank you for agreeing to be my wife," he whispered. "I love you."

For the next week Barbra made herself scarce around the apartment. The only time she was there was when Courtney and I weren't. We could see her messy trail as she made her way through the apartment. We could only guess that she was staying with Travis.

We had signed a six-month lease on the new apartment, and I worried that Courtney would be moving in with Ted before they got married. Even though the rent was much lower than we were currently paying, I couldn't afford it on my own.

"Have you set a date yet?" I asked, hoping she would fill me in on what her plans were.

"The lease for our new place is for six months. I figure it

will take that long to plan a wedding. My mom is coming over from New Mexico to help with the plans, but it will still take that long." She gave me a hopeful smile.

"Love seems to be in the air lately. First Doctor Weber and Janice announced that they've been married all these years. Now Ted and I are getting married. Maybe you and Rex will make it three?" Her voice lifted at the end, turning it into a question.

"We don't talk about it," I admitted. "We're waiting to see if I ever remember my past."

"Don't waste your life waiting for something that may never happen." Her words echoed the same advice Doctor Weber and Janice had given me. "You love him, don't you?"

"Yes, of course, but…"

"But nothing," she interrupted. "Grab onto happiness with both hands, and don't let go."

"I was going to say he's only said he loves me in general terms." My heart clenched slightly. Was he waiting until my case was solved? What if they never figured out who had tried to kill me? Would our lives always be in a holding pattern?

"He's said it in everything but words, girl. He's so in love with you he glows every time he looks at you." Her statement intruded on my worried thoughts, startling me.

"But he hasn't asked me to marry him."

"So what's stopping you from asking him?"

"What? I can't do that."

"Why not? We aren't living in the dark ages where the woman has to wait around for her man to make up his mind. Go for it, girl."

I laughed nervously. I wouldn't dare, would I?

CHAPTER TWENTY

Moving day was at hand! We were taking our time moving into the new apartment. We had very little furniture to move, so it wouldn't take long. Courtney and I were trying to coordinate it so we moved out at the same time Barbra did. Leaving her there alone to clean up after she moved out would be a disaster. She might destroy things just for spite.

Ted's house had been rather sparsely furnished when I first met him. With Courtney's help, he had acquired a few new pieces of furniture. Once we had our apartment picked out, she bought a couch that would fit in with Ted's things. The store would deliver that after we moved in. I wondered if they had subconsciously known where their relationship was leading them.

Barbra had finally gotten over her snit, and even congratulated Courtney on her engagement. "I'm happy for you both," she gushed. "When's the big day?"

"In the spring," Courtney hedged. She didn't want to give the exact date. Barbra was being too nice. She was up to something.

"You're going to be a beautiful bride." She turned to me with a big smile. "What are your plans? Will you and your hunky detective be getting married as well?"

"No plans," I said, giving my head a shake. He hadn't asked me, and I hadn't gotten up the nerve to ask him like Courtney suggested.

"Well, don't fret, it won't be long. He's crazy about you." She walked off without cutting down either of us.

I looked at Courtney, bewildered by how nice she was acting. "What's up with her?" I asked in a whisper. "She's never said a nice word to me before."

"She's only nice when she wants something, so be careful." An hour later we figured out what she wanted.

"I'll be moving in with Travis this weekend, but I don't

176

have any way to get my things to his house. I was wondering if you would ask the guys if they would help me."

My mouth dropped opened in surprise. For the last three months she had gone out of her way to be nasty to all of us. Now, because she wanted something from us, she was all sweetness and light.

"What?" She looked at me like I had grown another head. She didn't curb the waspish tone now.

"Nothing." I shook my head. "If you want the guys to help, you'll have to ask them yourself." My backbone was becoming stronger every day.

"I just need you to ask them to help me," she whined. "They haven't exactly been nice to me. I thought they would help me out if you girls asked them." Tears shimmered in her eyes.

"You haven't exactly been Mary Sunshine either," Courtney countered. "Why don't you rent a truck and move the things yourself?"

"You expect me to lift all this furniture myself?" She was shocked at the suggestion.

"What about Travis's friends at the hospital? Can't he get some of them to help you?"

It was a losing battle. The waterworks came on in full force at that suggestion, tears streaming down her face. "The other doctors at the hospital are jealous of Travis because he's a much better doctor than they are. They wouldn't lift a finger to help him. We're just asking for a little kindness from those closest to us."

Those closest to them? I thought. She couldn't be serious. She wasn't close to either Courtney or me, and Travis certainly didn't like Rex.

~~~

Parked across the street, he watched them loading up the trucks. Where was she going? He hadn't heard anything around the hospital about her leaving town. His gut twisted. Had she remembered where she was from?

He quickly dismissed that thought. The hospital grapevine

would have spread that kind of news in a flash. Was she moving in with that damn detective? Again his stomach churned. If she moved in with him, he'd never be able to put her out of his misery. He chuckled at his twist on the words.

All he needed was one final score, and he would be out of here, never to be seen again. After that, she could remember everything that had ever happened to her and he wouldn't care.

It would be better if he could eliminate her before he left, but he'd almost given up on that possibility. Living with those nurses made it difficult to catch her alone. Living with the detective would make it impossible. She had more protection than the president.

Fury spread through him. It no longer mattered to him if she remembered what had happened to her. He wanted her to pay for the mess she had made of his life. He should be on a beach in Cayman, sipping Pina Coladas instead of staking out her apartment to see where she was going.

"Damn bitch," he growled as the object of his hatred came out of the building carrying another arm load of clothes. How many clothes does she have? She stopped beside the same late model car as before, placing the clothes in the backseat.

He hadn't been aware she had her own car. The detective even took her to work when she wasn't riding with Courtney. An evil smile spread across his normally handsome face. That could be the answer to all his problems. Blow her up when she drives off, and he'd finally be rid of her. Nothing could save her then. He even knew just the person to set it up. His underworld connections were going to finally pay off.

He started his car, pulling slowly into traffic. Tomorrow was another day, and he would make sure it was a good one.

~~~

"Why did we let her guilt us into helping her?" Courtney shook her head, her blonde hair swaying around her face. "I should be immune to her tricks by now."

I pushed at my hair to get it out of my face. It was finally long enough that I was in need of a haircut. The summer sun had lightened it so that it was more strawberry blonde than red now. I kind of like it. "If this gets her out of our life, I'm willing to pitch in." We'd each made three trips downstairs with clothes to load them in Barbra's car. "How can one person have so many clothes?" I wondered. "Where does she wear them since she wears a uniform to work?"

"She wouldn't want to be caught wearing the same thing twice," Courtney joked. Turning serious, she asked, "What's she doing upstairs? She should be helping out."

"She's the one passing out orders. I'd like to know what Travis Dean is doing. Shouldn't he be pitching in?"

"You wouldn't want him to do anything that might harm his hands, would you? After all, he's a big time surgeon. His hands are his livelihood." She was repeating the excuse Barbra had given for him not doing any of the heavy work. "The last I saw him, he was giving the guys instructions on how to load the furniture. If he isn't careful, he might end up with a knuckle sandwich from one or both of them." We laughed, but there was a grain of truth in her statement. The guys were getting fed up with his superior attitude.

"One last night in this place," Courtney looked around the nearly empty apartment. She was a little melancholy at leaving. She must have had some good times here, as well as bad ones. The only things left to move were the beds. The guys would move them first thing in the morning while we finished cleaning. Getting Barbra to help with that task wasn't going to be easy, but maybe we could guilt her in to it. She had to have a conscience, right? I asked myself.

Almost too excited to sleep, I heard Barbra come home at midnight. She would try to say she was too tired to help with the cleaning in the morning. Oh well, after tomorrow we wouldn't have to put up with her any longer. My eyes drifted closed with that thought.

~~~

A loud explosion rocked the building, bringing everyone out of a sound sleep. Tenants in the other apartments poured out into the hallway rubbing their sleep-filled eyes. "What happened?" "What was that?" "Is the building on fire?" It wasn't even six o'clock in the morning.

"Where's Barbra?" Courtney looked around at the crowd filling the hall. "She couldn't have slept through that noise. Did she even come home last night?"

"I heard her come in. She has to be here somewhere." I tried to see if she was somewhere in the crowd, but there were too many people. Everyone was pushing and shoving wanting to get outside to see what happened. Loud sirens suddenly filled the air. Someone had called the fire department. "I'll go back to get her up. If there's a fire, she needs to leave the building."

Screaming and yelling could be heard as people made it out to the parking lot stopping me from going back to the apartment. Something awful had happened. Following the noise and the crowd, I stepped outside. A car had been blown up, what was left of it was on fire. Even so, we could see what was left of the person sitting in the driver's seat.

Courtney grabbed my arm. "That's Barbra's car!" Her voice came to me as through a tunnel. "Who's that in her car?"

I broke away from her grasp, running back inside. Maybe she was still sleeping, I told myself. She had to be sleeping. That couldn't be her. Maybe someone tried to steal her car.

Throwing open her bedroom door, I saw that her bed was empty. She hadn't bothered to make it since someone would be here to move it in a few hours. So where was Barbra? The image of what was left of a body in her car flashed through my mind. "Oh, God, no. Please," I whispered. "Don't let that be her."

The rest of the morning was a blur. Rex showed up within minutes of the fire trucks. Several other cars had caught fire in the initial explosion, but they had been empty. Since Barbra wasn't in the apartment, we assumed it was her in the car. It would take time for the medical examiner to make the final determination. But we all knew it was her.

"What was she doing up so early?" Rex asked. He had

taken Courtney and me back to our apartment to question us. We looked at each other, shaking our heads. We shared the same thought. She was probably trying to avoid helping clean the apartment. We didn't put voice to that thought though. "Do you know when she got home last night?"

"I heard her come in, it was late," I answered. "How did this happen? Why did her car blow up?"

He drew a deep breath before answering. "The crime unit said someone had placed a bomb on the underside of the car. It was rigged to go off when the car was started."

We gasped, staring at him. "Who would do something like that? Why would they want to kill Barbra?"

Rex shrugged, keeping his thoughts to himself. There was something he wasn't telling us. I didn't know if he was trying to protect me, or if he didn't want to say anything in front of Courtney.

"Has anyone told Travis Dean yet?" Courtney asked softly. Before Rex could answer, Ted burst into the room. "Court, what happened? Are you all right?' We were sitting on the floor since there wasn't any furniture left in the apartment. He pulled her up, wrapping his arms around her in a crushing embrace. Relief and fear were written on his face.

After talking to us in the apartment, Rex was busy doing whatever it is a cop does in this situation. The crime scene unit went over every inch of the car. It wasn't until the tow truck left with the burnt out remains of the cars before Rex was able to come back to us.

It took the better part of the day before the parking lot was cleared as a crime scene, and the burned out cars towed away. A big black spot marked where the car had exploded, the asphalt melted into a bubbling mess. It would be a constant reminder of what had happened there.

Until Barbra's parents could be notified in New York, the identity of the victim wasn't released. The media milled around trying to get information, and interviewing everyone who would talk to them. No one had any insight into why this happened or who the victim was. This was one time it was a good thing that Barbra hadn't been friendly with any of the neighbors. Courtney and I refused to talk to them. I wouldn't know what to say.

It wasn't until the middle of the afternoon before Travis Dean showed up. He looked upset, but not devastated by what had happened. "His girlfriend was blown up, and he's just now showing up," Courtney whispered to me. "The man is devoid of feelings or he didn't really care for her."

"The police don't want her name released yet. Maybe he was told to stay away for a while. Maybe he just isn't the kind of person to show his emotions." At least I hoped that was the reason. I was making excuses for him, I didn't want to think he cared so little for Barbra.

Rex was the one who had to make the notification. Considering the fact that the men didn't like each other, it couldn't have been easy.

Rex was afraid to let me out of his sight, and insisted I go home with him that night. I didn't know what the bomb in Barbra's car had to do with me. If he thought the same person who tried to kill me had killed her, I didn't understand the connection.

"This is the most inept killer I've ever come across," Rex said as he paced around his living room. "He's got to be feeling the pressure since he hasn't been able to close the deal." He continued to mumble and pace. I didn't think he was aware I was in the room, or that he was thinking out loud.

I didn't understand what he was talking about. The man had just killed Barbra. That seemed pretty efficient to me.

"What are you talking about?" I finally got his attention by stepping in front of him. "He killed her. What more do you want?"

For a minute he stared at me like he had forgotten I was there. "Don't you see what happened?" he finally said. When I shook my head, he pulled me into his arms. "Babe, he's killed two people, but he's after you." I jerked in his arms, but he held me tight. "He's tried to kill you four times, but he can't get it done. Right about now, he has to be feeling pretty frustrated." If Rex was right, the same person had killed the orderly from the hospital.

My stomach rolled. "Are you saying the maniac who has been trying to kill me for whatever reason killed Barbra in my place? Why would he do that? What did he have against her?" Although I didn't like the reasoning of killing Bobby Morrow, I understood he was hoping to get the heat off himself. What reason would he have to kill Barbra?

Rex drew in a deep breath, rocking me against his chest with the breath, exhaling slowly. "I have no proof that Bobby Morrow didn't kill himself, or that this maniac was after you with the bomb, but if I'm right, that's exactly what he was aiming for."

"Why would he think that? It was her car. That doesn't make sense."

"This whole thing doesn't make sense," he agreed. "But in a way it does."

I pulled back to look up at him. "What do you mean? Do you know why he tried to kill me?"

"No, but I know Bobby Morrow isn't the one who did that to you. His death was set up to look like a suicide so we would stop looking for the real killer. He wanted the cops to drop their guard hoping to be able to get at you."

"But why did he put a bomb in Barbra's car? Why would he think that would kill me?"

"I'm guessing, but he probably thought it was your car."

"That doesn't make any sense either." I was trying to follow his reasoning, but failed miserably "I don't even have a car, so why would he think it was mine?"

"Think about it. Who was the one loading that car with clothes yesterday?"

"Me." The word came out in a whisper. This mad man was still coming after me, and he didn't care who else he killed in the process. Would the nightmare that was my life never end? "You think he was watching us while we were moving out; that he's been watching me all along." It wasn't a question.

I pulled away from him, pacing across the room as those

thoughts swirled through my mind. "What's the matter with me? Of course, he's been watching me." I was talking to myself more than to Rex. I stopped pacing to stare at him. Determination filled my mind. "Okay, if he's frustrated and upset that he missed me again like you say; let's use that to our advantage."

Rex was confused now. "What are you talking about?"

"You said he was an inept killer, so put that in the paper. Let's draw him out. Make fun of him; announce to the world that he is incapable of accomplishing his objective." I started pacing around the room again as the idea took shape in my mind.

Rex grabbed me, giving me a shake. "If you think for one minute that I'm going to taunt this guy so he'll come after you, you're nuts, or you think I am. I'm not using you as bait."

"What if this is the only way to be sure we can catch him? You can protect me, and catch him when he makes his next move. So far, he's held all the cards. It's time we had the advantage for a change. We've been twisting in the wind long enough. I'm tired of looking over my shoulder, wondering if the next person I meet is going to kill me. I want this finished." I rested my head on his shoulder, my heart pounding in my ears. "Deborah was strong," I whispered, "and so am I." I wanted to be brave, but I was scared to death.

CHAPTER TWENTY-ONE

The mood was somber the next day when we went to work. By that time everyone knew Barbra had been the person who died in the car bomb. Although she hadn't been very nice to those she worked with, no one wished this to happen to her. Travis Dean took advantage of the situation to take the day off. I hoped it was because he truly did care for her, and not just so he could get a day off.

"Are you all right, Deborah?" Chaplain Winston was in the chapel early, waiting for anyone who wanted to come in for grief counseling.

With a heavy sigh, I nodded my head, lifting my shoulders at the same time. I didn't have an answer for him. "I can't believe someone would do something like that." I still hadn't convinced Rex to go with my idea. He said he would run it by his superiors, but I wasn't sure he really would.

"Have the police said anything to you about a motive? You're still seeing that detective, what does he have to say?"

"I get the standard reply they give everyone else. He can't comment on an ongoing investigation." I didn't say anything for a minute. "I feel guilty," I finally said.

"Whatever for? This wasn't your fault."

"I didn't really like her," I whispered. "I wasn't always nice to her." That was only a part of the reason for my guilt. I wanted to tell him the truth behind Barbra's death, but I couldn't give out that information. Besides, it was only a theory behind the crime. As yet, there was no evidence that I was the intended target

He cleared his throat several times before he spoke. "I understand your feelings, but you shouldn't feel guilty about that. Not everyone is loveable."

"Did you know her?" I looked up at him.

He shook his head. "No, but I've spoken to a number of people who worked with her. She was...a hard person," he finished.

A weak smile tilted the corners of my mouth. "That she was. Still I feel bad. I didn't try very hard to be friends with her."

"You can only be friends with someone who wants to be friends. I understand that we are to love our enemies, but sometimes they don't want our love. Don't let guilt eat at you, Deborah. We each make our own choices, and I don't think she made very wise ones about a lot of things. My prayer is that she knew the Lord." He sounded doubtful though. For several minutes, we sat in silence.

"How is everything else going for you? Have you been able to remember anything from your past yet?" He switched subjects.

I shook my head. "I can do almost everything except remember what happened to me before I woke from the coma." I sighed in frustration. "I automatically do certain things that I have no memory of ever doing before. Doctor Weber calls it muscle memory. If I can do those things, why can't I remember something as simple as my name? Shouldn't that be muscle memory as well?" I had almost given up knowing who I really am.

"Medical science isn't perfect," he said. "You can't live your life looking for the past. There are a lot of people who love you, build your life around that." A lot of people had been telling me the same thing lately. Maybe it was time to listen.

As I left the chapel, Jerry Edmonds was standing around trying to look busy. The man seemed to be everywhere. I wondered how he managed to get any work done. "How are you this morning, Deborah?" Instead of his usual jovial self, he was as glum as most of the other employees.

"Upset," I answered simply. I didn't know what else to say. How did people think I was? I didn't like Barbra, but she was still my roommate.

"I understand," he nodded his head gravely. "As everyone is, but she wasn't easy to like. She wasn't a very nice person."

My mouth dropped open at his blunt statement. I was

surprised that he would voice that sentiment. Most people would reserve such things for their closest friends.

Seeing my disapproval, he shrugged. "At least I'm not a hypocrite like a lot of people around here. I don't believe in saying she was a nice person simply because she's dead. I didn't like her, and she didn't like me. In fact, she didn't like most of the folks around here, including her patients. The universe has a way of evening things out." With that, he turned away, stalking off. His usual swagger was missing this morning.

The universe? What did the universe have to do with what happened to Barbra? I stared at his retreating back. Did he think she deserved to be blown up simply because she wasn't very nice? The man was slightly creepy the way he appeared out of nowhere at times, but I never thought he was cruel.

Turning away, I bumped into Doctor Collin Riley. Why were people sneaking up on me today? Was he hanging around the chapel, thinking of going in to talk to the chaplain? "I'm sorry, Doctor. I should have watched where I was going." We did a little dance as we tried to step around each other.

"Want to dance?" He chuckled. "How are things going?" He asked, repeating the question I'd been asked numerous times already this morning. His close scrutiny was unnerving.

"Things are just peachy," I said sarcastically. "Now if you'll excuse me." I headed down the long hallway for the stairs. He acted like he hadn't heard about Barbra's death. Everyone was acting odd today. Maybe he was trying to hide his true feelings. I'd never seen him with Barbra, but that didn't mean he wasn't upset about her death.

~~~

Panic gripped him by the throat. How had she escaped again? Was she some sort of supernatural being, slipping away from danger, placing someone else where she should be? Either that or she is the luckiest person alive. She should have died months ago, yet she was still alive.

He'd beat her within an inch of her life, tried to run her down with a car, and now tried to blow her up. What more did he have to do to be rid of her? His hands shook as he combed them through his thick hair.

"Get a grip," he whispered. "She's as human as you are. She can die just like anyone else. She will die," he insisted. Three strikes and you're out. The refrain ran through his mind again. "No, damn it. I'm too close to the finish line. No one is going stop me."

This wasn't his fault. That idiot must have put the bomb under the wrong car. That was the only possible explanation. He told the gangbanger which car was hers, and he put the bomb under the wrong car. She had spent the day bringing clothes out of the apartment and putting them in that car. Barbra Johnson hadn't been out there all day. In fact, he hadn't seen her at all.

He slapped his forehead. It was the right car; just the wrong person owned it. In his haste to do away with her, and disappear, he was getting careless. He should have known Barbra Johnson was too lazy to actually do any of the work involved with moving if she could get someone else to do it for her. There was no way all those clothes could have belonged to an aide when she had no money to buy them.

He shrugged. It was too late to do anything about it now. He needed to wrap this up before that gangbanger did something to get caught. He wouldn't hesitate to rat him out if it would save his own skin.

His mind was preoccupied with these thoughts when the object of his hatred walked into the cafeteria. He'd spent the past few months avoiding her in an effort to hide his hatred. That hadn't done him any good. He hated her more every day. The bitch was everywhere. Watching her with her detective almost sent him over the edge. He wanted her out of his life once and for all, but it didn't look like that was going to happen. He left the cafeteria before he crossed the room and strangled her with his bare hands.

~~~

"What did your boss say about my idea?" Rex joined me

in the hospital cafeteria for lunch. If he thought he could get away with it he'd be right beside me all day. The tuna sandwich wasn't too bad, considering it was hospital food. "Are they going to let you tell the media that whoever this person is, he is incompetent? That I was the intended victim?"

"They didn't like it any better than I did. There is no proof that Barbra wasn't the intended victim. She wasn't very well-liked. She made enemies everywhere she went."

"That's beside the point!" I said harshly, forcing myself to keep my voice down so others in the cafeteria couldn't eavesdrop on our conversation. "No one had threatened her. No one had tried to kill her. Logically, I was the intended victim."

"We have to work off of the evidence, not conjecture. There simply isn't any evidence to indicate that the bomb was meant for you." He sounded as frustrated as I felt. "We don't know if someone had threatened her."

"You really think she wouldn't have been all over the police, demanding protection if she had received a threat?" He couldn't argue with that point. She would have wanted the entire police force protecting her if she thought her life was in danger.

"So what happens now?" I asked. "We wait for this maniac to try again? How many chances does he get before he accomplishes what he set out to do months ago?"

"I'm not going to let anything happen to you, Babe, but I'm not using you as bait either." His grip on my hand was almost painful. "I won't put you at risk like that." He stroked my wrist where my pulse beat rapidly.

I know he meant what he said, but he couldn't be with me twenty-four/seven. What if this person put a bomb in Courtney's car next time? I couldn't take that chance; I *wouldn't* take that chance. I wasn't sure what I was going to do, but I knew I wasn't going to sit around waiting for him to blow up someone else in my place.

That night Courtney and I cooked our first dinner in our new home. If this hadn't happened to Barbra, we would be celebrating in our new apartment, but it felt wrong to celebrate after what had happened. "How long before we stop feeling guilty?" she asked. "We didn't do anything wrong, so why are we feeling guilty?"

"You feel guilty too?" I looked over my shoulder at her. I was standing at the stove turning the chicken in the frying pan. Fried food must have been a staple for me in my former life because I could fry just about anything, including deep fried dill pickle spears dipped in beer batter. "I thought I was the only one feeling that way."

She nodded her head. "No, I think a lot of people are feeling some form of guilt. We were so happy to be rid of her," she whispered. "But I didn't want her to die."

I couldn't think of anything to say. That wasn't exactly why I was feeling guilty though. It was supposed to be me in that car, not Barbra.

"Who would do something like that? Why put a bomb in her car?" She drew a deep breath. "I know she didn't treat people very nice, but I can't imagine anyone wanting to blow her up because of that."

I wished I could tell her what Rex was thinking, but I had to remain silent for now. Not telling what he thought about Bobby Morrow's faked suicide hadn't accomplished anything. I didn't think keeping his suspicions about Barbra's death to himself was going to get the desired results either.

Whoever this person was, he had to know the police would keep looking for a motive for placing a bomb in her car. When they didn't find a reason to kill Barbra, they would look for another intended victim. Since there had been multiple attempts on my life, I was the logical person for them to consider next. How many more times would he try to kill me before he got the results he wanted?

Dinner was subdued as we sat on the couch with TV trays in front of us. The dining room set that Ted and Courtney picked out was in his house. I still didn't have enough money to buy furniture. When they got married, I would have to come up with the entire rent. I would have even less money for furniture then. *If I managed to live that long*, I thought morosely. The fact that someone really wanted me dead had been driven home with a bang.

"All right, enough of this gloom and doom," Ted said, breaking in on our thoughts. "I'm sorry about what happened to Barbra, but we can't let that take the joy out of our lives. We have a wedding to plan." He reached across the small space between the trays to take Courtney's hand. "If this hadn't happened, we would be making all sorts of plans. Let's not let it spoil things for us."

"He's right," Rex agreed. "I'm sorry about what happened to Barbra, and I'm going to do my best to catch whoever did it. For now, let's put it aside and enjoy ourselves." He grasped my hand, bringing it to his lips to kiss my fingers. Courtney gave me a sharp look, and nodded her head at Rex. Her message was clear. He didn't have to say the words for me to know he loved me. She didn't want me to wait for him to propose either. She wanted me to propose to him. I hadn't worked up my nerve to do that yet.

"I wish you would agree to stay with me, at least until I catch this guy," he whispered later while we said a lengthy good night at the door. "You could stay in the room you slept in last night. I promise I won't come sneaking into the room in the middle of the night to ravish you." He wiggled his eyebrows comically. "At least I promise to try to control myself." We laughed until he pulled me into his arms. "I'm in love with you, and I'm not going to lose you. I know Ted would be more comfortable if Courtney moved in with him."

I was half tempted to agree. If I wasn't around Courtney, she wouldn't end up being collateral damage when this guy came after me again. And he will come after me again, I told myself. I had little doubt of that. That would put Rex in danger though. I couldn't allow that either. I didn't know how I could protect everyone I cared about while the killer was still running loose. If I went away, they would be safe, but I had nowhere to go.

"What would we do about the lease on this place?" I halfheartedly asked. "It would be a waste of money to pay rent here, and live somewhere else."

"Money be damned," he growled. "I want you to be safe." His lips claimed mine possessively. I wrapped my arms around his neck, leaning in to him. That was all the invitation he needed to deepen the kiss. He swept his tongue in my mouth, dueling with mine in an age-old lovers dance.

When we finally pulled apart, we were both breathless, our hearts pounding in unison. I couldn't deny that I was in love with him. I no longer cared if there was a husband out there somewhere. I wasn't sure how the law would treat me if that ended up being the case, and Rex and I got married. But then, he hadn't said anything about marriage, just living together. Could I be brazen enough to ask him?

"I love you, too," I finally managed to make my voice work in a soft whisper.

A big smile spread across his handsome face. "Will you marry me?" We spoke at the same time. "What?" Again we spoke at the same time, then we laughed.

"You're serious?" He looked down at me, searching my face for an answer. "You really will marry me?"

"I still don't know who I am. Doesn't that bother you?"

"No, it doesn't. I don't care if you're Deborah or Dora. Either way I love you, and I want to spend the rest of my life with you. So, will you marry me?" He dropped down to one knee in front of me as he pulled something out of his shirt pocket.

"I've been carrying this around with me for weeks waiting for the right moment. Deborah Winston, or whatever your name is, I love you with all my heart. Will you do me the honor of agreeing to become my wife?" He held up a beautiful ring.

A gasp was all I could manage for several beats, then I whispered, "Yes, yes I'll marry you." I pulled him up so I could wrap my arms around him, placing a kiss on his lips.

"Okay, you two, come up for air." It was several minutes before Ted's teasing voice drew us apart. "You got something you want to tell us?"

Without answering, Rex lifted my hand, sliding the ring on my finger before sealing it with a kiss. "We're getting married," he finally said, a huge smile lit up his face like it was Christmas.

CHAPTER TWENTY-TWO

Life at the hospital slowly returned to normal. Travis Dean was back at work acting like nothing had happened. Apparently his feelings for Barbra had been superficial at best. I knew we couldn't dwell on her death, but I felt bad that so few people cared about her in life or death.

Her parents had come out, demanding answers from the police that they didn't have. They were understandably upset about losing their daughter. Still I wondered whether their concern was genuine. It didn't take much imagination to guess where Barbra had come by her materialistic attitude. They wanted everything Barbra had moved to Travis's apartment, and even expected him to pay to have it shipped to New York. Good luck with that, I thought. He didn't strike me as being that willing to part with a dollar unless it benefitted him.

A small memorial service was held in the chapel for the employees to attend, which few did. It was further indication how little people had cared about her.

Within a week, it was like she had never worked there. Other nurses filled in the shifts her death left vacant. Her name was seldom mentioned. It was a shame that so few people would miss her, but you really couldn't blame them. Her selfishness hadn't drawn people to her.

"The guy who placed that bomb in Barbra's car wasn't exactly competent," Rex announced over dinner. Courtney and Ted were shopping for caterers for their wedding, and we were alone in the apartment. He didn't discuss his cases when anyone else was around.

"What do you mean he wasn't very competent? He killed her."

"Well, I'll grant you that." He nodded his head. "But he left some evidence that the crime scene techs were able to find. There was also a partial print on the underside of the car where the explosive device had been planted."

"You know who did it? Does that mean you've arrested him?" Excitement shot through me. I reached out and took his hand. "Did he tell you who I am?"

"Slow down, babe, I said a *partial* print. Real life isn't like a cop show on television. We can't run a partial print through the system and come up with a suspect. If we had someone in custody, we could say there was a high probability that the print belonged to them. It still wouldn't be definitive." I felt like a balloon with all the air let out; deflated and defeated.

"What happens next?" I wanted this over with before we got married.

"We keep digging for more information." I thought there was something he wasn't telling me. How much was he allowed to reveal about an on-going investigation?

"What can you tell me about Barbra's activities around the hospital?" His question was so off-the-wall that I stared at him for several seconds.

"What do you mean? She was a nurse. She took care of the patients." I shrugged.

"I know, but was she there at odd hours? Did she leave her station very often?"

"Okay, what aren't you telling me?"

"Can you answer my questions without asking any right now?" He didn't look any happier about this than I felt.

"I didn't work with her, so I can't answer those questions. You need to talk to Janice Able. She was Barbra's supervisor. Any of the other nurses on her floor would be able to tell you more than I can."

"Did she leave the apartment at odd hours when she wasn't working?"

He was beginning to freak me out with these questions. Did he suspect that Barbra had done something wrong? "After I moved in with them, she never left her place on the couch unless she had a date. She wanted to make sure I didn't touch anything of hers."

"She was that territorial? What was she hiding?"

"I guess you could call her territorial, but I think it was

195

more selfish. I don't think she was hiding anything. She just enjoyed being nasty." I clamped my hand over my mouth. "I shouldn't have said that. I'm sorry."

He reached for my hand. "You can't whitewash the way she was just because she's dead." He echoed Jerry Edmonds' sentiment the day after she died. "What else can you tell me? Did she have a lot of boyfriends before she started dating that doctor?"

"You know she was dating Ted before he and Courtney got together. From little things Courtney has said, Barbra was also dating other guys at the same time, but I don't know who they were. At the time I moved in with them she didn't have a steady boyfriend. When she started dating Travis Dean, she was gone a lot. But you know that. What's going on?"

Instead of answering me, he asked another question. "What can you tell me about him?"

"Nothing. He's a doctor. Until they started dating, I only talked to him at the hospital about patients or my own medical condition. He spent a lot of time trying to impress Doctor Weber. That's who you need to talk to about him."

"Is there anyone at the hospital who has been acting out of character lately?"

Jerry Edmonds and Doctor Riley came to mind. The day after the explosion they had acted like Barbra deserved what had happened to her. Did that qualify for what he was looking for? Everyone had been in shock, so that could explain their reaction. I shook my head. "After the initial shock wore off, everything went back to normal. I don't know what else I can tell you." I lifted my shoulders in a shrug.

He was quiet for a few minutes before asking more questions. "Was she extravagant with money, spending more than she earned?"

Again I had no idea how to answer him. "She kept any and all personal information to herself. She would have handed me my head if I even hinted at wanting to know about anything like that."

"How did she buy all the things we were transporting to

Dean's place? I didn't think we were ever going to finish with that."

I shook my head. I had no idea. "It was all in the apartment when I moved in. Everything was hers. Courtney's former boyfriend took almost everything she had when he took off."

"How did she afford everything? Her clothes didn't look like knock-offs. They had to have cost her a bundle. Do you know if her family was wealthy?" He was totally focused on Barbra.

Again I didn't have an answer for him. I had only met her parents once. They didn't strike me as extremely wealthy. If anything, I thought they probably lived well above their means. Putting that thought into words would make me sound as nasty as Barbra had always been.

"What about her friends? Can you tell me their names?"

"I don't think she had many friends, certainly not around the hospital. But you're asking the wrong person all these questions. She was Courtney's roommate for a lot longer than I was. Are you going to tell me what this is all about? Why so many questions about her finances? What does that have to do with someone putting a bomb in her car? I thought we agreed I was the intended target, not Barbra."

He gave a careless shrug. "I just need to get some background on her." I knew that wasn't the complete truth.

I took his face between my hands, forcing him to look at me. "Why all the questions about her finances and her friends? I thought the bomb was meant for me. Are you thinking this wasn't about me after all? Are you saying that maybe she had been into something illegal?" Barbra was too self-centered to do something that might land her in jail.

He drew a deep breath, releasing it slowly. "Besides the partial prints, there were traces of drugs on the explosive device. He didn't bother wearing gloves to hide his prints. Drugs were in use wherever the bomb was assembled. Like I said, the guy who put it there wasn't very good at what he did. We're trying to figure out if this was somehow related to drugs."

A wave of dizziness swept over me at the mention of drugs. "Not Barbra, no way." I rubbed at my aching head. "She was too much of a narcissist to have anything to do with something that seedy. She wouldn't put something like that in her precious body." I hadn't known her all that well, but I knew she wouldn't do something that might ruin her good looks. "Besides, getting involved with something like that would have hurt her chances of marrying a doctor. That had been her top priority."

"She didn't have to be taking them. Maybe she was selling them. Crossing someone higher up the chain of command is a sure way to get killed." Someone had been trying to kill me for months. Was that because I was somehow involved with drugs? The thought was shocking. Barbra had said I was a bad luck omen for the hospital. What if it was more than that?

At the sharp pain in my head, I rubbed at the scar where I had been hit the hardest during the attack. This time the dizziness caused me to sway slightly. Each time this happened, the dizziness and pain were more severe.

"Are you okay?" Rex caught my arms, to steady me. If we hadn't been sitting down, I would have fallen over.

"I have a headache; it made me a little dizzy." I rubbed my head again as the pain began to subside leaving behind a dull ache. "I'll be fine."

"Do you get headaches often? Have you told Doctor Weber? You need to get it checked out." He pulled me against him, placing a soft kiss on the spot I'd been rubbing. "It could be something serious caused by the attack." His concern made him forget all of his questions about Barbra.

I'd come this far. I didn't want to think that suddenly something more serious than amnesia would come up. Besides, it only happened when drugs were mentioned, or when I went near the pharmacy.

Lying in bed a short time later, I tried to figure out what it was about the mention of drugs that caused such a reaction. Until the drugs had turned up missing at the hospital, the only time I had a headache was when I had to go to the pharmacy.

Even thinking about it now caused my head to throb.

What if it wasn't Barbra who was involved in the drug trade? What if it was me? Tears filled my eyes. That would account for the attack. Drug deals going bad usually ended violently. When the bombing first happened, Rex thought the person behind the attacks on me thought Barbra's car belonged to me. If that was true and drugs were involved, I must have been involved with them.

Please God, don't let that be true, I prayed silently. *I don't want to be a criminal. I want to be a good person.* Tears flowed from my eyes, flooding my ears as I lay in bed.

Tossing and turning, sleep eluded me for a long time. When sleep finally did come, drug dealers chased me through the desert, bringing me awake with a start. If I was involved in something like that, I had to end my relationship with Rex. Being tied to someone like that would ruin his career. Tears once again flooded my eyes. I really did love him.

Groggy and out of sorts the next morning, I tried to reason out what Rex had told me the night before. Since Barbra's death there had been no mention of drugs missing from the hospital. What was the significance of that? Had the person behind the theft decided to stop since the police had been questioning everyone about the bombing? Or had the theft stopped because Barbra had been the one taking them? Could it have been a clerical error instead of theft, I thought hopefully? Thinking about it still caused my head to hurt, and that couldn't be a good thing.

Rex had never mentioned the missing drugs at the hospital. Was he keeping that to himself for a reason? Was there some significance to his silence? Did he really suspect me, not Barbra? Was this all a ruse to catch the real thief? My heart ached along with my head. I needed to talk to someone. There was one person I could trust; Chaplain Winston.

I had to be careful how much I told him. I couldn't repeat anything Rex had told me. But I could tell the chaplain about the headaches and dizziness. "You need to tell Doctor Weber," he said, concern showing on his kind face. "This could be something serious from the beating you sustained."

I shook my head. "No, you don't understand." I wasn't doing a very good job of explaining myself. "This only happens when..." I stopped to draw a deep breath before plunging ahead. "When someone mentions drugs, illegal drugs," I clarified. "Or when someone mentions the missing drugs here at the hospital," I finished lamely. "That's when I get dizzy and my head hurts."

"What missing drugs?" He frowned like this was the first he'd heard about that.

"Drugs are missing from the hospital pharmacy and different drug cabinets on the floors," I whispered, rubbing at my head. "Why does my head hurt just when something like that is mentioned?" Why didn't he know about the missing drugs? The initial reaction of the others here at the hospital was like it was no big deal. Had the administration even reported the theft to the police?

I'd think about that later. For now, I needed to know what the chaplain thought of the possibility of me being involved with selling drugs. "When a drug deal goes bad, someone usually ends up dead. What if I was attacked because of something like that?"

"Are you suggesting that maybe you had something to do with the drug trade in your former life?" Chaplain Winston asked, shock registering on his face. I nodded my head, unable to make my voice work. He shook his head. "I refuse to believe that, and so should you. Why would you even consider that possibility?"

"Because my head hurts only when drugs are mentioned. I can't even walk past the pharmacy without my head hurting and getting dizzy. There has to be some sort of significance to that. I just don't know what."

He was silent for so long, I was afraid he now believed it was true. Finally, he shook his head again. "I don't believe you were involved with something like that. You have a good heart, a heart for God."

"What if the hit on the head didn't just take away my

memory? What if it caused a change in my personality as well?"

"Is that even a possibility?" he asked. I shrugged, unable to answer that. "Have you spoken with your detective about any of this? He might be able to ease your fears if you would talk to him."

"No," I whispered. The thought of telling Rex what I was thinking caused my stomach to hurt as well as my head. "If I really am a criminal, I can't marry him. It would ruin his career. I don't want to say anything to him until I know if it's possible." I twisted the engagement ring he'd given me such a short time ago.

Chaplain Winston laid his hand over my trembling fingers. "You need to confide in the man. He's in love with you. He needs to know what you're thinking. You also need to talk to Doctor Weber about these headaches. They might not be connected to drugs, but what happened to you."

"What does Detective Booker have to say about the missing drugs here?"

"Nothing, I'm not sure he knows. Why didn't you know about that?"

"I'm not in a position to know about a lot of things that go on around here. Sometimes it's frustrating to be a part of the hospital, but not really be a part of it, if you know what I mean." He sighed. "Anyway," he smiled encouragingly at me, "you need to talk to Detective Booker and Doctor Weber about what's going on with you. I'm sure they both can help you. I'm sorry I haven't been much help. I will pray that you find the answers you're looking for." He took my hands, and we both bowed our heads.

When I left the chapel a few minutes later, I felt like a heavy weight had been lifted from my shoulders. I still didn't know the answers to what caused the headaches and dizziness, but I knew I wasn't alone in this. The thought of talking to Rex about it still upset me, but I could only pray that everything would be all right.

LOST MEMORIES

CHAPTER TWENTY-THREE

Anger and frustration rode him like a hound from hell. Thoughts of killing that woman consumed him, but she was harder to kill than a cockroach. He chuckled at that comparison. She was a bug in his life.

Mentally reviewing his options, he decided he had to cut his losses, and disappear while he still could. All I need is one more big score, he told himself. Then I'll be set for life, never to be seen again.

He had already set his plans in motion. His plane was gassed up and ready to fly. His new identification and passport were in his 'Go Bag' ready at a moment's notice. He chuckled at that term. It sounded clandestine, which was exactly what this part of his plan was. He'd been looking for other positions, this time out of state, as his reason for leaving. He had enough experience with Weber to beef up his resume.

But it really didn't matter. Any position he secured was nothing but a smoke screen, just for show, to throw anyone looking for him off his trail. He would announce that he was leaving, and walk away free and clear. If anyone checked up on him, the new position would be real. Instead of actually taking the position though, he would simply disappear, and no one here would be the wiser.

He chuckled as he imagined the surprise on the old man's face when he told him he was going somewhere else. The man never understood why doctors wanted to leave his tutelage. He certainly had a high opinion of himself, probably encouraged by his wife willing to stick around all these years while he played the big man getting his ego, and probably a whole lot more, stroked by all the doctors and interns who came to worship at his feet.

He shook his head. This was the second time he'd worked for the man, and he'd never guessed he had a wife. Why had

202

they kept it a secret other than it would detract from his image of being all consumed by his work?

He shrugged the thought away. It didn't matter. He was done with all that. The only thing that mattered now was getting out of here before she remembered. Once he was gone, she could remember everything, and it wouldn't do her or anyone else any good. He would have vanished into thin air. If she never remembered, he would still be gone.

Ending her existence wasn't his top priority any longer. He needed to get away. Her medical skills were coming to the surface more and more each day. Even the old man was taking notice. There was talk around the hospital that he had put her in for one of the hospital scholarships so she could go to school for her nursing degree. He chuckled at that. A doctor becoming a nurse, instead of a nurse becoming a doctor. He laughed at the irony. Quite a come down for you, Doctor Sanders.

Too bad she fell for that detective. I could have had a lot of fun with her before I finally put her out of my misery. He gave an evil chuckle.

~~~

It was another two days before Rex and I were alone long enough to talk about anything serious. I decided to go see Doctor Weber while I waited. Maybe the chaplain was right, maybe the headaches and dizziness had a medical cause connected to the attack.

"Headaches and dizziness?" The doctor frowned at me. "When did that start?"

I couldn't tell him it started the same day as the rumor that the drugs had come up missing at the hospital. "About three weeks ago." It was hard to believe it had only been three weeks. So much had happened in a short amount of time.

"Why didn't you come see me immediately?" He picked up his phone without waiting for an answer. "I want a full head CT done on Deborah Winston. STAT." He snapped out the order. "She'll be there in five." He was running up unnecessary hospital bills, bills I couldn't pay. But I couldn't stop him without explaining about the connection between my symptoms and the missing drugs. I was afraid of what his reaction would be. I was being a coward, but I couldn't help myself. I tried to tell myself that this was just a precaution. I didn't want any further complications because of the attack.

As I suspected, there were no blood clots or tumors causing my problem. Doctor Weber scratched his chin as he looked at the negative results. "It's always better to be safe than sorry." He gave a sigh that sounded like relief. "The blood tests might show something. For now, I want you to rest. Take a few days off."

"No, I can't do that. I need to work. Please, I'd rather be here. Can I ask you a question?"

"Of course, anything. What's bothering you?"

I drew a deep breath for courage. "Can a traumatic head injury cause a change in personality?" I had mentioned that to Chaplain Winston as a possibility, now I needed to know if it really could happen.

"Certainly, why? Are you beginning to remember things that don't fit in with your life now?"

"No, I was just wondering if it's possible for someone, me," I corrected, "to have a totally different personality after a serious head injury."

"Well, of course, there could be small changes in your personality, but not a complete reversal. You would still be you if that's what you're thinking."

A sigh of relief escaped my parted lips. Maybe I hadn't been a bad person before this happened, after all. "What kind of changes are you talking about?" I pressed for more information. I didn't want to be blindsided if I finally recovered my memory.

He chuckled. "I've seen people change their career choices after a head injury. But it didn't necessarily mean it was a change in their personality. It just means they no longer wanted to be one thing, and decided to do something else with their life."

When I fell silent, he stood up. "I want you to take it easy until we get the results back from the blood tests. If you begin feeling dizzy, you need to lie down. Falling could cause even more problems." He scowled at me to enforce his order.

Courtney was moving ahead with her plans for a double wedding in spite of my objections. Even without my fears of being involved somehow with drugs in my forgotten past, I couldn't let her pay for my part. I didn't want Rex to pay either. That would smack a little too much of Barbra's agenda, having someone else always footing the bill. Somehow I had to convince both of them that our wedding would be small and inexpensive.

I wanted to help Courtney pick out her dress, but I wasn't ready to try on wedding dresses myself. "I'll be one of your bridesmaids," I promised. "Let's let it go at that for now. I need to save money before I can get my own dress." She started to argue again, but I pleaded with her. "Please." I gripped her hand, silently willing her to understand.

With a sigh, she nodded her head. "Okay, we can look for a bridesmaid's dress for you. But I'm not giving up on the idea that we'll make it a double wedding. There are still five months on our lease. That gives me plenty of time to work on you." She chuckled at the dirty face I gave her.

The press had been allowed to assume that Barbra was the intended victim in the bombing, and no one was discouraging them from that idea. Meanwhile, the police looked for evidence that Barbra was either somehow involved with drugs, or the bomb was meant for me. There was little evidence either way.

"Rex, I need to talk to you. I want you to listen to what I have to say without interrupting or arguing. Can you do that?" We were finally alone so we could talk.

"Uh, oh, it's got to be serious when you use my name instead of calling me Honey." He tried to make a joke, but I didn't laugh. When I didn't say anything, he sat back on the couch, propping one ankle on top of his knee. "Okay, I'm listening. I'll try not to interrupt or argue until you're finished." He seemed nervous. "First, tell me that you aren't going to break off our engagement."

"When I'm finished, you might be the one to break it off." I drew a deep breath. "You need to take another look at me as the intended victim of the bomb."

"We haven't ruled that out." I gave him a dirty look, and he held up his hands. "Sorry." He made like he was turning a key in a lock on his lips.

I started to pace across his living room. "You're trying to find some connection between the bomb and some sort of drug gang. That the bombing had something to do with a drug deal gone bad." He nodded, but remained silent. "But you also think the bomb could have been set by the same person who has been trying to kill me." Again, he nodded. "What if both of your theories are correct, but with the wrong person dealing drugs?"

"Huh?" He looked confused. Once again I wasn't doing a very good job of explaining myself.

I drew in another deep breath, plunging ahead before I lost what little courage I had. "Do you remember when you told me about finding traces of drugs on the explosives, and my head hurt and I got dizzy?" He nodded, but looked even more confused. "That happens every time drugs are mentioned, or I have to go to the hospital pharmacy. Maybe that's because I was the one involved with a drug gang. Maybe that's why someone wants to kill me." The faster I talked, the faster I paced.

He sat forward, opening his mouth like he was going to argue, but I held out my hand in a stop motion. "Every time the missing drugs at the hospital are mentioned, I get the same headache and dizziness. It has to mean something."

"Whoa, stop right there." He stood up, stepping into my path. "What missing drugs? When did this happen?"

I shrugged. "I don't remember the exact date. About a month ago, I guess."

"So, it was before Barbra died."

Nodding my head, I let my reddish hair fall over my face. I didn't want to see his reaction when I continued with my explanation.

When I started to say something, he stopped me. "No, it's my turn now. I don't know anything about missing drugs at the hospital. We'll get to that in a minute. But right now, you need to understand something. You were not involved with drugs at any time. There was no indication that the attack on you was drug related, so you can put that right out of your head."

"How can you be so sure?" I whispered. "We don't know who I am."

"There were no drugs in your system. There was no drug residue on your clothes or around where you were found. The only people involved with drugs in the desert are drug smugglers from Mexico. If that was what your attack was about, you wouldn't have survived to be brought to the hospital. They also wouldn't have tried to kill you with insulin or run you down with a car.

"The bomb," he shrugged. "That sounds more like something gangs would be involved with if they were double crossed. That's why we're looking at Barbra. She seemed to be living rather large, well beyond her pay grade. Now you tell me there are drugs missing from the hospital. Why wasn't that reported at the time it happened?"

I shrugged. "I thought it was."

"Is it still going on?"

I shrugged again. "I haven't heard any more about it."

It was his turn to pace across the room. "I think it's time I had a talk with Doctor Weber."

I sank down on the couch, rubbing my aching head. "People always acted like it was no big deal. I don't even know how much is missing." Talking about this still made my head hurt, and I rubbed at the scar.

All the tests Doctor Weber had insisted on having run to find out what was causing the headaches and dizziness came back negative. There was no physical reason behind them. It was a relief while at the same time it gave me more reason to worry. If there was nothing physically wrong with me, it must mean something in my past caused them whenever drugs were mentioned.

Rex had his talk with Doctor Weber about the missing drugs, but it wasn't very fruitful. Frustrated, Rex threw himself onto the couch only to bounce back up again. "How can he be so casual about missing drugs? Why would they want to sweep it under the rug and not report it? Those drugs are probably on the street right now, poisoning a bunch of kids."

"Is it still going on?" I rubbed at the ache in my head.

"He wouldn't say. He seems to think it's an employee feeding his own habit, or maybe someone trying to stay awake during a long shift. That would mean only small amounts taken at a time." He shook his head. "That's a poor excuse for letting theft go unchecked.

CHAPTER TWENTY-FOUR

Doctors come and go in a hospital, but everyone was surprised to learn that Jerry Edmonds was leaving. There had always been something about him that didn't fit in. I never could decide exactly what it was though.

"You're moving to Tucson?" He was making his rounds, telling people good-bye. I couldn't decide if he was hoping people would make a fuss over him, or if he was just wanted to say good-bye. His friendly nature had made him a lot of friends.

He shrugged his broad shoulders. "Yeah, it's time I went home." I frowned, not understanding what he meant. "My wife wants to give our marriage another try."

My mouth dropped open. "You're married?" I couldn't hide the shock in my voice or on my face. The man had asked every unmarried nurse out. "I didn't know you were married."

His handsome face colored slightly. "I wasn't telling people because I wasn't sure how long I'd stay that way after she kicked me out. She said I'm a flirt, to go away until I got it out of my system."

"You are a flirt." The words came out before I could censor them.

He chuckled, his face turning a brighter shade of pink. "What can I say, I like women, but I've discovered I love my wife more."

"So you have all that flirting out of your system now?" I lifted one eyebrow. Somehow I doubted that.

He laughed out loud. "I'll probably flirt right up to the time they put me in the ground, but that doesn't mean I'll ever follow through with anything. It's just a game." He leaned down to whisper to me. "Don't tell Weber, but learning about his marriage mishap, I've decided I don't want to wait twenty years to find out the woman I had is the one I want."

I offered him my hand. "Good luck, Doctor."

Before I could guess at what he intended, he pulled me

209

close, placing a gentle kiss on my cheek. "I hope things work out for you, and you get your memory back soon."

I pulled away from him, giving him a dirty look. "You might want to stop doing things like that if you're serious about making things work out with your wife. She might look unkindly on something like that."

He chuckled. "Just a friendly peck on the cheek. Good luck to you, Deborah. You're going to make a great nurse. You'd make an even better doctor though. You've got all the right instincts, plus a boat load of compassion." He walked off with that same swagger that I had found creepy before. Now, I had to laugh. He really was a born flirt. Hopefully, he'd learned his lesson, and wouldn't carry the flirting too far. I had confused his swagger with arrogance when he was really a sweet guy with a flirting problem.

His parting statement left me bewildered. Yes, I had instinctively known what to do for Mrs. Taylor, but that didn't mean I would be a good doctor. Everything I did as an aide seemed routine, like I had done it all before. Would it be the same with the classes Doctor Weber had signed me up for here at the hospital?

Did that even have any significance? Maybe I'd been a nurse somewhere before all this happened to me. That could explain why I could do so many of the things at the hospital. But where had I worked? Why hadn't anyone reported me missing? The questions just kept coming.

If all hospitals took the same stance on drugs missing from the pharmacy or drug cabinets, would that explain my reaction to what had been happening here? I still had no knowledge about Arizona beyond what I had learned since waking from the coma. Did that mean I hadn't worked in Arizona before? How did I get in the desert? I shook my head. Since my memory remained stubbornly blank, I had no answers.

~~~

After beginning the classes, I started working a split shift; four hours in the morning, classes in the afternoon and four hours at night. I tried to sleep during the day, but it wasn't always easy. The hospital was quiet during the late night shift. I still had plenty to do, but without the doctors making rounds and visitors coming and going, I had enough free time to study while the patients were sleeping.

After Barbra died, I had transferred to Janice Able's floor. The older woman was nothing like Barbra had portrayed her to be. She encouraged her staff, giving praise where it was warranted, while gently correcting any mistakes that were made. Under her guidance, mistakes were few and far between.

Like everything I did for the patients, the classwork also seemed routine, like I could do it in my sleep. Maybe with this schedule I was on, I would be doing it in my sleep. Working full time and taking the additional classes left little time for sleep.

The small chapel was always open, and I took advantage of the quiet each day before work. Chaplain Winston wasn't there unless a family was in need of his services, but God's peace was there. That's what I needed most of all. I had all but given up trying to remember who I was before the attack. No one had reported me missing, so either I had no family or no one cared enough to miss me.

Even late at night, I used the stairs to avoid going past the pharmacy. Going to that cursed room was not something I wanted to do. Going there in the middle of the night was the stuff nightmares were made of. There were still times I couldn't avoid picking up meds for new patients. Each time, a wave of dizziness swept over me, and the scar on my head throbbed.

Rex refused to believe I'd had anything to do with something illegal in my forgotten life. But how else could I explain what had happened to me before, and what was happening now? "I've checked every criminal data base available," he explained. "Your fingerprints aren't there. I've also run your DNA. You've never been a victim or a suspect in any reported crime."

"Reported crime may be the operative phrase," I argued.

211

"Maybe whatever I was involved in was never reported. Or maybe my part in the crime wasn't known."

"Do you want to be a criminal?" Frustration made his voice sharp. This was the only area we argued about.

"Of course not, but what am I supposed to think? Someone wanted me dead. They've killed two other people because of me."

"We don't know that," he interrupted.

"Okay, I'll give you that. We don't know whether the same person who killed Bobby Morrow also planted the bomb under Barbra's car. But we do know whoever killed Bobby tried to kill me many times, otherwise why would he leave that faked suicide note?"

"Do you love me?" Rex asked. He was fighting unfairly now.

"Yes, you know I do."

"Do you still want to marry me?"

Tears burned in my eyes. "Why are you asking me this? You know the answer."

"I want to hear you say it. I *need* to hear you say it." His gray eyes pleaded with me.

Placing my hands on either side of his face, I pulled him close, kissing his lips. "I love you with all my heart and I want to be your wife. But not if it would do you any harm. If I had been involved with people willing to kill, I don't want anyone else getting hurt."

A light bulb seemed to go on over his head. "That's why you insisted on taking the bus to work after the bomb was put under Barbra's car." With a shake of his head like he couldn't believe he had missed that, he pulled me into his arms. Looking down into my eyes, he said, "You didn't want anyone harming Courtney or me in the hopes of killing you."

It took him long enough to figure that out. Barbra died more than a month ago. Even Courtney had put the pieces together, and she had stopped arguing with me on that issue.

She was still insisting we have a double wedding though. "Is it because you don't want to share your special day with anyone else?" she asked for the third time in a week.

I felt like they were ganging up on me. They didn't understand I was trying to protect them. "That has nothing to do with it, you know that. I just don't want anything to ruin your day. What if this lunatic decides to blow me up on my wedding day?"

"So you're not going to marry Rex after all?" She sounded horrified now. "Does he know you're backing out of the wedding?"

"No, I didn't say that." I ran my fingers through my hair in frustration. I'd kept it short while the small patch that had been shaved grew back. It was finally all the same length. Maybe now I could let it grow out. I don't like short hair.

The thought stopped me. "I don't like short hair." I spoke the words out loud, drawing a confused frown from Courtney.

"Huh?"

"Don't you see?" I said, excitement bubbling up inside me. "I don't like my hair being short. I've always had long hair." When I woke up in the hospital, my hair had been long except for this one spot. I touched the place that had been shaved. "I've never had short hair until now. I remembered something." I could even see myself pulling my hair up in a ponytail or clipping it up off my neck during the hot, humid days in the south.

"So do you remember being a criminal?" she asked. I'd finally had to admit to her where my fears had led me.

"No, of course not, but that doesn't mean anything. I can't remember anything else either." In spite of the few memories that had surfaced the week before, I still wasn't one hundred percent convinced that I hadn't been involved with something illegal.

Maybe I'd been dating a criminal, and had tried to get away from him. That could explain why he wanted me dead. I hadn't thought of that until now. It was a comforting option to what I'd been thinking all this time.

~~~

"A new patient is being brought up from the ER," Janice

Able told me. "The list of meds he'll need has been called in to the night administrator. He'll meet you at the pharmacy." She handed me the form that I needed to give the administrator. With shaking hands and an aching head, I headed down the stairs. Would I ever figure out what caused this reaction?

Expecting the hospital administrator on night duty to meet me at the pharmacy, I was surprised when there was no light on behind the frosted glass. I rubbed at my aching head, willing the pain to go away. "Hurry up," I whispered. I wanted to get the meds and be gone from this hated room.

A small light flickered behind the glass. Someone was in there. My fingers felt like they were encased in ice as I reached out to turn the door knob. Being quiet as a mouse, I pushed the door open enough to see inside the room. Light from the hallway flooded in, surprising the man standing behind the counter. It wasn't the hospital administrator.

"You again," the man screamed, lunging at me from across the room, diving across the counter to grab for me. For what felt like a lifetime I stared at him, frozen in place, my feet rooted to the floor. At the last possible second self-preservation took over. As his big hands wrapped around my throat, I pulled the stun gun out of the pocket of my scrubs.

Blinded by hatred, he failed to see what I had in my hand until it was too late. Before he was able to cut off my breath, I pressed the silver points on the small stun gun to his throat. When I pulled the trigger, he jerked and twitched. His hands convulsed around my neck. For a second I thought he wasn't going to let go. I kept the prongs of the gun pressed to his neck while I continued to pull the trigger.

With the longer contact to his neck, he finally fell down, jerking around on the floor. "You b...bitch," he stuttered, his voice quivering.

A constant scream followed me as I ran from the room, and I finally realized I was the one screaming. People were gathering in the hall, looking to see what was happening. When someone grabbed my arms, my shriek went up several

214

octaves.

"Miss Winston, what's going on here?" The night administrator gave me a shake, shutting down my scream. "I'm sorry I got delayed. What's going on here?" he asked again as he looked over my shoulder at the man still twitching on the floor. His muscles hadn't recovered from the extended electrical shock from the stun gun.

"It's Brianna Sanders." The words came out of my mouth without any thought on my part. "Doctor Brianna Sanders." Realization finally hit me, and my mouth dropped open. Excitement bubbled up in me. "I know my name; I know who I am. I remember everything." I whirled around to face the man who had attacked me.

He had managed to pull himself up, and was moving away through the crowd, trying to escape. "Someone stop him. He tried to kill me. He killed Bobby Morrow and Barbra Johnson."

"Hold it right there, Doctor Riley." A security officer took hold of his arm. "We need to have a talk." He struggled to pull away but the officer tightened his grip, giving the doctor's arm a shake. "You aren't going anywhere, so just calm down."

"Do you know who I am?" he asked indignantly. "I don't know what she's talking about. She must be having a breakdown due to the trauma she went through." His eyes moved through the crowd gathered around us. Even at two in the morning there were plenty witnesses to this little drama. "You need to call Doctor Weber. She might have an aneurism or something that could be causing a problem for her."

"No, I remember everything you did to me. You tried to kill me." I punctuated each word by poking him in the chest. "Someone please call the police."

"Already did that," the officer said. He looked around at the people still standing in the hallway. "Okay, folks, the show is over. Go about your business." He turned to me. "Let's take this in my office, Miss Winston."

"My name is Brianna Sanders," I stated firmly. "I'm a doctor, and he tried to kill me." I wanted to impress that on everyone listening.

"She just tried to kill me with that stun gun," Doctor Riley insisted. "I was getting meds I needed for a patient when she stormed into the pharmacy. She shocked me with that thing." He pointed again at the stun gun I was still holding.

He shook his head, putting on a sad face. "Can't you see that she's clearly delusional?" He tried to pull his arm out of the security officer's firm grip. "She needs to be examined to find the cause of this dramatic change in her personality. I was one of her doctors when she was brought in here. Let me take her upstairs."

Panic struck me. What if the officer believed him, and turned me over to this man? He would kill me as soon as we out of sight.

"No one's going anywhere until the police get here, so settle down, Doc. We'll let the police straighten this out." He pushed Doctor Riley into a chair.

"You don't understand the urgency of this." Doctor Riley pulled himself up to his full height. "This could be life threatening. She needs immediate medical attention. She's been looking for her name for so long, she's grasping on to anything. There isn't such a person as this Doctor Betty Saunders that she claims to be."

"It's Brianna Sanders, and I do exist." I turned to the administrator who had followed us into the security office. "You can check with the medical center in Tucson. I was to start working there the day after he attacked me. This is the second time I caught him stealing drugs. He's the one who attacked me at the hospital in Tucson. I remember everything." I kept repeating myself, hoping they would believe me.

"No, she's lying. I would never do anything like that. I'm a doctor. I save lives, I don't take them. You all know me."

"I'm also a doctor," I insisted. "I can prove it." I wasn't positive about that statement. I didn't know what had happened to all the things I'd left in a storage facility in Tucson.

Rex charged into the office. "What the hell is going on?" He glared at Doctor Riley before leaning down to place a kiss in my hair. "Are you all right?"

"I'm fine now. My name is Doctor Brianna Sanders." It felt so good to be able to say my name again, my real name. "He tried to kill me because I caught him stealing drugs at the hospital in Tucson. I caught him again tonight."

"She's delusional." Collin Riley acted offended. "I have never stolen anything in my life. Can't you see she's not quite right in the head? I think she might have a problem because of the attack she sustained. If you won't let me examine her, you really need to call Doctor Weber. He might be able to help her before it gets too bad." His arrogance was slipping. Sweat dotted his forehead, and his hands were shaking.

"I can prove who I am, Doctor Riley. Can you prove you weren't stealing drugs tonight?"

"That's ridiculous. Why would I steal drugs? I told you I was getting meds for a patient."

The administrator stepped forward. "The only order for meds tonight came from the third floor. Miss Winston…"

"Brianna Sanders," I corrected him. I finally knew my name, and wanted people to use it.

"Yes, of course, my dear. I'm sorry. Miss Sanders…Doctor Sanders," he corrected with a chuckle before I could interrupt again. "Doctor Sanders was to come down to get the meds. What were you doing in the pharmacy with the light off, I might add?"

"I…it was an emergency." He fumbled for an answer. "I needed the meds immediately. I couldn't wait to go through channels."

"How many drugs did you need, Doctor?" The security officer had stepped out of the office without anyone realizing it until he held up a bag. Turning it over, he dumped the contents on the desk. A gasp erupted around the room.

"You're under arrest for murder, attempted murder, assault, and drug trafficking." Rex pulled the doctor's arms behind his back, placing handcuffs on him as he read him his rights. He handed the man over to the uniformed officer waiting in the hall to be taken to the jail. We could hear his denial all the way down the hall.

~~~

"You're really a doctor?" Courtney asked. "I can't believe it all came back just like that." She snapped her fingers.

I laughed. "Yes, I'm really a doctor." The following day, the four of us were in the living room of our apartment. Everyone had questions for me. "I was supposed to start work at the medical center in Tucson the day after he attacked me." I shook my head. "If I hadn't gone there that night to get a feel of the place before I started work, none of this would have happened."

Rex was holding my hand, giving it a squeeze now. "I'm sorry for all that you've gone through, but since it did, I'm grateful that you ended up here." A worried frown drew his light-colored brows together. "You do remember everything that's happened since you came out of the coma, right?" He was afraid that recovering my memory of my former life had blotted out my memory of what we had been building together.

I lifted his hand to my lips. "Yes, I remember everything. We're getting married." I wiggled my ring finger to show off the engagement ring he'd given me.

"Why didn't anyone report you missing when you didn't show up for work?" "Courtney asked.

I shrugged. "You'll have to get the answer to that from Collin Riley or someone at the hospital in Tucson. I hadn't reported to work yet. No one knew me there."

"Why didn't your family report you missing when they didn't hear from you? Where are you from?" He frowned at me. There were still a lot of unanswered questions.

"I was born and raised in South Carolina, but I don't have any family." I lifted my shoulders in another shrug. "I was raised in foster care. I was in so many different homes I never had time to make friends." I could feel my cheeks turning pink. "I didn't want to spend the rest of my life living off the system, so I studied hard in school. Some of the other kids made fun of me for that, but studying hard paid off with scholarships."

I sighed. "When I finally aged out of the system, I tried to forget everything about that part of my life. I thought I'd made it with that job in Tucson."

"Are you going to want to go back there? Do you think the job will still be waiting for you?" The worry was evident in his voice.

"No," I laughed. "I think this is where I'm supposed to be." For a long moment, I was silent. "All of the foster homes I was in had one thing in common; all the kids had to go to church. I can't say I'm happy about the way I came to Phoenix, but I think God placed me here because he knew this is where I'd find the family I've always wanted."

EPILOGUE

It didn't take long to finally retrieve all of my belongings from the storage facility in Tucson. I'd paid for three months of storage. It was three months beyond that now. The storage facility is allowed to auction off the items left in storage after six months without payment. I didn't have much, but what I had, I cherished. My diplomas were all there proving who I was, and that I was indeed a doctor.

Pay it forward was no longer a foreign concept to me. So many people had helped me when I needed it most. I couldn't do anything less for those around me in need. I didn't want to be like some of those I'd recently met; only concerned with the money to be earned from being a doctor. There were a lot of people who needed a doctor, but they can't pay the high prices charged by hospitals and medical centers. That was something I could help with.

Doctor Collin Riley was still maintaining his innocence. Of course, none of what happened was his fault. Against his attorney's advice, he tried to lay the blame for everything on Bobby Morrow. There was no way that Bobby had been behind the attack on me, or the drug thefts. I would testify to that.

It would be months, if not longer, before Riley finally faced trial. Besides, aggravated assault, attempted murder, and theft of drugs from two hospitals, there were also the murders of Bobby Morrow and Barbra Johnson. I would have to testify against him. I wasn't sure how much evidence the police had that would convict him of murdering Bobby Morrow. Hopefully, circumstantial evidence would carry the jury to a guilty verdict.

The gangbanger Riley hired to place the bomb under Barbra's car wasn't all that smart. He'd bragged one too many times about getting away with murder, and another member of his gang turned him in. As a result, the gangbanger turned state's evidence in exchange for a lesser sentence. He was singing like a canary. Hopefully, Collin Riley would spend the rest of his life in prison. Maybe he would put his medical training to good use in the prison system. Somehow I doubted he would do that though. The extreme arrogance he'd shown from the start wouldn't let him stoop that low.

After a lot of digging, and some excellent detective work, the police found the plane he kept in the name of his alter ego. The bank accounts he had set up in Cayman were turned over to the government. Too bad the money couldn't be put to use helping those in need.

Courtney got her wish. Our double wedding is tomorrow. Doctor Weber is walking me down the aisle. He's the closest thing I have to a father. After a lifetime of no friends, just acquaintances, I will spend the rest of my life with the man of my dreams and friends that are now family. I didn't know I could be this happy. I've come to realize that God uses the evil of others for His good. I am so grateful for everything He has given me.

ACKNOWLEDGEMENTS

I thank God for the many wonderful gifts He has given me in this life, among them are my wonderful family. He has answered my prayers, allowing me to tell my stories and publish my books. I am so blessed.

My thanks and gratitude also goes to Gerry Beamon, Sandy Roedl, and KaTie Jackson for their suggestions, editing skills and encouragement. I can't forget about all the information retired Phoenix Police Detective Ken Shriner has given me on police procedure. Thanks for your patience with me, and for answering my many questions about law enforcement. I apologize to Ken for taking literary license with police procedure in an effort to move the story forward. Patricia Young, a retired RN, has helped me with all things concerning the activities in the hospital. Again I took literary license to move the story along. Any mistakes or exaggerations were mine, not Pat's. Thanks to everyone who helped me through this process.

OTHER BOOKS BY SUZANNE FLOYD

Revenge Served Cold
Rosie's Revenge
A Game of Cat and Mouse
Man on the Run
Trapped in a Whirlwind
Smoke & Mirrors
Plenty of Guilt

Dear Reader:

Thank you for reading my book. I hope you enjoyed reading it as much as I enjoyed writing it. If you enjoyed Lost Memories, I would appreciate it if you would tell your friends and relatives and/or write a review on Amazon.

Follow me on Facebook at Suzanne Floyd Author, or check out my website at SuzanneFloyd.com.

Thank you,
Suzanne Floyd

P.S. If you find any errors, please let me know at: Suzanne.sfloyd@gmail.com. Before publishing, many people have read this book, but minds can play tricks by supplying words that are missing and correcting typos.

ABOUT THE AUTHOR

Suzanne is an internationally known author. She was born in Iowa, and moved to Arizona with her family when she was nine years old. She still lives in Phoenix with her husband Paul. They have two wonderful daughters, two great sons-in-law and five of the best grandchildren around. Of course, she's just a little prejudiced.

Growing up and traveling with her parents, she entertained herself by making up stories. As an adult she tried writing, but family came first. After retiring in 2008, she decided it was her time. She still enjoys making up stories, and thanks to the internet she's able to put them online for others to enjoy. When Suzanne isn't writing, she and her husband enjoy traveling around on their 2010 Honda Goldwing trike. She's always looking for new places to write about. There's always a new mystery and a romance lurking out there to capture her attention.

Made in the USA
Charleston, SC
01 August 2016